A
Harlequin
Romance

THE POST AT GUNDOOEE

by

AMANDA DOYLE

HARLEQUIN BOOKS

Toronto • Canada   New York • New York

THE POST AT GUNDOOEE

First published in 1970 by Mills & Boon Limited,
17-19 Foley Street, London, England.

Harlequin Canadian edition published April, 1971
Harlequin U.S. edition published July, 1971

Standard Book Number: 373-51486-7.

Printed in Canada

CHAPTER 1

LINDSAY DUTTEN pushed a tendril of brown hair back from her forehead, and sighed.

It was straight hair of an unremarkable colour—brown, mouse—and inclined to be difficult in the humid summer heat of Sydney. She was resigned to its contrariness, though, in much the same way that she was resigned to the fact of her orphaned status in life, and her unwelcome but unavoidable dependence upon her cousin Carleen, with whom she shared this unit.

Her sigh, just then, carried a burden of resignation for almost *everything*, Lindsay acknowledged wryly to herself in a spurt of self-honesty. She was one of the doormats of this world, she supposed. There were the givers and the takers in life, and in the same way there were the doormats and those who walked upon them, without sparing a thought that, in cushioning their own feet, they might be trampling a fellow-mortal, more sensitive and inarticulate than they.

Lindsay wondered, as she carefully spooned small mounds of caviar on to the canapés she was preparing for Carleen's party tonight, if it were possible to be a doormat *and* a taker at one and the same time. Lindsay didn't think such a combination either likely or frequent. In her experience, the doormats were destined to give—sometimes unstintingly—while the takers took as though it were their right, and often stepped heavily upon the doormats' fingers even as they clutched greedily at the offerings which were being proffered.

Lindsay's lips were pursed in a suddenly uncharacteristically mutinous manner, as she pushed her recalcitrant hair back again, and surveyed the trays of dainty and exotic bouchées which she had prepared. About two dozen people, Carleen had said. That meant there weren't enough yet.

5

'Make them attractive, but as substantial as possible, will you, darling. I hate stingy eats.' Carleen's cool, commanding voice rang in her cousin's ears, and Lindsay did her best to shut out the memory, as she began to fill tiny vol-au-vent cases with a mixture of creamy smoked blue-cod.

Carleen hated stinginess, enjoyed luxury, to such an extent that her demands upon Lindsay's own monetary contribution to the weekly budget had increased out of all proportion to her own just lately.

'After all, it's my flat, Lindsay,' Carleen had pointed out reasonably, with that peculiarly one-sided reasoning of which she was sometimes all too capable, 'and it's only out of a sense of duty to Mother and Father that I'm letting you share. They'd have worried about you on your own, and goodness knows, you've been enough of a bother to them one way and another, without stringing yourself around their necks all your life. I know you didn't *ask* for your parents to dump you in this world all alone,' she added judicially, aware of Lindsay's uncomfortable flush. 'Car accidents can happen to anyone. But it was quite decent of Mum to take you in, considering you were only her cousin's child—and not even her favourite cousin, at that. Anyway, I do think you could contribute more than you do to the running of this place, I really do!'

'But, Carleen, I already give you nearly two-thirds of my salary. Shorthand-typists don't get as much as models, remember! With what I give you, I'm only left with a few dollars for clothes and things.' She gestured vaguely. 'Why can't we be a bit less extravagant when you—when we entertain?' she suggested with some temerity. 'You didn't *have* to have oyster cocktails to start with the other night, when that photographer came. I could have done it far more cheaply for you, and just as nicely, with some iced consommé and——'

'Darling, that photographer, as you call him, happens to be the best in the game in this whole city at the moment,' Carleen interrupted coldly. 'He's the entrée to the big time, so far as I'm concerned, and if I say you'll give him oysters, then you'll *give* him oysters, do you hear?'

'Yes, Carleen.'

Her cousin studied her nails critically. They were long nails, beautifully kept, oval, perfect—so perfect that Lindsay suspected that the critical, annoyed appraisal they were receiving was not meant for them at all, but for Lindsay herself!

'I'll need another three dollars at least from you, Lindsay.'

'Three dollars!'

'At least. I ought to make it four. You haven't got half the incidental expenses that I have myself. In my profession one can't afford to let appearances slide, whereas nobody notices a nondescript little typist to-ing and fro-ing, you must admit. Why, you don't even need to go to the hairdresser, or anything, do you? They'd only tell you that that dead-straight mouse of yours is best kept clean and brushed, and you can do that just as well yourself at home. You're lucky.'

Lindsay had fingered the 'dead-straight mouse' doubtfully.

'I've never thought myself particularly *lucky*,' she stated dubiously.

'Then it's time you started counting your blessings,' Carleen replied tartly. 'In the first place, you were lucky that Mum and Dad took you in at all, and I personally think you've fallen on your feet being able to share a unit like this with me. You could have ended up alone, couldn't you, in some crappy boarding place?'

Lindsay scraped the last of the New Zealand blue-cod from the bowl, and placed the last lid, with some finality, on the last vol-au-vent. Blindly she stared out of the window as she rinsed her hands under the kitchen taps and dried her fingers absently.

Carleen's unit, high up on Dover Heights, had a breathtaking view of the harbour. The water today was green rather than blue, choppy with the salt-spumed restlessness of foamy 'white horses' that broke before the stiff sea breeze. Yachts of all descriptions scudded about. Sails of many colours darted and dipped, hoist by every type of craft, from the jauntily weaving dinghies to the thrusting eighteen-footers and the more stately twelve metres leaning into the wind. The headlands loomed above, jutting like stone-struck warriors on guard, impressively aloof from the dizzy gaiety enacted by the myriad craft in the sparkling water below, impervious to the suck and swell of the Pacific breakers that pounded hungrily against their feet.

Lindsay was oblivious to the splendour of the scene.

Her eyes—large, luminous green eyes that were her one singular claim to beauty—were misted and suddenly dreamy. Her mouth—generous and expressive, but too wide and vulnerable altogether—softened into a gentle curve of nostalgia, the mutiny gone. Her tip-tilted nose wrinkled under its scattering of freckles.

Almost she imagined that she could smell the bush!

Not the Sydney bush. Not the harbour fringe of eucalypt, nor the mangrove of the northern inlets, nor the banksia and bottlebrush of Kuringai. Not any of those, no.

What Lindsay imagined for a moment that she could smell was the scent of the *real* bush—the country place where she had been born. She had only been six years old when her parents had met with that fatal accident and she had been taken away to the city by her mother's dutiful cousin, but still she could remember those warm, earthy, country smells. There had been a grove of citrus trees at the side of the house, oily and pungent when the leaves were wetted by rain; sweet-perfumed wattle on dark-trunked, blue-foliaged boughs, all fuzzed with clusters of golden-yellow balls; delicate gum-blossom, creamy and fragile. The orchards had been riotous with scented blooms, cerise and pink and white, and after that there had been the fruit, clinging lavishly to sagging branches—apples, peaches, nectarines, apricots, warm to the hand, juicy and luscious—and after those, the plums and winter pears.

Her recollections, dimmed by her youth and the passage of time, had taken on a Utopian quality. Her childhood now seemed to her to have been one of happiness, of super-abundance.

It was difficult to know exactly which of her memories were real, which imagined. She was almost certain that she could remember a pony, a squat little skewbald fellow called Taffy. There had been several dogs, too, living in kennels under the trees at the back of the house. She had been secretly afraid of their bouncing enthusiasm when they ran up to lick her. She could remember tractors, gay with bright paint, droning monotonously over the paddocks as their ploughs churned the soil to a rich tilth, and she still carried in her mind the vague image of a man called Bill, who had allowed her to ride on the footplate as he ploughed, and who had given her boiled sweets from his pocket.

Lindsay could not recall a single jarring note in that secure life in the country. If there had been any unhappy moments, they had been confined to mere trivialities, such as her secret fear of the dogs.

Her real unhappiness had come later.

Mulling it over, she could only conclude, in fairness, that no one was to blame—certainly not the cousins whom she now called Uncle and Aunt, and to whom she would always feel a measure of gratitude for the way in which they had stepped into the breach. They had never actually complained about the additional commitment her presence represented, and it was almost certainly unintentional that they had made Lindsay conscious that she was a nuisance from the very outset. They had placed her in a boarding-school—not the exclusive establishment to which they had sent their own daughter, Carleen, but a quite adequate institution which gave her a proper education, and attended to her physical well-being and development while conveniently ignoring the spiritual wilderness into which a small, lonely child had been plunged.

Even at school, Lindsay reflected, she had been a doormat. Shyness, uncertainty, and a total lack of affection at her aunt's house, had all combined to render her withdrawn and self-effacing. She was demonstrative and warm-hearted by nature, but soon learned to curb and suppress these qualities in herself, for fear of a rebuff. She had been unremarkable on the sports field, average in the classroom. In her final year, the headmistress had advised a business course, as Lindsay would be expected to support herself at the earliest opportunity—the uncle and aunt had made this clear in an interview relating to vocational guidance, and Lindsay, who had no particular strong bent in any direction, had been glad to

9

avail herself of her senior's advice. She had worked diligently, yearning for the time when she could regard herself as independent, no longer a burden upon her relatives. She had followed up her school commercial course with a year of advanced tuition at a special college, and when she passed out, she was proficient not only at shorthand and typing, but also at book-keeping and elementary accountancy.

The position which she held at present called for neither of these latter qualifications. Perhaps, if she had had a more positive personality, she might have projected herself better at all those interviews, she thought now, wistfully. Instead, she had been miserably shy and over-anxious, terrified that she would be turned down, that those other, more confident applicants would be accepted in her stead.

They were, of course!

Lindsay was learning the hard way!

She knew she had only herself to blame. She had gone home in a mood of bitter self-reproach, and in a fit of reckless despair had blued her entire savings on a natty little linen suit—the sort which her rivals had been wearing at those interviews! It was a basic suit of uncluttered simplicity and excellent cut, and Lindsay was surprised at its improving effect, not only upon her physical aspect, but upon her morale. Gazing at her reflection in the mirror, she had seen a slender, well-proportioned figure, of medium height, dressed in a subtle shade of muted olive that livened the green in her wide, beautiful eyes. Her fly-away hair was flattened submissively against her ears. Her legs, encased in pretty, honey-coloured nylons, seemed depressingly long and coltish to her critical appraisal, but quite neat, nevertheless, and she had lightened her old shoes with a new sand colour to match her cotton gloves.

The overall effect pleased Lindsay. Her wide mouth curved into an approving smile. Perhaps a touch of lipstick? Those other girls had! Carefully she rouged her lips with a soft peach colour and went, almost gaily, to her next interview.

Half an hour later, her gaiety had subsided, but an aura of confidence remained. Lindsay knew it was that pretty suit!

She also knew that, when she took it off and placed it back on its hanger, the new-found poise would probably get hung up along with the suit. But who cared? For the moment—and *that* was what mattered!—she knew that she felt good and looked good.

Another half-hour, and Lindsay had acquired a passable job as a stenographer with a respectable firm, and when she took off the olive linen that night, she smoothed it out with careful affection before putting it away, because she knew that its magic had procured her her independence.

At least, she had *thought* her independence was assured—but her uncle and aunt had had other ideas.

'That's nice for you, Lindsay,' they had said when she told them. 'Now that you can support yourself, you will be able to move in with Carleen. What a good thing she has that extra room!'

'With—*Carleen?* But I thought——'

Lindsay was dismayed. Carleen, five years her senior, had never treated Lindsay with anything but scant civility, or in her kinder moments, amused patronage. Her beauty, poise, and assurance served only to highlight Lindsay's own feelings of inadequacy, and since she had become established in the top flight of models, she had scarcely bothered with the younger cousin who, to use her own frequent description, had been 'foisted' on them.

'What did you think?'

'Well'—Lindsay hesitated, striving for tact—'I thought that at last I would be able to strike out on my own, and relieve you of your responsibility for me. You've both been wonderful, and I'm enormously grateful, Aunt, but you have your own lives to lead, things you both want to do, and I just thought I'd like to be—well—self-supporting as soon as possible.'

'You *will* be self-supporting.' Aunt Evelyn sounded impatient. 'Naturally you will contribute to the upkeep of the flat. It will be far more economical for Carleen to run it on two salaries than one, and a great comfort to us to know that you are there to do things for her. A model's life is extraordinarily demanding, and you know how hopeless that dear child has always been at anything domestic. In her position, she has to entertain a great deal—one has to keep up appearances, you know, and you will be able to relieve her of some of the more mundane tasks in the flat. You're much better at them than she is.'

Lindsay stared soberly at the woman who had taken her into her home so readily. (Where might she be otherwise? An orphanage?)

'I do think you might be more gracious about it, Lindsay,' pursued Aunt Evelyn crisply. 'After all we've done for you, surely it's little enough to expect of you? You need not mix with Carleen's friends—in fact, I'm sure she would prefer you to keep in the background. You're hardly their type, and you've always liked to efface yourself whenever possible, so it should suit you both very well. Your uncle and I have this cruise to Japan coming up shortly, too, if you remember. I shall shut up the house, and go away with a peaceful mind. Surely that's not too much to ask for? A little peace of mind, after all we've done for you? If you *are* enormously grateful, as you say you are, then now is your chance to prove it.'

'Very well, Aunt,' Lindsay had replied quietly. 'Does Carleen know? When shall I move my things?'

'Yes, she knows. We've discussed it with her, and she agrees that you share with her, so long as you do your bit. Remember, not many young girls are able to go to their very first job from a luxury flat, so it's to your advantage, too.'

'I'll do my best,' she had been assured with all the sincerity at Linday's command.

And I *have* done my best, Lindsay told herself now, wearily surveying the trays of food which she had come home early to prepare, Carleen having warned that she herself would be late because of a hair appointment.

She *had* done her best, but she was not quite sure how much longer she would be capable of carrying on like this.

Life with Carleen was anything but easy. It was a time-consuming job on its own, without trying to combine it with an office situation. After more than a year of it, Lindsay felt tired to her very bones, and she knew that her work was suffering. Often she dragged herself home through the peak-hour bustle, only to have to whisk around the unit, tidying up Carleen's clothes, ironing garments which her cousin had left laid out with a note pinned to them—'Be a darling, Lindsay', those notes always pleaded disarmingly—hurriedly preparing innumerable dinners à deux, from which she knew she was expected to efface herself with some tactful excuse when Carleen's swain of the moment should appear, or more frequently, like tonight, assembling an array of food and cocktails for 'some of the crowd'. Here again, Lindsay was discouraged from putting in an appearance.

'That's marvellous!' Carleen could be generous with her praise. 'They look perfectly delicious, Lindsay! Now, don't you bother hanging around. You don't really hear much noise from your room, do you, sweet? A good thing it's furthest from the lounge. See you in the morning, then— if I'm awake before you leave for the office. Or would you like me to bring you a coffee later—we'll be making some, I'm sure?'

'No, don't bother, Carleen. Goodnight.'

Lying in her bed, listening to the hubbub of voices, the laughter that sometimes reached screaming point, and which kept her awake far into the night, Lindsay often felt like screaming herself—only it would not have been a scream of merriment, but of sheer hysteria and desperation! She would try to close her mind to those disturbing sounds. Endeavouring to coax herself into that evasive state of sleep, she would conjure up childhood memories of peaceful country life—of lucerne plots with fat sheep grazing, willows trailing their green fronds in the slow-running creek, the lonely cry of a mopoke in the still bush dawn.

It was always the same after one of Carleen's parties. Lindsay's alarm would rouse her, and, heavy-eyed, she would crawl from the sheets, dress hurriedly, and attack the mountain of washing-up which Carleen had stacked in the kitchenette. Before she left for work, she generally managed to empty the ash-trays, put away the spare glasses, and marvel at the way in which Carleen contrived to sleep through the din. How lovely she looked, with her long blonde tresses spread around her, one arm outflung—like a sleeping Prin-

13

cess, Lindsay thought wryly, except for the scattering of dainty, brief undergarments flung carelessly on to the foot of the bed. A Princess would doubtless have had a servant to remove them and tidy the bed-chamber, but Lindsay herself had no intention of going as far as that!

This evening, Lindsay found herself asking the same old question. How much longer could she go on? Carleen had been more demanding of late, and was not slow, when Lindsay tried to make her see how much she already had to do, in reminding her of her debt to her own parents. It was the cruellest form of moral blackmail, but Carleen did not hesitate to apply it whenever it suited her to do so.

Tonight, more than ever before, Lindsay experienced a quiet sense of despair, of longing to escape. As she stared bleakly from the window, up there on Dover Heights, watching the yachts returning to their moorings in the gathering darkness without really seeing them at all, a poem which she had always loved came unbidden to her mind:

'In my wild erratic fancy, visions come to me of Clancy
    Gone a-droving down the Cooper where the Western
        drovers go;
    As the stock are slowly stringing, Clancy rides behind
        them singing,
    For the drover's life has pleasures that the townsfolk
        never know.'

Lindsay spoke the next verse aloud, savouring each line.

'And the bush has friends to meet him, and their
        kindly voices greet him
    In the murmur of the breezes and the river on its
        bars,
    And he sees the vision splendid of the sunlit plains
        extended,
    And at night the wondrous glory of the everlasting
        stars.'

Preoccupied as she was with her 'vision splendid', she had

not heard Carleen's key in the lock, and was unaware of her presence until a prolonged sigh of exasperation sounded from the kitchen doorway.

'Lindsay, what *are* you doing? Have you got everything ready? They'll be here soon, you know.' Carleen's voice was sharp.

'Yes, I know.' Lindsay came out of her trance.

'Well, stop standing there spouting Banjo Paterson—if you've nothing better to do, you may press my blouse. And for the love of God, don't moon around quoting poetry in front of my friends, will you? They'll think you're odder than they already do—and in any case, Paterson's positively old hat, or didn't you know?'

Without waiting for an answer, Carleen took the garment to which she had referred from the laundry basket, handed it to her cousin, and disappeared. Moments later, Lindsay could hear the shower running, and Carleen's voice humming the latest hit as she turned herself beneath the spray.

Abstractedly, Lindsay switched on the iron, pulled the board down from its wall supports.

How had the rest of the poem gone? She couldn't remember the next few verses.

'And something, something, something—something, something, la, dee, da,' she muttered, spreading the blouse over the board.

Yes, that was it!

'And I somehow rather fancy that I'd like to change
    with Clancy,
  Like to take a turn at droving, where the seasons
    come and go,
  While he faced the round eternal of the cash-book and
    the journal—
  But I doubt he'd suit the office, Clancy of the Over-
    flow.'

Lindsay's generous mouth curved a little bitterly.

No, he wouldn't have suited the office, any more than she

15

did herself. She was a misfit, just as Clancy would have been if he had had to forsake the freedom of the plains for her sort of nine-to-five employment in the city.

> *'And I sometimes rather fancy that I'd like to change with Clancy.'*

Oh, *how* she would like to change! Only Lindsay herself knew how trapped she felt, here in this unit with Carleen. She was just a cypher, really—a pair of hands that did things which were useful to her cousin, uncomplainingly, unquestioningly, because of that debt. *Always* there was that debt! Lindsay was asking herself now how long it took to pay off a debt of such magnitude. All of your life, maybe?

She shuddered at the prospect. She could imagine herself as an old, bent woman, still stooped over this very ironing-board, saying, 'Yes, Carleen,' 'No, Carleen.'

'Haven't you finished?' Her cousin spoke from the doorway, wafting a cloud of French perfume into the small kitchen.

Carleen's hair was still confined in a shower-cap, and there was cream on her face, but standing there in her quilted housecoat and swansdown-trimmed mules, she managed to look as glamorous as though she were posing for some perfumerie commercial.

'Thanks'—as Lindsay handed her the blouse—'Have you put those pastry things in the oven? Well, switch it on, for goodness' sake! Another few minutes, and they'll be starting to arrive. What *has* got into you tonight?'

Lindsay was wondering the very same thing. Whatever had possessed her to go into a dream world like that, when there was so much yet to be done? How could she possibly have forgotten to switch on the oven? Oh dear! She'd be caught now, most probably!

In feverish haste, she took glasses from the sideboard, assembled bottles together, carried through the plates of savouries, and put olives and mixed nuts into small bowls which she dotted about the lounge. After that, she got ice from the refrigerator, crushed it, and placed it in its own thermally-protected container.

She was in the act of carrying this through when the door-bell rang.

'Drat! Someone's early!' Carleen's voice, muffled and annoyed, came from her bedroom. 'Answer that, will you, Lindsay. I'll be out in a couple of minutes.'

Lindsay glanced from her apron down to her old shoes. Then, with a shrug, half humorous, half despairing, she went to the front door.

Carleen's photographer—the one for whom Lindsay had made the oyster cocktail a few evenings ago—took in her shabby appearance with one comprehensive sweep of his light-blue eyes, and then averted them politely.

They were quite nice eyes, really, and his smiling mouth was pleasant, if not exactly strong. Lindsay decided that Carleen had sometimes done a lot worse!

'Good evening. Am I too early?'

'No, not at all. Won't you please come in, and I'll give you a drink while you wait. Carleen won't be long, and I dare say some of the others will arrive soon, too.'

He followed her along the hall to the sitting-room.

'You must be the little cousin,' he observed quite kindly. 'The one who hates parties and people.'

'Yes, that's right.' Lindsay forced a stilted smile. Was that what Carleen told them? Oh well, what did it matter? There was nothing to be gained by defending herself to this man. It was pure chance that she had not managed to escape before he arrived, and his definition of her, while strangely hurtful, was of no real consequence, after all.

'Martini? Or would you prefer something here?' She indicated the bottles on the sideboard.

'Martini would be very nice. Dry, please.' He watched with interest as she speared an olive, and laid it deftly across the filled glass. 'Tell me,' accepting his drink, 'what have you got against people? Or parties either, for that matter? You seemed to do that with the efficiency of long experience.'

Lindsay flushed.

'N-nothing. Nothing, of course,' she declared with hasty politeness.

'Then why not honour us with your presence this evening—just for once? I don't mind being left alone while you go and change—not that you aren't perfectly charming as you are,' he added, with what to Lindsay appeared to be spontaneous gallantry.

'Oh no, I couldn't! I mean——'

'What *do* you mean?' He was studying her closely.

'Well, I mean, I just couldn't. I've—er—things to do.'

'Don't you want to?'

'N-not particularly. I don't know any of Carleen's friends,' she pointed out lamely.

'Has anyone ever told you that you have an interesting face, little cousin?' His abrupt change of topic took her by surprise. 'That bone-structure would photograph well.'

Lindsay smiled. What a line! All Carleen's friends had a line, one way or another. You expected it of them. They were given to extravagant statements and exaggerated phrases, and their conversation was usually quite generously spattered with 'darlings' and 'sweethearts'.

Knowing this, she simply smiled, making no attempt to reply.

'There has to be first time, doesn't there?' he persisted. 'What are you smiling at? You look as enigmatic as the Mona Lisa! Why not come tonight—with my support, of course! I've helped launch countless young lovelies into society, you know.'

'Lindsay can't possibly come.' Carleen's voice came sweetly from behind them. 'Such a pity! She has other things to do, haven't you, pet? Now, do let her go, John. It's not fair to the poor girl to let her get caught by the others looking like that, is it? You, of all people, should know women's little vanities by now. We hate to be discovered without our *face* on, darling.' She gave a tinkling laugh.

'Some faces can stand it.' Lindsay caught his words as she fled from the room, thankful to take the opportunity to escape, but her cousin's reply was lost in the chinking of ice as Carleen helped herself to a drink.

Soon after that, the bell rang again, and for some time the front door remained open while 'the crowd' poured in.

18

The same old routine followed. As the party gathered momentum, the hum of conversation caused the flat to literally vibrate with the buzz of human voices. The sounds of speech and laughter, the clink of glasses, the beat of the record-player, chased each other in and out of Lindsay's brain as she moved about her room, and finally went to bed.

Her clock showed her that it was two o'clock before the noise began to diminish. She could hear goodbyes being called every now and then, and the bang of the front door as people departed.

Soon there were only two voices left—Carleen's and the photographer's.

'Coffee, John? Let's make some in the kitchen, now that we're alone.'

'Sounds cosy,' the deeper voice agreed.

They were there for quite some time, and Lindsay relaxed. The low exchange of talk had an almost soporific effect on her after the previous abandoned din, and she was on the very brink of sleep when Carleen and the man passed her door again on the way to the lobby.

'—wonderful evening, sweet.' His voice. 'Make it by twelve-thirty if you can, tomorrow, will you, Carleen?'

'I'll try, darling. I hope I wake up. I mustn't be late if Sarino himself is to be there, must I? It's my big chance!'

'Wrong, my pet. I'm your big chance, and don't you forget it! Although I'll admit Sarino's handy with a lens.' A pause. 'Why don't you bring that little cousin along with you when you come? She's got a challenging face—a sort of *undiscovered* quality, quite appealing—and those green eyes are remarkable. Green as the sea itself. In fact, that's what I see her as—a seascape. One of those *gran turismo* poster backgrounds, if you like—you know, the cliff road winding away, and in the foreground the sophisticates, watched from a distance by this green-eyed water-nymph in the briefest little bikini you ever saw—all big green eyes and green sea spray——'

'Darling, you've gone quite, quite mad. It must be the champagne.' Carleen's voice was dry, amused. 'She'd be utterly hopeless. She would freeze at the mere thought, and

19

you'd embarrass her. She's full of inhibitions, you know.'

'She didn't strike me as quite that.'

'Well, she is. In fact, she's as dull as ditchwater. Quite the dreariest flat-mate possible.' There was a bite in that cool, floating tone. Lindsay, now sitting upright in her thin cotton pyjamas, listened with a sort of awestruck compulsion, shivered. She wished she hadn't begun to listen, because now, to her horror, she found she couldn't stop. Even in her humiliation, something drove her to it!

'Don't you like her? Why have her, then? Why not get someone else to share—someone who *isn't* as dull as ditchwater?'

'Oh, John, I'd love to, you know that, but she—well—Carleen's voice became honeyed, almost, one might say, *sacrificial*—'I can't let her down, John, the poor child. Do you know, she actually *begged* me to take her in, and what was I to do? My parents had had her for years, and I couldn't let them do it for ever, could I—limit their lives in that tedious way? No, I decided that it was my turn to offer her a roof, even though she cramps my style, too, just the teeniest little bit. I told her that she could stay here for just as long as she needed me,' Carleen finished on a positively magnanimous note.

John's voice came.

'Or you needed her.'

'*What* did you say?'

There was a rich, amused chuckle—the man's.

'You heard me, darling,' he said smoothly. 'I said, for as long as *you* need *her*. Oh, come off it, Carleen, be honest! We're birds of a feather, and I can read you like a book. We're both unscrupulous, and we both *use* people, so why not admit it? We're even going to *use* Sarino tomorrow, aren't we? You're using your dull little cousin for all the nasty little domesticities that you yourself can't bear, and so long as she copes with the sordid, everyday domestic routine, you'll keep her. Well, I want to use her, too—or her eyes, at any rate. That's all I want, sweetie, just her eyes, so you needn't worry that she'll spoil things for us.' He adopted a more persuasive tone. 'You have my word, Carleen—from

20

one rogue to another! So take that jealous look off your pretty face, you little spitfire. Of course, I'll have to play her along just a little bit at first, to get her co-operation. You and I will both know it doesn't mean a thing, and it shouldn't be too difficult. I don't think your little cousin has ever had much attention from the male of the species, and I can be quite devastating when I like. *You* should know that! And remember, my interest is solely professional. If you don't bring her along, I'll be really disappointed.'

'She'll be working. How do you expect me to get round that?' Carleen's voice was sullen.

'You'll get round it, sweet, just as you get your way in other things.'

'And if I don't?'

'Then *I'll* get round Sarino.'

'You wouldn't!'

'I would. If I'm to be disappointed, then I'll make certain that you are, too.'

'Then I'm afraid you'll just have to *be* disappointed, *both* of you,' came Lindsay's strangled interruption from the doorway.

She had meant to sound calm, even sarcastic, but instead her voice was husky with hurt, as she stood there confronting them, heedless of the ridiculous figure she must present in her checked cotton pyjamas, with bare feet and ruffled hair. Her whole body was shaking with outrage and humiliation. It was no use trying to carry the thing off with elaborate sophistication—such a measure was quite beyond Lindsay just then!

'Lindsay!' Carleen uttered shrilly, then, collecting herself—'Darling, did we wake you up, you poor sweet?'

Lindsay threw back her head and met her cousin's eyes. There was about her a curious air of dignity, as if some hidden force had taken possession of her and was guiding her actions, telling her just what must be done, what must be said.

'No,' she returned evenly, 'you did not wake me up, and I am not your sweet. I am merely your dull flat-mate, whom you told could stay here just as long as I needed you—wasn't

21

that how you put it? Well, it will be a relief to you to know that I *don't* need you any longer, Carleen, so you can start looking for someone else to share straight away. I shall be out of here by the end of next week.'

'But, *darling*——'

'As for you'—Lindsay addressed herself now to the man—'there is just one thing that I would like you to know. You were quite right in thinking that I've had little attention from the male of the species, and having just heard your own sickening revelations, I count myself lucky to have been spared. Goodnight!'

'Well done, Green Eyes! I guessed there was a bit of hidden spirit under that submissive little exterior. How about that, Carleen!'

'Shut up, John!' Carleen snapped. 'You keep out of this, you'll only make things worse.' She advanced towards Lindsay, arms outstretched placatingly. 'Lindsay darling, you don't really mean that. You're tired and a bit put out. I'm sorry we were so noisy. You've every reason to feel irritable, but you can't be serious.'

'I'm perfectly serious, Carleen. I'm leaving in a week.'

'Dear, don't be *silly*. Where would you go?'

'I don't know yet, but I'll find somewhere,' Lindsay retorted hardily.

'I think Green Eyes really *is* serious, sweetie! Could be you have a problem on your hands.'

'John, for heaven's sake, go, if all you can do is to stand there being clever!'

'Don't hurry away because of me,' Lindsay told him politely, although inside she felt quite numb with shock, 'because I'm going back to bed in any case.'

Not waiting even to observe his reaction, she went blindly in the direction of her bedroom, and once within its sanctuary, turned the key in the lock and huddled miserably between the sheets.

Her heart was racing at a threatening pace, and tears, unshed, stung her eyelids. When Carleen banged and rattled on the door some minutes later, she was thankful that she could pretend to be asleep.

CHAPTER 2

NEXT morning it was no surprise to Lindsay to find that she looked as dreadful as she felt!

That beastly photographer would not give twopence for her green eyes today, she decided grimly, observing their puffed lids and reddened rims in the mirror as she dragged on her clothes.

Her eyes! That was all he had wanted—to *use* her, or a part of her, just as Carleen did!

And she had actually been foolish enough to be warmed by his evidence of sincerity, had thought him quite charming when she had shown him in last night. She had permitted herself to be flattered by his complimentary phrases, only to discover that he had not meant them—or, at least, not in the way she had supposed. There was no kindness in him after all, only ambition and selfishness.

Lindsay patted her face with a cold, damp flannel, and shivered at the extent of her own gullibility. What an idiot she had been! And how pathetically little she knew about men! Familiar as she was with Carleen's spiteful ways and catty remarks about her fellow-creatures, she had stupidly thought that men were above such feline artifices, that those were confined to a woman's world alone. Now she knew better! She had been far too ready to be deceived, because nobody had ever praised her in such a warm fashion before. She had even been stupid enough to believe the man had wanted her at the party because he had found her attractive. Even though she had refused, it had been encouraging that a sophisticated friend of Carleen's had actually begged her to stay—that he had sought her out because he found her own particular brand of shy charm irresistible.

Something inside Lindsay shrank with humiliation as she recalled the extent of her disillusion. She had responded as a flower might to the promise of sunshine, unfurling its petals tentatively to those warming rays, only to find itself drenched and frayed by a sudden douche of icy rain. For Lindsay, the effect was as bracing and astringent as a slap on the face.

Her longing for independence had hardened into resolution to actually achieve her freedom from Carleen and her kind. Bitterness was useless, a corroding emotion if ever there was one. Distrust, though, was harder to eradicate. It would be a long time, if ever, before Lindsay would believe in other people, but right now it was supremely necessary to believe in *herself*.

The realisation of that need enabled her to face Carleen's ensuing pleas and tantrums with an equanimity she was far from feeling. The other girl begged, cajoled, and finally theatened, but Lindsay remained adamant. After a prolonged bout of sulks and silence, Carleen resorted to sarcasm.

'Who'd want you, anyway? You won't find it easy to get someone to share with you. It's like living with a saintly dormouse, heaven knows!'

'I'll find a place,' returned Lindsay imperturbably, pleased to find her newly acquired courage a foil for Carleen's venom.

'I'm not so sure.' Carleen smiled rather waspishly. 'Word has sort of got around that as a flat-mate you're a dead loss, darling. The general impression seems to be that I've finally turned you out.'

'But'—Lindsay blinked in bewilderment—'that's not true! You know it's not, and so do I. And so does Mr—er—what was his name, the photographer?'

'John?' Her cousin's laugh was brittle, taunting. 'He's forgotten all about the other night. I asked him to, and he agreed, so long as I do things his way professionally. Why should that bother me? He's the tops, after all.' She shrugged. 'Haven't you ever heard of honour among thieves, pet? It's very convenient at times.'

'Sydney's a big place.' Lindsay tried to appear sanguine, to stop the flutterings of apprehension inside herself. 'It's ridiculous to suggest that you can influence a whole city against me, Carleen.'

'Maybe.' The other lifted her shoulders again, lit a cigarette and leaned back in her chair, blowing a thoughtful smoke ring. 'On the other hand, most people will ask where you've been living before, won't they, and with whom?'

'I can live alone.'

Sitting in the bus later, wedged between a hard-faced businessman immersed in the financial pages and a plump housewife who smelt strongly of onions, Lindsay prided herself upon the dignity of her reply. It had been an effective exit line, at any rate, she thought, recalling with a sudden spurt of fun the expressions that had chased themselves across her cousin's lovely face as she picked up her handbag and walked to the door. Dislike, frustration, helpless rage had distorted Carleen's classic features, and yet she managed, as always, to appear incredibly beautiful in a quite frightening way. She had usually succeeded in getting her own wishes met in everything, simply because of that ineradicable beauty, and she had been none too pleased at having her way challenged by Lindsay, of all people.

It was stuffy in the bus, although a welcome shaft of air from the platform fanned the long rear seat into which Lindsay had squeezed herself.

They jolted down into Double Bay, with its gay boutiques and pavements alive with shoppers, and then up the hill towards Edgecliff. At the Cross the housewife got out, and her place was immediately taken by another of the standing passengers. The businessman never raised his eyes from his paper, dedicating his entire attention to it in the way that regular commuters do, oblivious to his surroundings, incurious as to his fellow-travellers. No doubt a sort of built-in radar would tell him when his own destination was near, and he would fold up his newspaper with automatic precision, preparatory to leaving the bus, without even bothering to glance about him.

He had finished the financial columns now, and had turned another page, folding the paper back upon itself to render it more manageable in the confined space.

Lindsay's eyes wandered over the newsprint only vaguely,

her mind absorbed in her own problems.

Advertisements, he was at now.

Registered teacher. Works Superintendent. Cost Accountant. Salesman with Ambition. Deputy Director of Public Relations. The next advertisement was enclosed in a neat black square, and printed in heavier type.

Somewhere in Lindsay's inattentive brain, a little bell rang. It was an unexpected little bell, but it rang loudly enough to bring her eyes, already passing on to Stationery Representative and District Midwife, back to the message inside the neat black square. The message was to the effect that Gundooee Station was needing a book-keeper, experienced, single preferred, salary negotiable on appointment. It also told the reader how many sheep and cattle and sub-bores Gundooee Station had—the first two were in thousands, the last in single figures. Sub-bores, whatever *they* were, came a poor third on Gundooee Station, decided Lindsay whimsically.

She read on.

'Airstrip eighty miles west of Emmadanda. The successful applicant will be responsible to the station manager, but personal initiative rewarded. Enclose qualifications, own handwriting. All communications answered.'

Well, Lindsay asked the little bell reprovingly, what is there to ring about in that? It was, after all, just another advertisement, like the Cost Accountant and the Salesman with Ambition.

The bus groaned on, and the businessman turned to sport. Races, mostly.

Gundooee.

What a strange name! Lindsay wondered what it meant. Perhaps it did not have a meaning at all. Maybe it was just a name, but it had a nice friendly sound. Emmadanda, too, was pretty and quaint. Lindsay thought she could imagine the sort of place Emmadanda would be. It would be tiny and clean, with narrow streets lined with jacaranda trees, all mauve and drooping, a pretty country town held in the arm of a willow-fringed river.

Lindsay's green eyes became soft and misty.

Even sitting here, she could smell the cool, wet willow smell of that river, could hear the shallow singing of the rippling water, feel the caressing tree-clad shade of its peaceful bends. There would be orchards and lucerne plots and a neat, red-roofed house somewhere nearby, and that house would be Gundooee. At least, it would be *quite* near. Eighty miles, the advertisement had said, but it had implied that Emmadanda was desirably close, hadn't it?

Lindsay sighed.

Gun-doo-ee. What a pretty, friendly name! A 'bush' name, with a 'bush' sound of friendship and welcome.

> *'And the bush has friends to meet him, and their*
> *kindly voices greet him.'*

She pushed the haunting words to the back of her mind and stood up as her own stop came in sight. Other alighting passengers jostled, propelling her forward, as she made her way rather dreamily to the exit.

All along the street, that refrain seemed to echo, her own footsteps keeping time with it. It was a lilting measure, that one of Banjo Paterson's, easy to walk to. *Too* easy! At lunchtime, it was still with her, when she bought coffee and a sandwich, and carried her paper cup and packet to the park bench in the gardens opposite the office block in which she worked.

'Emma-danda, Emma-danda,' trilled a bird in the bushes behind her seat. 'Gun-doo-ee, Gun-doo-ee,' whispered the lapping water at the base of the near-by fountain.

Some madness seemed to have taken possession of Lindsay. I'm crazy, she thought, even as she was buying a copy of that newspaper and stuffing it into her hold-all.

They'll want a man, anyway, she was telling herself all the way home on the bus. It's meant for a man, quite obviously, although they don't say.

But why should it matter, to *them*? coaxed a tiny, persuasive voice within, as she walked towards the lift. So long as the 'someone' can keep books, why should *they* mind?

With a name like Lindsay, it could be either, couldn't it?

suggested the small, persistent devil inside her again, as she pushed the button and swept upwards to the top of the Dover Heights unit-block.

Lindsay Hallingham Dutten. There was definitely a masculine ring to that name, especially if you couldn't see the luminous green eyes, sensitively curving mouth, fly-away brown hair, and fragilely coltish limbs of its indubitably feminine possessor!

Thank goodness for Grandfather Hallingham! breathed Lindsay, as she fitted her key in the Yale lock and let herself into the flat. There had been times when she'd hankered for a 'Jane', or 'Margaret', even 'Adelaide' or 'Euphemia', but now there was a satisfyingly nondescript sound about her middle name that gave her cause for gratitude. If anything, it leaned slightly to a suggestion of male ownership rather than complete sexlessness, she decided, and for her present purpose that was all to the good!

Lindsay made herself a cup of tea to still the fluttering unease within herself at the boldness of her intention. It was difficult to sit in the kitchenette, perched up there on the heights above the harbour, watching the yachts and ferries and hydrofoils in the sea below, when already you could feel the peace and stillness of the bush about you, smell the gum-trees, see the paddocks full of sheep in the country sunshine.

Presently she got up, rinsed her cup and saucer, and went to the bureau in the lounge. It was gratifying to find that all but one of her certificates made no mention of her actual sex.

She put the offending one aside, and studied the others thoughtfully.

'This is to certify that the bearer Lindsay H. Dutten has satisfied the Board of Examiners——'

'that Lindsay Hallingham Dutten has passed with merit the required examination in Advanced Book-keeping——'

'A Pass with Credit has been awarded to Lindsay Hallingham Dutten by the Examining Board of the College——'

She was sitting on the floor, with the certificates still spread out around her, when her cousin came in.

'Don't tell me they've sacked you from the office as *well*?'

Carleen spoke almost with relish as she took in the scene.

'No, but—Carleen, I'm going to try for another post. Look!' In her enthusiasm and excitement, Lindsay could not sustain her own antagonism, even in the face of Carleen's unfriendliness. She opened the newspaper, and pointed out the advertisement. 'See that? I'm going to try for it, Carleen. A job in the country—just what I've always longed for!'

The other girl read the item, handed it back.

'You must be out of your tiny mind, Lindsay. That's obviously a man's position, you twit! Why don't you look in the Governess column if you're determined on country life——' She yawned. 'Boring as it is, it might just suit you down to the ground.'

Lindsay flushed, half defiant, half guilty.

'It doesn't *say* it's for a man, Carleen. It just says it's for a book-keeper, doesn't it?'

'Darling, you know perfectly well it's for a man,' drawled Carleen. 'Why pretend? For heaven's sake, come down to earth.'

'But they don't *say*, do they? And I need never have realised, need I? If I could land it, they wouldn't know until I got there that I wasn't a man, and once they saw that my work is efficient, they wouldn't mind, I'm *sure*. All they want is a book-keeper, and with a name like Lindsay, I could be either, couldn't I, anyway?'

Carleen raised one eyebrow. It was a very expressive eyebrow, neatly shaped, and she lifted it quite beautifully, in a way that suggested scepticism, amusement, and a certain element of surprise.

'Well, *well*! What duplicity, from a saintly dormouse! I didn't think you were capable of such deception. Don't tell me you're human, after all? You can hardly accuse John and me after this little revelation, can you?'

'It's not really deception,' mumbled Lindsay damply, red-cheeked and a bit miserable now. 'I mean, they don't *say*——'

Carleen studied her uncertain face, shook her own head.

'You aren't likely to get it, anyway, so why waste time talking about it? By the end of the week, you'll doubtless have come to your senses, and will realise what a good wicket you're on here with me. I'll be quite prepared to overlook your quite atrocious and embarrassing behaviour of the other evening, Lindsay, and we'll just go on as before, so long as you pull your weight about the place.'

With this magnanimous utterance, Carleen went to her bedroom, leaving Lindsay more unhappy, apprehensive, indignant, and determined than she had been before.

'I can't bear it,' she muttered to herself. 'Not another week!'

A few minutes later she was writing with desperation.

'Credentials are enclosed herewith. I am accustomed to positions demanding trust and initiative, and furthermore am free to take up the post immediately. Salary is not of paramount importance, providing employment and surroundings are congenial, and I should be prepared initially to accept the minimum award of remuneration as per scale at present pertaining. I have former experience of, and a marked preference for, country life, and trust that you will seriously and favourably consider my application.

> Yours faithfully,
> Lindsay H. Dutten.'

She signed her name with a flourish, and addressed an envelope to The Manager, Gundooee Station, Via Emmadanda.

Her step was swift and assured as she walked along to the local Post Office and slipped the letter through the slot. It was something to manage a spring in your step, when your palms were actually moist with fright and your heart thudding like a bongo drum!

A week later, Lindsay was walking the same route, but without quite such a spring. She was walking the same route because it was not only the way to the Post Office, but to the taxi stance as well, and the lack of spring was partly because of the weight of the suitcase she carried, but also because of Carleen's farewell scene.

Lindsay's knees trembled as she recalled it.

Her petulant cousin had been unbelievably nasty in every way. Her final reprisal had been the taking back of any clothes which she had bestowed on Lindsay over the past eighteen months. Even though they had been given in a spirit of patronisation, Lindsay had been grateful for them, and had spent a good deal of time shortening hems, mending seams, and sewing on buttons, to make them fashionable and presentable. They had comprised the better part of her wardrobe, and it had been something of a shock to find Carleen snatching them all from their hangers and dumping them on her own bed in a fit of rage when she saw that Lindsay was really serious about leaving.

'I—I thought you'd given them to me,' she had protested rather stupidly, aghast at her cousin's malicious action.

'I *loaned* them to you, which is a very different thing,' Carleen had retorted coldly. 'If you choose to go, you forfeit them, naturally. They'll probably come in handy for my next flat-mate. I shall make sure they go to someone who *appreciates* them, at any rate!'

Lindsay had swallowed her dismay, resumed her packing.

There had not been very much, after that, to put into her cases, and by dint of some rather ruthless cramming, she had been able to fit all her possessions into the one bulging suit-case which she now carried. At least Carleen had saved her the burden of a lot of luggage, she told herself as she panted on her way, smiling half grimly. And if the manager of Gundooee Station was really expecting a male book-keeper in trousers, it could hardly matter to him if the female one who turned up instead had only the suit she stood up in, one cotton sun-dress, and a faded denim skirt to her name! Just so long as she was the perfect *book-keeper*, it couldn't matter at all!

Because it was so early in the morning, there was a taxi waiting at the rank. The city was scarcely astir, the streets almost empty. The rising sun cast long-fingered shadows upon the great columns of sky-scrapers, and the air was warm, gently suffused with the pink light that foretold another hot humid day.

'The station, please—Central.'

Lindsay heaved her case into the taxi-driver's hands and collapsed thankfully into the back seat.

'Central Station,' the driver echoed nasally, and let in the clutch.

Lindsay sat holding her fingers tightly together to stop herself from trembling. She was on her way! This was the final, irrevocable step!

Away down to her right, the harbour could be glimpsed from time to time, calm tracts of sparkling water today, ink-blue, with passing views of jetties and boat-houses, and occasionally a peep at the majestic grey arch of the famous Bridge, now challenged for pride of place among Sydney's landmarks by the petal-shaped domes of the Opera House.

She sank back against the worn leather upholstery and marvelled anew at the miracle of having been chosen, recalling her wonder upon opening her own self-addressed envelope and discovering, not only her returned certificates, but a memo which told her that she had been engaged, and giving travelling instructions as well. It had been signed in a pretty, feminine hand—Vera E. Manning (Mrs.).

Lindsay supposed that Mrs. Manning must be the manager's wife. Perhaps, with the temporary absence of a proper book-keeper, she had been handling his correspondence for him. In that case, they would be very glad to see Lindsay! For her, the fact that it had been Mrs. Manning who had replied was an added guarantee of her own welcome.

'Thank you.'

She paid the driver, and picked up her case again, made her way to the ticket office.

'The end of the line, eh?' the clerk grinned as he punched the date on to her ticket and handed it over.

She was aware of his curious, good-natured scrutiny. Perhaps her hair was flying away again, although it had been smooth when she left the unit. She had kept the window open in the taxi all the way to the station, though, so it was probably in a mess.

She hoped this pretty linen-textured suit would create the same good impression upon Mr. and Mrs. Manning as it had upon her last employer. She would have to take care not to spill anything on it in the train, since it was now the only decent article in her wardrobe! Luckily it was virtually non-crushable, and the muted olive colour was at once cool and practical for travelling. She had wrapped her sand-coloured gloves in a piece of tissue and tucked them into the side pocket of her hold-all. They had been washed last night for the occasion, and Lindsay intended to put them on at the very last minute, just as she arrived at Gundooee, so that they would add to her feeling of neatness and poise.

The train was crowded. By noon the carriage was swelter-ing and stuffy, in spite of the open window and draught from the corridor. Smuts and flies, sticky paper, children crying with heat and exhaustion, a wedge of sunlight across one's face and knee, so fiercely penetrating through the glass that it was sheer relief each time the train changed direction and the burning wedge momentarily disappeared.

Lindsay stared out of the window, determinedly directing her concentration to the passing landscape.

They were over the Great Dividing Range now, the Blue Mountains with their magnificent, plunging gorges and majestic peaks, the ochre-crusted escarpments and impene-trable, eucalypt-choked gullies were behind them.

Memory stirred, painfully, uncertainly, in Lindsay, as they traversed the lower slopes of the west side. Her childhood hovered, half imagined, half recognised. The creeks, the poplars, small lush paddocks, lucerne, orchards, lanes. The same, yet not the same. Familiar enough, though, to imbue in the fragile-limbed girl, looking eagerly out of the window, an almost exquisite sense of homecoming. Her green eyes shone with warmth and expectancy.

Some hours and a couple of hundred miles later, the same green eyes were shining no longer. They were strained with fatigue, wide with dismay, and just the tiniest bit alarmed, too. Lindsay had found her childhood—and lost it again! It was away back there—*hours* and *hours, miles* and *miles*, back there—and the distance between her and it was increasing with every minute that she was being tossed from side to side, alone now in a compartment that swayed with speed as the train seemed suddenly to gather urgency, as if it, too, was

33

wishing the journey over.

And who could blame it? Not Lindsay, certainly!

She closed her dust-rimmed eyes against the blatant glare of the endless wastes outside the window. No more friendly hills and little creeks, warm soils and shining kurrajongs. No more pretty green willows and elegant, slim poplars, lively townships, and well-stocked paddocks.

Here, there was nothing but flat, hard plain, and to Lindsay's apprehensive eyes, it appeared devoid of vegetation and life, except for the odd patch of twisted scrub, and those funny little dumpy bushes that looked desiccated and unattractively steely in colour.

Once her heart was gladdened by the sight of a profusely blooming sea of golden mulga blossom, but for the most part the landscape seemed to her desolate and monotonous and awesomely lonely. The occasional austere railway siding, and sometimes a fettler's hut or high-banked ground tank and windmill were the sole indication of possible human habitation. The few sheep she saw were depressingly lean and wrinkled, with prominent shoulder bones, starved necks and drooping flanks, quite unlike the plump-quartered lambs she thought she could remember.

Once, at a distance, she caught sight of a larger mob, moving slowly along in a cloud of dust, with a drover's plant bringing up the rear, and as the carriages clanked noisily over the sleepers—lickety-split, lickety-split, lickety-split—a kangaroo raised his head, on the alert, and rubbed his furry stomach with his fore-paws.

As the light faded, Lindsay evidenced the strangest metamorphosis in the scene about her. The sky became scorched with flame, seared with gold and scarlet, as the sun sank lower on the ever-distant horizon. The sky colours were harsh in their clarity, but the reflection on the plains was incredibly, wonderfully soft and misty, lending the stretches of gibber and grotesque, stunted trees a rosy dimension of breathtaking beauty.

Lindsay was entranced. Her spirits lifted a little. This could almost be Clancy's 'vision splendid', she thought, wiping the gathering beads of perspiration from her forehead with a handkerchief which in the morning had been crisp and white, but was now as limp and dusty as its owner. She must be nearing journey's end, too. Emmadanda could not be far now.

Emmadanda. That pretty, *pretty* name! Soon she would arrive there, and then there was just a little hop to Gundooee, and then she would be among the friends and kindly voices of the bush, just like the poem had said.

The thought of a long, cold drink, perhaps a salad, and a refreshing bath, almost made Lindsay groan aloud with pleasant anticipation.

With the lowering of the sun, the air became alive with birds—great flocks of brightly coloured parrots, banking clouds of pink and grey galahs, chains of wild duck, all were returning with the coming of night from their daytime feeding grounds to their resting places at the water-holes. In the gathering dusk, a couple of emus, startled by the noise of the train, went pelting off into the scrub with a queer, ungainly, rocking gait, their long legs splaying out in all directions like puppet attachments to their big, plumaged bodies.

At last the pace slackened. When the train finally stopped, Lindsay took down her case, collected her handbag and hold-all, and climbed stiffly down on to the platform.

Not Emmadanda's platform. Lindsay found herself gazing blankly at a completely unfamiliar name.

'Emmadanda?' The man she asked was one of two who had got out of the next carriage. They seemed to be the only other people left on the train besides herself. 'Emmadanda?' He stroked his unshaven chin, peered at her curiously. 'Yer gotta take the motor-train to Emmadanda. It's the end of the line, see. You arst that bloke over there when 'e's leavin'. It's generally about 'arf an hour, once 'e transfers 'is supplies, see.'

'Oh, I see.' Lindsay forced her lips to smile. 'Thank you.'

'Any time.' Her informant spat neatly into the space between the siding and the train, and sauntered after his mate. 'Say, Herb,' she heard him call to the man already busy loading crates and boxes into a single-carriaged motorised affair, 'you gotta passenger fer Emma—a sheila, too, yer lucky coot!'

'That right? You want to swop?' They exchanged grins in the half dark, but Lindsay's own presence now precluded a further exchange. The second man threw a couple of canvas bags into his little motor-train, and then turned to Lindsay.

'*You* wouldn't be L. H. Dutten, I reckon,' he stated tentatively.

'That's right. Lindsay Dutten.'

'Dinkum?'—sceptically. 'Then, in that case, this message is for you.' He fished in the breast pocket of his soiled khaki shirt. 'There's more light up in the cab if you can't see it too good.'

'Er—thanks.' She took the scrap of paper, unfolded it, read the message, her eagerness wilting.

It had no beginning. No end. It simply said—

'Stay at pub in Emma overnight. Mail-plane leaves for Gundooee 10 a.m. Don't miss it.'

'Message received and understood?' The driver slung her case into the rear van compartment, slammed the door.

'Yes, thank you. Understood,' Lindsay mumbled. She felt numb with tiredness, unable to think of anything except this terrible sense of anti-climax. It was, after all, a very crude note, she excused herself.

'Good-oh! It seemed quite clear when I took it over the transceiver, and then I began to wonder who in tarnation to give it to. I reckon I was lookin' out for a man—not that they *said*, one way or the other,' he added quickly, taking in Lindsay's quick flush and arrested expression.

'Is it far?'

'Eh?'

'Emmadanda? Is it far?' If it is, I'll never make it, she was thinking desperately. If it's far, I can't go on, even if it means missing that wretched mail-plane in the morning.

' 'Bout forty minutes, that's all. You must've come all the way, eh? Reckon you look plain tuckered out.'

She smiled wanly.

'Yes, I think I must be—er—tuckered out. I'm glad it's no further than that.'

'Hop in, then. Sit there near the window, and you'll get all

36

the breeze that's goin'.'

'Do you live in Emmadanda?' she asked, above the noise of the motor.

'Gawd, no! I come back here tonight. My missus and the kids is here, see. I just do this Emma run twice a week—to oblige the authorities, like.' He gave her his pleasant grin once more, and after smiling back politely, Lindsay relapsed into silence. Her legs were stiff, cramped, her brain somehow paralysed.

Never mind, she told herself bracingly, if you aren't at Gundooee tonight, with its friendly bush greeting and kindly voices, at least you'll be at Emmadanda. Just forty minutes to that pretty little town with the quaintly pretty name, nestling in the bend of a cool, green river. There might not be jacarandas lining the streets—because Lindsay realised that this was hardly jacaranda country—but there would be a real bush welcome waiting for her at Emmadanda.

> *'And the bush has friends to meet him, and their
> kindly voices greet him
> In the murmur of the breezes, and the river on its
> bars.
> And he sees the vision splendid of the sunlit plans
> extended——'*

Lindsay had seen the sunlit plains—desolate, awesomely lonely, she had been reluctantly forced to acknowledge their splendour in the light of the setting sun. Now the sunlit plains were behind her, and around her—out there in the dark, was only the solitariness of the great Australian bush, but Emmadanda lay ahead.

She eased her weary shoulders, lifted her cheek to the breeze from the window, and took a steadying breath of anticipation. Dear, quaint little Emmadanda was just around the corner—or rather, dead ahead, since there appeared to be no corners on these wide expanses of plain.

'Here we are, then.' The driver drew up without warning, hauling on the brakes, and there was an answering squeal of protest from almost every mechanised part of the motor. He opened the door, waved a hand vaguely into the darkness, and said grandly, 'Emma! There she is!'

'Thank you so much,' Lindsay breathed, to his retreating back, because he had already started to unload his cargo.

She stepped down, looked about her, blinked! Then she looked—and blinked—again. Disbelievingly.

'Is—is *this* Emmadanda?' Her voice was husky, but she managed, somehow, to take her case when the man passed it out to her.

'Mm?' He was totally preoccupied.

'The—the hotel?' she suggested, almost fearfully.

A jerk of the head. 'That's her—the pub. Hardly grand enough to be called a *hotel*, I reckon.'

Or even a *pub*, thought Lindsay bleakly, eyeing the long outline of a tin-roofed shack with misgiving.

'D-do I just go in?' She could scarcely whisper.

'Well, there ain't a commissionaire, if that's what you're waiting for,' came the laconic retort.

'G-goodnight. Goodbye.'

'So long, miss.'

Lindsay picked up her case, looked up and down the street. There was only one, so wide that it wasn't even a thoroughfare, really—just a bit of the hard-baked plain, with a few houses scattered about. They all had the same corrugated iron roofs, shining ghostly in the thin moonlight. One had a window full of tins. Lindsay could see the columns of stacked groceries in the building right next to her. Further down was a shed with two petrol bowsers close beside it.

The hotel, the pub, was in between. It was the only dwelling with a balcony, a hideous skirting of wrought iron, peeling and rusty, ludicrously Victorian in this setting. It sat on raised blocks to elevate it from its less important neighbours, which squatted disconsolately in the dust. Over the top was a long board with faded lettering. The word 'Welcome' stood out in black capitals, and underneath, in smaller print, Lindsay could discern 'Harry Meehan, Prop.'

She swallowed, lifted her case, went up the steps, along the veranda, past a window beyond which flickered a kerosene lamp, and into a narrow hall.

38

What followed was mercifully vague. Not that Harry Meehan and his wife weren't kind—they *were*! They welcomed her with interest, even excitement, since they did not get many visitors out here in Emma—'Plenty of boozers, but not *residents*,' Harry had explained. They plied her with tucker, because she looked dead beat—'Fancy a sheila, such a young slip of a one at that, comin' out here on 'er own, eh! Now you get some of that into you, and a good strong cup of tea, and you'll soon be jake.'

Lindsay found that her appetite had mysteriously fled. She made a gallant attack on the salt beef and fresh damper, but finally had to admit defeat. The tea was heaven-sent, and fortified her sufficiently to enable her to reach the room they pointed out, and to follow Mrs. Meehan on a conducted tour of the plumbing facilities.

'You stand under and pull on that rope and the water'll come down when the bucket tips, see,' Mrs. Meehan obligingly demonstrated the shower. 'Don't worry if the colour's queer, the tank's a bit low, that's all. We don't have it piped to the showers. Some of them blokes in the bar would be standing under it all day long to revive themselves after a bender if we did, and it's our scarcest commodity out here. Don't *you* worry, though—*you* just use what you want,' she told Lindsay generously.

At the door of Lindsay's room, she giggled.

'Don't forget to soap yourself before you up-end the bucket—it's a common mistake with beginners.'

'I won't. Goodnight, and thank you, Mrs. Meehan.'

By the time Lindsay had manipulated the strange shower, cleaned her teeth in the brackish water, drawn on her pyjamas, and crawled miserably beneath the mosquito net that graced her lumpy stretcher, she couldn't think at all.

Which was maybe a good thing!

CHAPTER 3

MORNING brought the birds back. They flew overhead, calling raucously, piercing deep into Lindsay's unconscious state. Plumbing the depths of her exhausted slumber, their sounds were like anguished screams from an avian Underworld.

She threw off the sheet and crawled out from beneath the mosquito net, poured water from an aluminium pitcher into the shallow pan on the washstand, and splashed her face. Then she dressed with care, paying more than her usual attention to her make-up. Whatever happened, she intended to meet her fate with outward composure, even though the leaden ball of anticlimax still rolled around slowly inside her stomach.

Gundooee could hardly be worse than this! From the small window in the dining-room, the view offered nothing more than the now hideously familiar brown distances, broken by a single clump of shade-trees near the pub, from which came the dismal and recurring carr-carr-carr of the crows that festooned the upper branches.

'They don't go away to feed like the others,' explained Mrs. Meehan, passing her a cornflake packet and a jug of reconstituted milk. 'Hang about 'ere all day, that lot will, waitin' for scraps from the garbage. Git out of 'ere, youse black scavengers, you!' she yelled, flinging the window wide and hurling one of the small stones that lined the sill, presumably left there for just such a purpose.

The birds lifted themselves out of range with harsh screeching cries, spread their wings and closed them again, sinking back on to their scrawny perches and eyeing the building patiently.

'See,' repeated Mrs. Meehan triumphantly, 'nothink'll move 'em!'

Lindsay guessed that the whole thing had become something of a ritual between the hotel proprietress and the crows, and that Mrs. Meehan would have been surprised and disappointed if her onslaught had had any other result than the one it habitually did. It was probably one small amusement with which to relieve the monotony of another day in Emmadanda, Lindsay thought, with a twinge of sympathy for the thin, sun-browned woman at her side.

'How often does the mail-plane come?' she asked presently, taking a piece of damper, now a good bit harder than it had been last night, and spreading it with tinned butter and home-made marmalade.

'It don't really call 'ere at all, as a rule. We're the end of the line, see. We connect twice a week with the rail junction, so we don't need a plane. It's only for the folks outback.'

Outback! Lindsay tried not to look at the desolate landscape, concentrated instead on the red and white checks of the shabby gingham tablecloth.

'You mean, it's calling specially for me?'

Mrs. Meehan shrugged.

'Reckon it is. They must 'ave arst 'im to, out at Gundooee, because they couldn't get in for you themselves. Better be ready, eh? 'E don't do it for everybody, but Gundooee's different.'

Lindsay longed to ask in what way Gundooee differed, but she could not bring herself to the point of speech on that particular topic. She was inquisitive, but now too fearful of what the answer might reveal to ever put the question. She could not make up her mind between those two contradictory proverbs—'Ignorance is bliss' or 'Better the Devil you know than the one you don't'—and in the final event, cowardice prevailed. She settled for ignorance!

Harry Meehan took her case out for her and left her there to await the plane. She stood beneath the shade trees, in a world that was hot and bright and suddenly very lonely now that even Harry had deserted her. Perspiration oozed from her pores, even in the shadow. The birds rustled and cawed above her head, cocking their heads at her cheekily. They were hard blobs of jet against a sky that was blatantly blue

41

and cloudless.

By the time the little silver plane came droning out of the blueness, the heat waves had set the whole landscape swimming with movement, and Lindsay was sagging against the mottled tree-trunk, wondering how she could bear to walk out into the direct rays of that relentless sun.

She was helped aboard, and they were off. The pilot, having bestowed upon her a surprised first glance and a laconic greeting, was obviously longing to be airborne again, and Lindsay, with a disembodied feeling of fatalism, was also anxious to be gone. Even though she had never flown before, it was something, at least, to be leaving Emmadanda!

The little plane rocked and bucked, plummeting every now and then with a suddenness that brought Lindsay's heart into her mouth. The pilot seemed to sense her tautness. He turned and grinned reassuringly.

'Sorry,' he said. 'Air-pockets. The heat's the trouble, flying this low. It's hardly worth getting above them when we've only eighty to go. Not too uncomfortable, are you?'

'No, no.' She smiled, but it was a pretty sickly effort, she knew.

'First time up?' He sounded kind.

Lindsay nodded.

'I see.' He pointed a thumb downwards. 'How's that for a panorama, then? A real bird's-eye view, eh!'

She peeped down, glad to take her mind off the bucking aircraft.

'What are those marks? They look like—sort of—pools.'

'Clay-pans,' he told her, 'not pools. We're still on the rim of the artesian basin here. The water's underneath, and you have to go down to get it. That's why you see so many bores. They tap the water down below and pump it up into the tanks with windmills—or engines, if there's no wind. There's one down there, you see. The bore drains take the flow—you can see the pattern they make, fanning out from the bore. Without these man-made watering places, the stock would die out in these parts. The finding of artesian water has been a key to development out here.'

'They look awfully thin—the sheep, I mean—coming out

42

on the train,' Lindsay offered diffidently.

'Ah well, they would be. They've had a bad go back there at Emma. Didn't get the rains that they got up this end. It's a nasty feeling, watching the storms skirting the horizon and giving you a miss, when you know other places, quite near, are getting a decent fall.'

Lindsay pondered over what he had told her. She was appalled at her own ignorance, at the cruelty, the irrevocability, the *challenge*, of the sort of country that she was seeing. She had never dreamed such tracts as this existed. It wasn't a bit like the 'bush' of her childhood dreams! This was a harsh reality that made her want to cry, because in its own way it was a moving experience just to see the enormity of it from above, like this. It was also humbling and frightening, because she didn't understand it.

There was not another bore for ages. Now that she knew what they were, she realised why, in the advertisement, the sheep and cattle on Gundooee had numbered thousands, and the sub-bores less than the fingers of her two hands.

Away to the west, she could see what she thought were hills—or was it all a mirage? There were plenty of those around, because of the wavering heat reflections, and they created weird and incredibly realistic images of water-filled lakes and shimmering seas.

No, this time they really were hills, the pilot told her. They were rough hulks of red and buff, thrown crudely upwards millions of years ago, when beyond the sandhills on the other side had been a great inland sea. Now there were only dried-up salt lakes for most of the year, and fossilised remains that told of the prehistoric animal and fish life that had once inhabited the central vastness of the Australian continent before the gigantic upheaval which had altered its entire geological and physical nature.

The awesome, rearing shapes remained distant, and the next time Lindsay blinked, they had disappeared altogether, and the plain was back. The shimmer of saltbush and blue-bush, mulga and gibber, ever-changing in its effects, was behind them now, and below was a seemingly kinder landscape, grassed with coarse herbage, dotted with sturdier specimens of

43

trees—ironbark, box and bloodwood.

The little plane banked low, circled over what looked like a small village, and descended gently towards an airstrip on the fringe. As they touched down, lifted, touched again, and ran smoothly along between the markers, Lindsay was aware of small knots of waiting people, and a variety of vehicles. There were jeeps, Blitzes, shabby utilities, all parked haphazardly around. Her heart fluttered nervously. A reception committee? Oh—*no*!

'Mail-day,' grinned the pilot. 'There's my mates, all waiting for me as usual. The most popular cove this side of the Alice, that's me!'

Lindsay expelled her pent-up breath. Of course, that was it! They were waiting for the mail-plane, not for Lindsay herself. How stupid of her!

No doubt the arrival of mail-day must be quite an occasion out here—such an occasion, indeed, that it might even be possible for Lindsay Hallingham Dutten, newly engaged book-keeper at Gundooee Station, to slip into her new role almost incognito, without anyone even noticing that the 'him' was after all a 'her'. There were enough folk around, goodness knows! It should not be hard to become one of the crowd, to identify with the knots of expectant people lining the strip with eyes only for their mail and supplies. Afterwards, when they dispersed, she would seek out Mr. Manning, and announce herself with the minimum of fuss.

Afterwards, Lindsay was to ask herself despairingly many time, how *could* she have known? Who would have thought that all those people—yes, every last one of them, with their Blitzes and jeeps and old tin trucks—belonged to Gundooee Station itself—that the whole village that she had spied from the air and upon which she and the pilot had swooped in the little silver plane was Gundooee homestead, and not a town at all.

How could she have guessed that all had come to meet the mail-plane, from their outcamps and boundary-riders' huts and well-sinkers' sites and from the village that was Gundooee homestead itself—all had come to collect their mail and supplies, and all appeared to know that a book-keeper

44

was expected along with the mail!

As Lindsay stepped out, she was first of all aware of the intense glare of light. She had to screw up her eyes to ward off the reflection of the sun on the galvanised roof of the hangar directly behind the waiting groups.

The next thing that struck her, quite forcibly, was that, apart from three lubras standing there flaunting gaudy cotton dresses, there wasn't a single other woman on that airstrip except Lindsay herself! They were all men, every one of them, save for Lindsay and the lubras. And what a collection they seemed to her astonished eyes!

They were as varied as a bag of liquorice allsorts.

A couple of young men, mid-twentyish, were scantily clad in khaki shorts, their bare brown chests glistening with sweat and rippling muscle. The older ones appeared to favour khaki trousers and yellowing singlets, while the dark-skinned members—the Aborigines—wore faded shirts of indeterminate colour, braces, and wide, sagging trousers, felted with grease, dust, and perspiration from themselves and their horses. The trousers, indeed, might well have stood up alone, without the aid of those tired braces! thought Lindsay fastidiously to herself.

The hats were much the same all round the group. They were wide-brimmed felts, depending for individuality upon the angle at which they were worn and the amount of battering they had suffered.

So were the boots alike. Pair after pair, all the same. Tanned leather stock boots, with elastic sides and defined heels, covered with fine yellow dust. All the same.

And so were the eyes, in one respect, at least. They all carried a certain gleam, apart from unconcealed astonishment, that was indefinable to Lindsay, but which made her feel every bit as uncomfortable as did the sudden, complete silence which ensued the moment she stepped down into their midst.

Only one man's eyes did not hold that peculiar gleam. Lindsay, registering the fact, found her own drawn back irresistibly to his. They were a clear, steady grey, this man's eyes, well-set beneath beetling brows in a lean, tanned face that was saved from narrowness by the width and strength of its clean-cut jaw. A rocklike physique, too, that went with the jaw. A six-footer, at least, with powerful shoulders and narrow hips, long agile limbs.

Lindsay. peeping shyly, saw now that there were several other things that were different about this particular man, things she had not noticed at first. Not only were his eyes narrowed upon her without any significant expression at all, when all those other eyes carried that discomfiting gleam, but she was aware that his clothes, too, were subtly different in a minor sort of way—narrow-legged moleskins, a many-pocketed bush shirt, a kangaroo-hide belt at the hips. His hat was just like the rest, but he was alone in raising it.

He did this with an unselfconscious brevity, a purely reflex action. Then he stepped towards her and said politely,

'May I be of any help? You look a bit lost.'

Lindsay was grateful. At last someone had spoken, breaking that sudden, oddly oppressive silence! She was so grateful that she summoned up courage to smile at the man who had taken the initiative, and her green eyes softened, reflecting the warm and friendly gratitude she was feeling.

'Oh, thank you, I wonder if you could? Help, I mean. I'm looking for Mr. Manning, the manager of Gundooee Station. This *is* Gundooee, isn't it?' How silly that sounded, out here in the middle of nowhere!

The men were all grinning, as if they were enjoying themselves, all except the big man to whom Lindsay had addressed herself.

'That's right'—his quiet voice was deep, abrupt. Puzzlement had crept into the clear grey gaze. 'But there's no Mr. Manning here, I'm afraid.'

'Oh, I see.' Lindsay fumbled, because she didn't see at all. 'I—I had a letter from—from Mrs. Manning, just last week, and I naturally thought——'

She tailed off, because the beetling brows were lower now, and they were drawing together in an irritable way. The man's voice, however, was still carefully polite.

'I am the manager, here at Gundooee. My name is Bennett, Rod Bennett. If I can help at all, Miss—er——'

'Dutten,' Lindsay supplied, rather breathlessly. 'Lindsay Dutten.'

'*Dutten!* You can't mean——?'

Oh yes, I can, said Lindsay under her breath, crossing her fingers in their nice, clean, sand-coloured gloves. That's just what I *can*, and *do*, mean.

'I'm Lindsay Hallingham Dutten,' she announced clearly and sweetly, with a confidence that belied the apprehension gathering within her, 'and I've been engaged as a book-keeper for Gundooee Station. And—and here I am,' she concluded less certainly.

The effect of this rather obvious pronouncement upon the entire group was prodigious. Jaws dropped, mouths fell open, eyes protruded—flabbergasted!

'Skin the rakin' lizards! A *sheila*!'

A man somewhere to her left, a man in a shabby singlet with a hole near the shoulder, bared his yellow teeth and spoke, seemingly for all, while another let out a high-spirited sort of cowboy yodel of unmistakable enthusiasm. Out of the corner of her eye, Lindsay saw his elbow come jabbing sharply into the ribs of the man beside him.

'Grey Eyes', alias Mr. Rod Bennett, must have spotted the gesture too, although Lindsay could have sworn his gaze had not shifted for one second from her own face.

'That'll do, Art.' The deep voice held a ring of authority. 'Get your mail and tobacco, all of you, and anything else you want. I'll take the homestead bag, Mac, and Mannie will give you tea up at the house as usual'—this to the pilot. 'Now,' he turned to Lindsay, '*you* come with *me*.'

How grim he seemed, yet curiously urbane. Lindsay quailed. There was something positively unnerving about Mr. Bennett's patient politeness in the face of his very evident displeasure.

'My—my things?' she squeaked.

'Bring them up to the side veranda, Mickie, will you?'

'Sure thing, Rod.' One of the young, brown-chested men stepped forward with alacrity.

As she turned to follow the manager, Lindsay heard whispering, quite distinctly, coming from the huddle of men who had immediately surrounded the one with her suitcase.

'No jumpin' the gun, now, Mickie, just 'cos you got a head start'—'We all start the same, mind'—'Odds or evens?'—'A fiver in, an' winner take all.'

'Cut it, all of you!' The big man ahead of her stopped so abruptly that Lindsay almost cannoned right into him. He thundered the words, and this time he really did seem very angry.

'We wasn't doin' nothink, boss—not 'ere.' Art sounded injured.

'Not here, not *anywhere*. Understand?'

'O.K., Rod.' The chorus was resigned.

The little group made way for Mickie and the suitcase, and gave their attention instead to the mail-plane and its cargo, and Lindsay turned once more in the wake of the big, brown, square-jawed man who was already striding away ahead of her over the bare, hot ground.

She had to run to catch up, and for a moment she tried to match her step with his in order to keep alongside of him. It was no use. The powerful strides were taking him away again, and he didn't even look around, or attempt to wait for her. He might at least have slowed down a little, she thought resentfully, finding herself almost running now to keep abreast of him.

'Were they—were they doing something wrong, your—er —the men?' she asked curiously, as she puffed along at his side.

He shot her a quick, incredulous look.

'Didn't you understand what they were doing?' he countered, in a carefully expressionless voice.

Lindsay shook her head.

'No,' she panted. 'Did you?'

'My God!'

The man lengthened his stride, and Lindsay broke into a trot.

What an odd creature! she was thinking. That was no sort of an answer at all, and her question had been perfectly civil. Whatever had she said to annoy him so much? Or was it only those men who had angered him? There was no way of

48

telling, really.

Soon he was slowing down, lifting the catch on the white wicket gate that was set in a pretty white paling fence, standing aside and indicating that she should precede him.

Lindsay did, and was instantly enchanted. It was like stepping into another world. Cool, green, buffalo lawns swept before her, close-cropped, still damp from the sprinklers that had been rotating over them. Bougainvillea tumbled rampant along the fence, and unfamiliar but attractive shrubs lined the borders around the house—mimosas, acacias, oleander, several species of palm. The house itself—the 'homestead', he had called it as he led the way once again—was vast, a low, rambling building with gauzed verandas running right around it. It had a white roof that dipped away at different angles in all directions, indicating its extensive and wandering interior, and in several corners were big round rainwater tanks, set up on stands, with cone-shaped lids and a tap at the bottom.

Mr. Bennett took the steps to the veranda in a couple of bounds, and held open the fly-screen door. Lindsay, exhausted, stumbled inside.

Out of the sun it was cool and dim. Oh, this blessed shade! she thought, leaning against a veranda column and savouring it. She felt on the point of collapse. All that standing about in the heat, under the shade trees at Emmadanda, waiting for the mail-plane, seemed to have sapped her customary energy. And out here at the Gundooee airstrip there hadn't even been a tree!

The man beckoned her to follow, and Lindsay dragged herself away from the support of the veranda-post and obeyed.

Perhaps he would offer her some tea, as he had done to the pilot. 'Tea as usual,' he had said, and, 'Mannie will give it.'

Lindsay's parched throat was crying out for moisture. She could think of nothing more acceptable, right now, than a good cup of tea. She could drink a whole pot full!

'In here, please. Sit down there.' He indicated a leather chair, placed his broad-brimmed hat on a wide, flat-topped desk, and began to pace about on the other side of the room, as if collecting his thoughts for some sort of verbal battle to come.

Lindsay wilted into the chair, hardly caring where she was, and not minding in the least if he never fired the opening volley, since she had a fair idea of what was coming. Her face felt pale and sticky, and her olive linen suit clung to her thighs and shoulder-blades, limply and unappealingly. She closed her eyes, and the pacing stopped immediately.

'Aren't you well?' How abrupt, unsympathetic, he was! A *brute* of a man!

'Of course I'm well,' she defended herself indignantly, wishing he would stop peering at her like that. 'But you must surely admit that it's quite—quite *warm*.'

As soon as she had uttered them, Lindsay wished the words unsaid. You could tell by the quick frown, the repressed line of his mouth, that book-keeepers, whether male or female, were not expected to complain of the heat the moment they arrived.

Rod Bennett, leaning over her with one hand on the tooled leather top of his office desk, opened his mouth to speak, apparently changed his mind, and left the room. Lindsay heard his heavy steps fading away along the veranda and closed her eyes thankfully again. Oh, for a cup of Mannie's tea, whoever Mannie was!

'Take these.' A curt command. The manager was back. He passed her a couple of pills and a pannikin of water. 'Go on, they won't hurt you, they're only salt tablets.'

Salt! Lindsay wasn't feeling like salt just now. She could think of nothing more thirst-making than salt! She screwed up her nose.

'Do I have to?' she asked doubtfully—and that was her second mistake.

The broad shoulders shrugged. 'No, you don't have to.' The deep voice was uncaring. 'I *could* leave you to die in your tracks, but I intend to get some answers first. Now, *drink up*!' A whiplash command suddenly supplanted the man's formerly lazy speech.

Lindsay did—hastily.

When she had finished the water, he took the empty mug

and said, 'Only an idiot, or someone completely inexperienced, would travel out in these parts without a hat.'

Lindsay flushed, patted her perspiring brow with her handkerchief, and decided to let that remark pass.

'You don't look altogether an idiot, so that leaves us with inexperience, doesn't it?' He hitched his moleskins, took the swivel chair on the opposite side of the desk, and placed his hands, palms down, on the leather top, eyeing her intently.

Lindsay quivered with nervousness. His eyes were unblinking. They were the most unswerving eyes she had ever come across, and they seemed to bore right into her, unwavering, relentless. His whole attitude was akin to the concentration of a tiger about to spring.

'Well?'

'Well.' She licked her dry lips.

'Let's have the story,' he said quietly. 'Why did you do it?'

'D-do what?'

'You know perfectly well *what*. Why did you apply for the book-keeper post here?'

Lindsay essayed a surprised smile.

'Because the post was advertised, and I happen to be a book-keeper,' she returned with commendable confidence. 'N-needing a p-post,' she added with something of a wobble, spoiling the whole effect. Oh, Lindsay, you ass!

'You were aware that the position required a man.' That wasn't even a question. The way Rod Bennett said it, it was simply a statement of fact.

It would take all her powers of persuasion to carry this off, Lindsay could see that.

'A—a *man*? Good *gracious*!' Now, *that* sounded convincing! She wondered whether to beat her brow in the best theatrical tradition, decided against it.

'You knew.' Again the statement.

'It—it didn't *say*,' she pointed out archly.

'It *implied*.'

'If it did, I'm afraid I wasn't aware of the implications.'

'And *still* aren't aware of them, by all appearances,' came the enigmatic murmur.

51

'How do you mean?' Lindsay gazed at him innocently.

He shot her that quick, incredulous look—the one he had given her outside. Then he passed his hand over his tanned, clean-shaven jaw, and paused. The pause lengthened.

Lindsay began to fidget. A pity that granite face was so unreadable. It would have helped, just then, to know what the man was thinking. As it was, she had no idea at all as to whether she was winning or losing.

Finally, Rod Bennett sat back, opened a drawer and took out a letter. He placed it carefully on the desk in front of him.

'As you can see, your own correspondence in the matter,' he told her, eyeing her with judicial sternness, as though she were a prisoner at the bar. He read—'"I am accustomed to positions demanding trust and initiative." How old are you, Miss—er—Dutten?'

'I'm twenty-one. Why?'

'An incredibly tender age to be so accustomed to positions of trust, don't you think?' he pointed out dryly.

Lindsay blushed.

'I don't know,' she muttered lamely, looking down at her hands. 'I'm completely trust-*worthy*,' she added, almost inaudibly.

'It's a different thing,' he asserted unkindly. Her adversary was giving no quarter. 'Now, let's see. Yes, here we are. "I have former experience of, and a marked preference for, country life."' He looked up. 'And you came out here— *without* even a hat—to a position which anyone with one shred of prior experience would have known was intended for a man?'

He eyed her sceptically, and Lindsay wriggled in her chair.

'I—I was *born* in the bush,' she told him. Torn between indignation and despair, the words came tumbling out. 'I was *born* in it, I tell you, and I do have a preference for it. I love it—I always have. I've been longing for ages and ages to get away from that horrid city. You can be so lonely there— lonely, lonely, even in all the crowds of people. I—I longed to escape, and that's what the advertisement was, an escape. Oh, can't you see? It was all because of Clancy, anyway.'

'Who?'

'Clancy. You know. "The bush has friends to meet him, and their kindly voices greet him"—that Clancy. I wanted the f-friends and the k-kindly voices.'

She faltered to a halt, ashamed to find that her throat was suddenly choked with threatening tears. She gazed at him helplessly with huge, wet-lashed eyes that were misty with pleading.

He appeared totally unmoved.

'Where were you born?'

'Near Batlow. It's down——'

'I know it. Orchard country.' His tone was contemptuous. 'How long were you there?'

'Six years.'

'And then?'

'My parents were killed, both of them.'

'And after that?'

'I went to the city, to a—a sort of aunt.'

'And?'

'How do you mean—and? I mean, I've told you. I hated the city. I've never liked it. I always longed for the bush again, for freedom. And then I saw——'

'Are you telling me'—Rod Bennett interrupted in calculated tones of sheer, cold, forbidding, incredulous fury—'that you remained in the city after you were six years old? That that was your sole encounter with the "bush", as you are pleased to call it? That on the strength of a few childhood years in a fertile, climatically equable, civilised area like Batlow—Batlow!—you had the presumption to apply as a book-keeper for Gundooee Station, eighty miles out from Emmadanda, beyond the Black Stump, at the back of nowhere, where the crows fly backwards to keep the dust out of their eyes? That you have the temerity to say, in addition, that you were experienced in station life?'

'C-country life, I said,' she corrected him fearfully.

He was standing now. He had left his chair and he had come right around the desk to tower over her. Colour had risen angrily beneath his heavy tan, and his grey eyes were dark, sparking with rage.

Lindsay was terrified.

'I've got all the qualifications, Mr. Bennett. Truly I have. If you'll give me a trial. Mrs. Manning seemed to th-think that my qualifications were acceptable.'

'Mannie can't be blamed for this! You misled her! She's in her seventies—an old family retainer. Unfortunately I had to visit another of our properties at short notice, and I instructed Mannie to choose an applicant on my behalf. She's not accustomed to engaging staff, but she'd have made a better job of it if you'd been on the level.'

'I was on the level, Mr. Bennett. My certificates are all in order. I can't see that experience really matters all that much—what I mean—' she qualified hastily, quailing at his deepening expression of grimness. 'What I mean *is*, book-keeping is book-keeping, and that's all that's to it. It's the same anywhere.'

'Is it?' The words were jaded. So were the lines about his mouth—jaded and cynical, as he sought in one of the flap pockets of his khaki shirt for the makings, and began to roll a cigarette, with calm, experienced, square-tipped fingers. Lindsay found her eyes fastened upon those steady fingers, mesmerized, as they tipped tobacco deftly, fashioned a neat cylinder.

Rod Bennett licked the edges of his smoke carefully, neatened the ends.

'Is it?' he repeated tiredly, as if he had had enough of the whole question. 'Have you ever stocked a station store, Miss Dutten, to cover the needs of a large and varied complement of men? All and every possible need, remember, since we have no shops around the corner out here! Have *you* ever been responsible for expensive and explosive fuels, and spirits that must be signed for? Handed out discretionary 'finger money' to black stockmen? Kept a check on the numbered drugs and replacements in a station medical chest? Relayed messages and orders over a transceiver? Helped men to write letters and fill in forms when they've forgotten what it's like even to read? Acted as general factotum, adviser, confidante, counter-hand, peacemaker, court-of-appeal, ombudsman over gambling debts and personal difficulties—I could go on

54

ad infinitum, Miss Dutten, and all *that* is before you even get out the cash book.'

Lindsay swallowed. Her hands were clutching themselves together, and her assurance had slipped, right down to her pretty sand-coloured shoes. She was badly shaken.

'I can *try*,' she whispered persuasively, willing her hopelessness not to show. 'I can try, if you'll only give me a chance. I'm here, aren't I, s-so you may as well. I'll do my best, I really will.'

He seemed not to have even heard her.

'And added to that, you're a *woman*,' he intoned bitterly. 'Not even a woman, a mere girl! That's the biggest complication of the whole damn lot, and heaven knows what I've done to deserve to be saddled with it!'

'But I can look after myself, I always have. I've done it for years,' she assured him eagerly. 'I won't be at all a bother, I promise.'

'A *bother*?' He ground out his cigarette end impatiently.

Lindsay took that as the signal to stand up. She felt positively frayed as a result of this unpleasant skirmish. All she prayed for now was that it would end quickly, whatever the outcome.

When she stood up, her action somehow brought her closer to him. Lindsay felt dwarfed beside that powerful, masculine frame. Not daring to speak, she nevertheless found herself forced to look up, right into the stern grey eyes that were so near, above her. For a long moment their gazes held, locked in challenge.

Impossible to tell what was going on behind that grim mask. Somewhere near the man's jaw a small muscle flickered, the merest ripple in his sunseamed cheek. Lindsay watched it, fascinated—took in, too, the crisp dark hair that sprang away from his temple, the imperious aquilinity of the nose and fine chiselling of the lips. She gulped, audibly, in an effort to clear the sudden nervous constriction in her throat.

The man appeared to come to a decision at last.

'I'll give you a trial, Miss Dutten, since you've come such a long way.' The words were deeply gruff, grudging, one might have said. 'You will receive the minimum rate, but on

the other hand I shall not expect—or indeed encourage—
you, a woman, to perform *all* the duties I listed a moment
ago. Your tasks and the area of your authority will be strictly
limited, and under my constant surveillance. Do I make myself perfectly clear?'

Lindsay nodded.

'Perfectly clear,' she hastened to agree huskily.

Rod Bennett turned, walked to the door and opened it,
standing aside to let her pass.

'Just one more thing.' A hand came down on her shoulder,
arresting her passage.

'Yes?'

'Just get one thing quite clear in your mind, Miss Dutten.
If I thought for one moment that you had *intentionally* deceived me as to your sex'—the manager paused significantly
—'I would pack you out of here in my own aircraft before
you could even say Ned Kelly. Do you understand that?'

Once again, grey eyes locked with green. It was the green
ones which wavered, slid down to stare instead at the man's
dusty stock-boots, planted there so near.

Lindsay couldn't trust herself to speak just then. She had
the feeling that words—*any* words—might be the wrong
ones, might alter the delicate balance of a danger-fraught
situation and plunge her over the brink towards instant
dismissal, back to the airstrip, back to Emmadanda, back to
that railway junction whose name she couldn't even remember, back to Sydney itself.

At the mere thought, Lindsay's head went up and down
several times, very smartly, to let the man know that she
understood.

She understood very well indeed, and she was anything
but sanguine about the outcome of her own incredible folly!

CHAPTER 4

LINDSAY followed the Gundooee manager back along the veranda, through the gauze door, and down the steps into the grilling sun once more.

Sitting on the white paling fence beside the wicket gate, swinging his legs idly against the rails, was Mickie, and planted in the dust beside the fence was her solitary suitcase. When Rod Bennett approached, the young man slid down nimbly and picked up the case, grinning openly at the flushed-faced girl who came panting back down the path in the manager's wake.

'Thanks, Mick,' the older man said briefly, picked up the case himself, and turned to Lindsay. 'Come with me. I'll show you to your cottage.'

'My cottage! Do you mean one of my very *own*?' she asked, intrigued.

'The *book-keeper's* cottage, Miss Dutten,' he elucidated repressively. 'It's down near the store, for convenience, you understand. The book-keeper sleeps and works there, but takes his meals at the homestead.'

'Oh. I see.'

He was walking briskly as he spoke, and again she found herself almost running in an effort to keep up.

They were taking a different direction this time. The airstrip and hangar were now on the other side of the big sprawling homestead, and Lindsay and the manager were walking away from it, passing an assortment of sheds and buildings which from the air had made her think that this was a clustered village, but which were in reality spaced quite a distance apart from each other when you were actually walking among them. She saw engine sheds, a power-house, station-hands' quarters with a row of open-sided shower cubicles at one end, feed stores, a blacksmith's

shop, a harness room, a fowl-yard, and in the distance a
long, low shearing-shed with yards and races surrounding
it.

'Just around this corner.'

Rod Bennett rounded the corner of the station store and
pulled up short in front of a neat pink weatherboard cottage
with a small canvas awning over its cement porch.

He stopped so abruptly that, this time, Lindsay *did* bump
into him.

A hard hand gripped her painfully above the elbow,
restored her balance, and let go. He hadn't even looked her
way, because his eyes were already busy elsewhere. They were
taking in the scene around the little weatherboard building.

It seemed to Lindsay that there were almost as many
people standing around it as there had been down at the
airstrip to await that plane.

The black stockmen weren't there, it was true, and neither
were the lubras in their bright cotton dresses—they had all
gone back to their humpies over at the creek, and even from
here, one could hear the yapping of their mangy dogs, the
crying of the piccanins, and the laughter of the women,
underneath the distant line of shade trees.

The aboriginal members of Gundooee Station had
apparently taken their supplies and gone, but most, or all, of
the others now seemed to be gathered about the precincts of
the book-keeper's cottage, busying themselves in a number of
ways. To her astonishment Lindsay registered the fact that
even Mickie was present. He must have taken an alternative
route after he had handed over her suitcase—a quicker route,
because he had reached the cottage before they did themselves, and Mr. Bennett had certainly set a spanking pace.

Mickie was apparently absorbed in lowering the striped
sun-blind to a more effective angle over the front steps. From
the attention Mickie was devoting to his task, it appeared to
be a tricky and absorbing operation.

A couple of the men were realigning the whitewashed
stones which flanked the path, while others made half-
hearted attacks on the weeds inside the old motor-tyres
which served to enclose small shrubs and saplings—the only

gesture towards any sort of garden that the cottage possessed. Further off, a singleted figure stooped to pick up a tin that glinted with metallic viciousness in the harsh noon light. To the left, yet another began to kick at a burr with the heel of his boot. One or two, unable to find some reasonable excuse for occupation, simply stood and scuffed at the dust.

Rod Bennett surveyed these activities in silence for a moment. Then—

'What's going on here?' he asked severely.

All the men stopped what they were doing, and the ones who were not doing anything stopped that, too, and regarded him somewhat sheepishly. Then they looked at each other, at Lindsay, at Rod, at each other. No one seemed to know how to reply, and therefore no one spoke at all.

'Well? What's going on?' Rod Bennett sounded stern. 'Mail-day's as good as over, didn't you know? Bluey, I thought you had a fence to ride?'

'Most certainly, boss,' mumbled a gaunt individual with an unruly thatch of bright red hair spiking from beneath his slouch hat. 'I just reckoned these stones could do with a bit of a shift, see. *You* know, they was kind of untidy, see.'

'I see more than you think! Barney? The number five bore?'

'Sure thing, Rod. I've got the casin' in the jeep. We just thought, I mean, these weeds 'ere are gettin' downright cheeky, they're comin' up that quick.'

'—just spotted this tin on me way to the quarters, Rod. Thought one of them blinkin' 'orses might shy at it if I didn't pick it up.'

'Collectin' up a bit of wire, I was——'

'Prickly little bastards, these burrs, eh, Rod?'

'We got the supplies up in the Blitz, Rod. I mean, you couldn't expect for a sheila ter be carryin' all them heavy packin' cases, could yer, now?'

'Quite, Herb,' agreed the man at Lindsay's side equably. 'From now on that can be your own job on mail-days. Part of the drill.'

Herb, a thickset man with a four-day stubble and a singular lack of teeth, received this news with some evidence of bewilderment.

'Yer don't mean *every* time, do yer, Rod?' he enquired in dismay.

'That's just what I do mean, Herb. *Every* time.' Rod Bennett smiled pleasantly at Herb's toothless gape. 'And you, Artie, can get a hoe, and cut burrs the *proper* way for the rest of the day. The horse paddock's getting pretty thick with them.'

'Aw, cripes, boss! Yer mean, all them burrs in the 'orse paddock? Stone the crows! There's acres of 'em!'

'That's right, Art. It's time they were done.' He turned his attention to the men kneeling beside the motor-tyres. 'You might as well weed all those beds, while you're at it. Even if the cottage is to remain empty in the meantime, it's as well to keep the place tidy, I reckon.'

'Empty?' The wail was a chorused protest, unanimous, heartfelt. To a man, they all stopped what they had been doing again, and blinked at Rod.

'Yes, that's right—empty. I was simply showing Miss Dutten the layout, the whereabouts of the store, and the place where the book-keeper used to stay.' His voice was deeply calm, utterly convincing—so convincing that for a moment Lindsay could almost have believed him to be serious. But hadn't he just *said* that she could have a cottage of her very own? That the book-keeper always slept and worked in his own cottage near the store? And it was such a dear little cottage, too!

Lindsay peeped at his set face. He appeared to be in deadly earnest. Very hesitantly, she plucked at his khaki shirt-sleeve.

'Excuse me, Mr. Bennett, but you just said a moment ago that——'

'Never mind what I said a moment ago.' Rod Bennett scowled down at her, as if her fingers on his arm were an unwelcome reminder of a presence that irritated almost beyond endurance. 'You can come with me,' he added, in the same sort of voice he had used at the airstrip, and which seemed to Lindsay to be loaded with forbearance. Then he picked up her case again and swung on his heel.

'But I thought——' gasped Lindsay, catching up with him around the corner of the store.

'Then don't. *Don't* think,' he rasped out briefly.

'But my cottage?' she panted. 'That dear little cottage? Aren't I going to have it, like the book-keeper always does?'

'No, Miss Dutten, you are not!'

'*Why* not? The other book-keeepers always did, so why not me?'

'Because you are not like the other book-keepers,' he told her curtly, opening the wicket gate and almost pushing her through in front of him.

'But you haven't tried me out yet,' protested Lindsay hotly, 'so how can you possibly know that I'm not like the others?'

Rod Bennett seized her elbow in a grasp that hurt, and practically lifted her up the steps and through the gauze door. Inside, he let her go, dumped her case down on the wooden veranda boards, pushed back his hat, and looked at her.

Lindsay gazed back, aware of the exasperation lurking in the grey depths of his eyes, the small white strip near his hairline where the suntan stopped, the glint of a couple of grey strands among the dark, clipped hairs at his temple, the brown strength of his throat in the open-necked shirt, the grim set of his mouth as he closed his lips upon whatever words he had been about to utter.

Lindsay's stare was limpid, green, and clear, and tinged with uncontrolled curiosity. She had never met a man of this type before—she hadn't, for that matter, met many men of *any* type!—and she found him both interesting and—well—*fascinating*, in a rather frightening sort of way. No wonder all those other men down there had positively jumped to do his bidding! He wasn't the sort of person to brook an argument when he issued orders, of that much one could be sure.

Rod Bennett's own stare was grey, candid, and uncomfortably penetrating. It seemed to search right into her own brain, to where her puzzlement and weariness and curiosity were mingling bewilderingly.

Lindsay watched the exasperation giving way to a tiny glimmer of some other, warmer emotion that she was unable to identify. Although he now looked slightly less dangerous, his mouth was still unyielding, however, as he stated positively,

'The others were different.'

'How do you mean?'

'The others were men.'

'Oh-h-h!' Lindsay's own lips pursed soundlessly. 'Does it m-matter?' she added after a moment, wishing that he didn't have to be quite so grim about it.

'It matters, yes.' He sent his broad-brimmed hat spinning into a deckchair impatiently. 'For two pins, I'd send you back. I *ought* to send you back.'

'But *why*?'

Brown fingers raked through his hair in a gesture of pure indecision. 'Those men——' he muttered.

'I thought they were being perfectly sweet,' Lindsay felt bound to defend them. 'After all, they were only trying to make things nice for me, weren't they? They meant to be friendly. My new bush friends.' She gazed out through the gauze at the sun-drenched lawn and shrubs, shimmering in a haze of heat, then brought her eyes back to his. 'They were the friends, the kindly voices—like in the poem.'

'The poem?'

'I *told* you. Like in Clancy.'

'Of the Overflow,' she felt bound to tack on, seeing his blank look.

'Ah yes. Clancy.' Rod Bennett's grey eyes flickered with amused irony. He fingered his chin. 'I don't suppose I could send you back, after that, could I? Not without a trial.'

'You *promised*, Mr. Bennett.'

He straightened up, sighed.

'That's right, I promised.' He picked up the case, for what seemed to Lindsay the hundredth time since her arrival. 'I'll show you to your room, and you can have a wash and join us for lunch. The dining-room is around that corner of the veranda. Mannie will get you some sheets and stuff afterwards, and you can make up a bed.'

'Thank *you*, Mr. Bennett. I really do mean that!'

He indicated a doorway, placed her luggage in what she hoped would now be its final resting-place, on the foot of the bed.

'I must be mad,' he grumbled deeply.

'I beg your pardon?'

'Lunch will be in a quarter of an hour.' Rod Bennett spoke abruptly. 'Please be punctual. Unpunctuality fouls up the cogs in a station's efficiency machine quicker than almost anything else.'

'Yes, Mr. Bennett,' she assured the broad, retreating back, sinking down weakly on to the bed beside her case, and listening to the beat of his heavy boots fading out along the veranda.

Phew! It looked as though she had made it, Lindsay reflected with relief. But only just!

For a while it had been touch and go out there, but now she felt that the first ditch had been safely negotiated. She was here, and she could stay, even if it was only on trial. She had bought herself a little time in which to prove to that strange, tough man that one's sex had no relevance whatever when it came to book-keeping. Once Rod Bennett saw what a neat, methodical set of books she could turn out, he would forget all about that one little drawback—the fact that she happened to be a girl.

Having become acquainted with the layout of the homestead precincts, Lindsay could not see that being a girl mattered even the tiniest little bit. She could soon learn to do all those other things too, the general factotum things that he had reeled off so blightingly.

Lindsay gave an involuntary shiver as she remembered the manager's eyes, how cold they had gone, when he said that bit about deceiving him. His eyes, indeed, had almost disappeared into cold, nasty, grey slits, and you'd have said there was a real hint of threat in his voice—

'If I thought for one moment that you had *intentionally* deceived me——'

Lindsay gulped. It was better not to recall how he had looked when he had said that. It made her feel apprehensive

63

and uncomfortable, all over again, just when she was beginning to recover her equilibrium. She thrust the recollection from her, and surveyed her surroundings with returning interest.

The room was pleasant—not as nice as the dear little cottage would have been, but gracious and spacious and homely-looking, with high, cool white ceilings and heavy Victorian furniture, a brass bedstead, floral curtains. The quilt she was sitting on was of white cotton, heavily fringed, and the mattress felt soft and springy. Lindsay would have liked to lie down on it right now, and drift off to sleep. She would like to forget all about Gundooee Station and its manager, just for the present, but Rod Bennett had said she must come for lunch, so she had better get ready.

She found the bathroom, washed her face and hands, came back to the bedroom and took off her pretty olive suit, hanging it up with care in the big wardrobe. Her mouth curled at the sight of its cavernous interior, and the rows of empty coat-hangers. Her suit and denim skirt and cotton sun-dress would not take up much of that room. Alas for all the pretty things which Carleen had snatched back so spitefully at the last moment! They would have gone some way, at least, towards filling up this generous space.

Lindsay put on the denim skirt now, buttoned her white cotton shirt, brushed her hair. Then she walked somewhat hesitantly across the hall to the dining-room.

Rod Bennett was there waiting for her. He made the fact that he was waiting obvious by looking pointedly at the watch strapped to one hairy brown wrist, and then he introduced her to the woman she knew must be Mannie, before putting her into her chair.

Mannie was already seated. She was thin and elderly, with wispy white hair and a complexion that was parched and drawn by the sun into a criss-cross pattern of wrinkles. They scored her cheeks, fanned about her eyes, corrugated her brow, lined her mouth. When she smiled they all changed direction, like miniature railway lines whose points had been changed. She smiled at Lindsay just now, and her beady brown eyes were alert, but also welcoming and kind.

Rod Bennett waved a hand between the woman and the girl.

'This is Miss Dutten, Mannie,' he told the old woman on his right. Then, to Lindsay, 'Mrs. Manning, or Mannie, as she prefers to be called.' He took his place at the head of the table. 'I have already prepared Mannie to expect a *Miss* Dutten instead of a Mister—isn't that so, Mannie?'

'Please just call me Lindsay. I'm not used to being called Miss.'

'Perhaps that is why you omitted it from your correspondence?' came the quick, sarcastic reply, and Lindsay felt quick colour tinting her cheeks.

'Now, Rod my dear, don't go on about it any more,' begged the old lady, unexpectedly coming to the girl's defence. 'As Miss Dutten—as Lindsay—is here, it's a *fait accompli*, isn't it, however vexed you may feel, so let's just make the best of it. In any case'—she twinkled deliberately—'it will be nice for me to have some feminine company apart from Sibbie and Bella, with all their skylarks.'

'Sibbie and Bella?' Lindsay was loth to speak at all in the face of Rod Bennett's own preoccupied silence as he got on with his meal, but as Mannie appeared to be in a more friendly and talkative mood, it seemed churlish not to join in.

'Yes, my dear. The lubras.'

'Do—do they work in the house?'

Lindsay had wondered about that. While she had been sitting on her bed, she had heard shrieks and giggles coming from somewhere at the back of the veranda, and the accompanying clatter and clash of cutlery and crockery told her that the sounds probably emanated from the kitchen.

'They do help—and hinder too,' smiled the old woman. 'I don't let them handle the food, and so I do all the cooking myself, but they do wash the dishes and peel the vegetables, and they turn the housework into a sort of fun session that can become quite riotous at times. You'll hear them soon, if you haven't already. They're apt to regard everything as a joke, which makes them the pleasantest possible people to have around one—when they *are* around.'

'Aren't they always?' Lindsay was moved to enquire politely, stealing another furtive glance at the stern figure on her right. He was eating with an abstracted expression on his face. Obviously his thoughts were engaged elsewhere, and he was quite oblivious of the women's conversational exchange.

'No, not always,' replied Mannie with a sigh. 'That's the one drawback. They can be somewhat irresponsible about turning up. One just has to be thankful when they do. They are a people of superstition, the aborigines, and a certain amount of religious rite and ceremony interferes with the living of their lives as the white man lives it. Things are changing gradually, of course, and not before time. I'm afraid we've done very badly by the people from whom the white settlers took Australia, and have, as a nation, realised our culpability rather late. Up till now, their fortunes have depended to a great extent on the sympathy or otherwise of the individuals who employ them, although recently the Government has taken a hand, and of course there are the Missions, which do an enormous amount of helpful work. Out here they still have cultural sessions of one sort or another, singing ceremonies, corroborees to celebrate spiritual events, and all kinds of ritual to do with their Dreamtime beliefs. Sometimes, too'—she laughed—'they just go walkabout for no apparent reason.'

'Walkabout?'

'They just move away, Lindsay—into the night, you might say. After being apparently quite settled and happy, they suddenly get the urge to wander, and they leave their gunyahs or humpies, the bark huts they make, and they just seem to disappear into nowhere. It's part of their inherent tendency to nomadism. But of course you'll know all this, anyway'—Mannie waved a deprecating hand apologetically —'I was forgetting that you have had previous experience of Outback ways.'

'Miss Dutten's previous experience has unfortunately been confined to the Batlow area,' put in Rod Bennett cuttingly. (So he *had* been listening, after all!)

'Batlow?' Mannie blinked. 'Goodness, isn't that the place where those lovely apples come from? Pears, too, I think.'

66

'*Quite.*' The manager succeeded in bringing a wealth of derision to that word.

'Yes, well'—the old woman glanced tactfully away from Lindsay's scarlet cheeks—'you'll have to tell me all about it some time, dear. Such pretty country, so I've heard. Will you be in for tea, Rod, or shall I pack you something? We're usually not so late as this on mail-days, you see, Lindsay. The men are almost always out for lunch, but with a new book-keeper coming—well, that's different.'

'It was certainly different today, anyway,' agreed the big man at the head of the table, holding Lindsay's eye as if delighting in her agonised expression. 'A few scones in my saddle-bag would be welcome, Mannie, thank you. I left it on the dresser in the kitchen.'

Rod Bennett got to his feet, smiled down and laid a kindly hand under Mannie's arm, helping her from her chair—not that Mannie was decrepit or in real need of such help. It was more a gesture of true affection and gallantry, Lindsay perceived with amazement, and the man's eyes were soft, considerate and fond, not remote and cool and disapproving like they were when they rested on *her*. Lindsay thought wistfully that it must be pleasant to have a difficult man like that on your side instead of against you, and to be the recipient of such a gentle, respectful look from those wide-set, expressive grey eyes.

It wasn't very likely to happen to her, though!

She cleared her throat.

'Er—thank you for meeting me at the plane, Mr. Bennett,' she mumbled. 'I'm sorry to have interrupted your day.'

'Not at all, Miss Dutten. It is usual, as Mannie has already said, for me to be on hand to meet a new employee, I assure you,' he returned formally.

'Don't you think it would be more friendly to say Lindsay, Rod?' interpolated Mannie with what seemed to Lindsay an awesome show of courage. '*I'm* going to—and you just call me Mannie, my dear. We all use Christian names out here.'

'I find the name Lindsay too equivocal in the circumstances, thank you, Mannie, to wish to use it,' stated Rod Bennett coldly. Scowling brows descended, turned the grey eyes into those nasty slits again. The slits were narrowed accusingly upon the girl who hesitantly started to collect plates, as the housekeeper was already doing. 'In any case, repeated use of her proper status might remind *Miss* Dutten that there are certain occasions when it is unforgivably remiss to omit the use of it with accuracy.'

Upon which quelling statement he strode from the room.

'Now what did he mean by that?' asked Mannie good-humouredly. 'It's not as if you did it on *purpose*.'

She continued her task with every impression of unruffled calm. Obviously Rod Bennett did not present the fearsome figure to her that he did to Lindsay, who now licked her dry lips tremulously and carried a pile of plates to the trolley with hands that trembled a tiny bit.

'I—I think perhaps he's still very angry, all the same. It's because I'm a girl, he's made that quite clear. Doesn't he like women?' She gazed apprehensively at the tall, retreating, slouch-hatted figure that crossed the yard outside the window with long, purposeful strides.

'Who? Rod? Of *course* he likes women—and they *adore* him!' averred the old lady indignantly, as though Lindsay had been guilty of casting some sort of aspersion upon her beloved employer. 'Why, he's got those lovely Brisbane belles eating out of his hand. They just fall over themselves to go out with him—he's *very* eligible, you know. It's a wonder he hasn't settled down with one of them before now, because some of them have been quite gorgeous. They sometimes come out here to stay, when the Races are on. He can pick and choose, really, Lindsay, a man like *him*, but I must say he's taking quite a time making up his mind. There hasn't been a single girl who has come out to stay at Gundooee who wasn't quite irresistibly beautiful and charming,' stated Mannie with pride.

Then it must be *her* that he didn't like, thought Lindsay sadly. Her, in particular, if it wasn't all women.

She sighed inwardly. Life was not going to be very easy if her employer had taken a dislike to her at the outset! Things weren't going to be easy in any respect, come to that. Lindsay was just beginning to realise how abysmally ignorant she was of all things pertaining to station life. This heat, for instance, when it was only just spring in Sydney. How much hotter would, or could, it get, when the summer really developed? Already her cotton shirt was clinging to her shoulders as she pushed the laden trolley through a long passage, across a narrow covered-way, to the kitchen block; through another gauze door, and into a large, surprisingly modern kitchen, warm in spite of the big whirring fans and the hum of an air-conditioning unit.

Sibbie and Bella were there already, chattering like magpies in the laundry off the far end of the room, giggling together as they washed the cotton overalls they had been wearing yesterday, and squeezed the soapsuds into amusing shapes with artful black fingers.

Every morning, when they came up to the homestead, Mannie would give them a clean overall to put on, and while they were waiting for the lunch dishes, they would wash the garments they had worn on the previous day. Then they would hang them out on the line, where the hot sun soon dried them, drawing out the bright, treasured colour in the process. When the colours became disappointingly faded from the constant washings, Sibbie and Bella would lose interest in the washing of their overalls, and become careless. Then Mannie would have to send them to the store for some new ones.

'This youngfella missus name belonga Lindsay,' Mannie was telling them now, and they clutched the wrung-out washing to their drooping bosoms, screeching with mirth as though Lindsay was quite the funniest name on earth. Their smiles were wide and beautifully white and unmistakably friendly, and Lindsay found her own mouth curving into a warm, answering greeting before following Mannie back into the kitchen.

'Shall I help with the washing-up?' she asked shyly.

'No, my dear, I wouldn't start that if I were you. It's best to leave them to the things they can do well, I find, and believe me, you'll have plenty to occupy your time once you settle in. I'm just going to get Rod's scones ready for his tucker-bag, and if I were you I'd unpack your things, and then go down to the store and check-in today's supplies.'

'Yes, of course. Just one thing, Mannie. I'd like to let my—er—cousin know that I've arrived safely, if that's possible.' Lindsay couldn't help sounding as dubious as she felt about that.

Gundooee seemed like the end of the world—or the deserted centre of it!—and short of sending a message by one of the crows that cawed hardily on the tankstand outside, there seemed little prospect of communication.

The city, and her life there, had already taken on the fragile substance of a dream. The present was the only reality —the drumming heat, the sweltering outbuildings, the rambling homestead with its green lawns, dim, air-conditioned interior, gauzed verandas; the brown, smiling, wrinkled face of the dear old lady here beside her; the suppressed giggling of Sibbie and Bella in the laundry beyond; the disapproving assessment of Rod Bennett's critical, unfriendly eyes—all these were real, involving her in a need for present thought and action.

The aunt and uncle, the spiteful Carleen, that hypocritical photographer, (whatever Rod Bennett might think of her, at least he wasn't hypocritical enough to *pretend*!) had all become faint, distant figures in her shadowed, unhappy past. Already she was finding that the miles that now lay between them had caused a subtle alteration in her relationship with those people. No longer had they the power to hurt her, as they formerly had. Almost, she could feel sorry for them, and the motives which drove them, and coloured their associations with their fellows. The jealousies, the comparisons, the petty quarrels that resulted, were washed into nothingness by the great blue vastness of the sky outside the window of the Gundooee kitchen. That sky seemed to dome itself right over its own world, shutting it off from the 'elsewhere'. It was a world that was inhabited by a comparative handful of people, forced by their very intimacy with each other to live by a different standard altogether, because the horizon they shared was frighteningly vast, lonely, humbling in its very magnitude.

'I don't suppose it's possible to send a message?' she said

again.

Mannie turned in surprise, laughing with genuine amusement.

'Of course it's possible!' she told Lindsay. 'We're very much in touch here, really, you know. You just write out what you want to say, and I'll send a telegram for you over the transceiver—that's what we call the modern form of pedal wireless, Lindsay, because they hardly ever use pedal sets any more. I don't suppose you needed them at Batlow, did you? Ah well, here we depend on them for almost everything—telegrams and messages, and to summon the Flying Doctor or the Air Ambulance, and of course we have the galah session, and the school of the air.'

'School? You mean, proper lessons?' Lindsay looked her surprise.

'Oh yes, proper lessons, just the same as if the children were in class together. Each pupil has his own call-sign, you see, and one by one the children are called in by the School-of-the-Air teacher. They participate in discussions, have questions and answers just as in a normal class—they even learn poetry and do plays. They have correspondence lessons by post, too, of course.'

'But that's marvellous!' Lindsay was impressed. 'And the galah session? Was that what you called it?'

'Yes, the galah—or sometimes it's termed the magpie. Now that's different again, and mostly for adults—housewives, in fact. They have an open session at a certain time each day, and all the women from near and far join in, swapping gossip and bits of news. There's nothing private about the Outback, Lindsay, even when you're miles from your nearest neighbour! Everyone knows what everyone else is doing, and the galah session is largely responsible. We call it that after those flocks of chattering pink and grey parrots, and believe me, the noise of human voices, the static, the calling-in of the signs, can sometimes be as noisy as any flock of birds! Even the tiniest detail can seem a meaty piece of gossip on the galah. It's the true bush telegraph!'

'They—they won't have heard about *me*?' asked Lindsay diffidently.

71

Poor Lindsay! Her ideas about bush life were being shattered every minute.

'Oh yes, they will—if not today, then tomorrow. Everyone knew that Gundooee was getting a new book-keeper. And very soon they will know that not only did the new book-keeper arrive, but that he turned out to be a girl instead of a man.' Mannie chuckled irrepressibly. '*That* should set them by the ears!'

Lindsay shuddered.

'W-will they know that Mr. Bennett was very angry when he found out?' she asked somewhat dismally.

Mannie's wrinkled face was still creased with humour.

'*Was* he angry?' she countered mildly. 'I don't think so. Rod is a very controlled person, and doesn't give away his feelings very easily. He has to be controlled, Lindsay, being in charge of a large number of people of such varying types, you see. It's a position of great responsibility, Rod's. He's got to know how to do everything he expects his men to do, and be able to do it better, so that they respect him. And he's got to be a bit of a psychologist, too. He often says it's part of his job to know what his men are thinking, almost before they know it themselves, and that way he can keep the path smooth, anticipating little troubles, and ironing them out before they can grow into big ones. I must say he's very good at doing that—almost uncanny, in fact—but on the other hand, it's very difficult to tell what's going on in his own mind. He's adept at concealing his feelings, and that gives him an immediate advantage in dealing with the grievances of others. All his men respect him, and depend upon his judgment to a greater or lesser extent, and his own temperament gives them encouragement to confide in him. I'd be very surprised to hear that he was angry—and in front of a mere girl, too!'

Mannie's paragon could apparently do no wrong in *her* eyes!

Lindsay swallowed, remembering.

'He was angry, all right,' she asserted feelingly.

'You were probably tired and a little overwrought, and imagined it,' Mannie told her comfortingly. 'In any case, although *you* will have been mentioned on the galah, nobody would dare to discuss Rod or his affairs so frivolously. They have far too much respect for him to do such a thing. They'll only have heard that Mr. Dutten turned out to be a Miss, and after all, what harm is there in them hearing that? It was a most unfortunate misunderstanding, nothing more.'

'Er—yes—most unfortunate.'

Lindsay moved her slender shoulders as if thereby she could ease her miserable load of guilt. If only Mannie knew! If only Mannie could guess how little misunderstanding there had really been! If only she could know how calculated had been Lindsay's deception from the outset! And if *he* should ever suspect—well, he'd pack her out of here on his very own plane before she could even say 'Ned Kelly', and it didn't take very long to say *that*!

'The message, dear?' came Mannie's gentle interruption to her thoughts. 'And you can follow it up with a more detailed letter on mail-day. Right?'

'Yes, thank you, Mannie.'

What a kind and helpful person Mannie was, reflected Lindsay to herself as she completed the unpacking of her meagre wardrobe later.

Mannie had told her that she used once to be governess to the Bennett family when they were small. Rod had been the youngest of three brothers, and when his parents died he had invited Mannie, who was by then widowed and struggling to maintain herself on a small pension, to return to Gundooee to act as his housekeeper. She had been grateful to accept. The old days spent at the station held happy memories for her, and now that she was in real need of a home and companionship, she could think of no place she would rather be.

There was little enough that she could do for Rod in return, she had confided to Lindsay, but he never allowed her to feel beholden in any way. Indeed, the reverse was the case. He acted as though Mannie herself was doing him a great favour in just being there, making her own quiet contribution to the running of the property. He had actually *wanted* Mannie to return to Gundooee, thought Lindsay wanly, even though she happened to be a woman. He had wanted—and invited—her.

He hadn't wanted Lindsay though. He hadn't exactly invited her, either, she had to admit. In a way she had invited herself, Lindsay supposed. She had gone into this with her eyes open, except that she had imagined that all country places were the same. *That* had been her big mistake. She had been thankful to leave the city behind her, had revelled in the scenery over the Mountains and through the Central West, had actually enjoyed herself until the train angled off into the 'never-never', (or what seemed to Lindsay's inexperienced observation to be the 'never-never'!) and at the end of that frightening and lonely journey, Emmadanda had been a surprise, and not a pleasant one.

Gundooee now seemed like an oasis in the desert of her hopes. She knew instinctively that she could be happy here the very moment she stepped out of that plane. Even the peculiar gleam in the eyes of all those men couldn't detract from the welcome in their smiles, could it? They had been the bush friends, about to greet her with their kindly voices, only something had spoilt it all, something had prevented them. Some*one*. The man who hadn't had a smile for her. The man whose grey eyes had held no strange gleam. Rod Bennett himself. And he had turned out to be the Boss.

Lindsay placed her nylon tights carefully in one of the big mahogany drawers, and mourned her luck. Why had she to run into such a man as he? Things could have been so different, except for him. Instead of a new, happy, 'bush' atmosphere, he made her feel virtually stateless, unwanted. She had cut the other ties that bound in order to come to Gundooee, and now the manager was going to try to freeze her out with his cold words of censure, his chilly grey gaze, his thoroughly unfriendly attitude, his *Miss* Dutten! Why, he had already refused even to let her have that dear little cottage that the book-keeper had always had. And it wasn't because she was a woman, whatever he liked to pretend. Hadn't Mannie told her that he *liked* girls, as a rule? All those lovely Brisbane belles—he must like those girls, mustn't he, to invite them out here to Gundooee for the Races just as he must like Mannie to have asked her to live here.

He liked those other girls, and he liked Mannie, too. It was Lindsay he *didn't* like! His antipathy was almost a living thing between them, and there was little that Lindsay could do about that.

She stood up, smoothed down her denim skirt and walked over to the mirror, gazed wistfully at her reflection.

What she saw was strangely depressing—a slender, girlish figure in a white shirt, a schoolgirl outfit!—guileless green eyes, wounded and apprehensive; coltish bare legs and arms too skinny to ever be seductive; an innocent mouth; bright brown, unmanageable hair that refused to be coaxed into a more elegant coiffure.

No, she certainly was no belle, but an ugly duckling for sure. And as for those clothes——! Clothes didn't make a beauty, but they certainly must help! If only she still had some of Carleen's, they might have helped a little bit towards a more sophisticated image.

She had so wanted to be liked, to find herself among friends. She *had* found some, too—Mannie, with her wrinkled, gentle face, Sibbie and Bella with their watermelon smiles and gay giggles, all those men who had surrounded her when she stepped out of the plane.

All except for one person alone.

Slumping disconsolately down upon the bed, unable to understand herself or the reason for her own misery, Lindsay admitted to her chagrin how unkind Fate could be—admitted that the very person whose friendship she would *really* like to have was the man whose antagonism was so chillingly obvious.

Rod Bennett.

CHAPTER 5

LINDSAY got up early next morning, mainly because she could not sleep. Depression gripped her, but she could also admit to an underlying determination to make a good impression on her boss at the first opportunity.

Sun-up was preluded by the whining and whimpering of the dogs in the settlement down at the creek. Their barking reached Lindsay's ears even before the first traditional crowing of the cock in the fowl-run or the shrill chattering of the birds which nested in the shrubs and saplings outside the window. She slipped from her bed and padded quietly out on to the veranda.

The birds' noise seemed to be concentrated around the banks of the big ground-tank beyond the garden. In the first faint light, Lindsay could not see the birds themselves, only the raised edges of the tank and the silhouette of the windmill that towered at one end. The sails were stirring lazily in the breath of dawn. The shaft of warm air from the plains could hardly be called a breeze, and was not sufficiently strong to blow the sails into revolutions, and the pump-rod groaned every now and then—a deep, baritone interruption to the trilling and cheeping of the birds—as though frustrated by its own inactivity.

A splash at the far end of the tank sent the birds chittering away into the trees. Lindsay pressed her nose against the gauze and peered out curiously.

Someone was swimming in the tank.

She could just discern a dark head moving, arms cleaving the water with long, easy, powerful strokes that scarcely disturbed the surface. That head, and the foot-splash, told her that whoever the swimmer was, he was certainly moving fast, up to one end, then back, then up again, without apparent effort.

76

After a time the figure stopped swimming, climbed out of the water and towelled itself perfunctorily. Then it came towards the house.

Lindsay waited only long enough to perceive that the dawn swimmer was none other than Rod Bennett himself, clad in brief black trunks, his tanned body glistening with wetness, the towel that had only half performed its task slung carelessly around his neck.

As he approached, she turned quietly and hastened back to her room. It would be awful if he caught her spying on him!

After she had dressed, she walked down towards the store. In the pocket of her denim skirt she carried the keys of both the store and the little cottage. The manager had given them to her the previous afternoon with an off-hand suggestion that she had better 'get started', and Lindsay had wondered, as she eyed the rows of unfamiliar bottles, cans, packs, and tins, the assortment of clothing and bedding, the drugs and chemicals, just where one *did* start, and how!

She had locked the store again hastily, and had gone instead to the cottage, relieved to find herself in the more familiar world of accounts, receipts, and statements.

Today she planned an early assault on the problem of that store. There was little to be gained by putting off the evil moment any longer. After all, it was possible that someone might ask for something at any time, and she would feel very stupid if she had not at least familiarised herself with the layout.

Lindsay hummed under her breath as she walked, her depression gone. There was something about this fresh, Outback morning that induced optimism, banished apprehension. As she neared the station-hands' quarters, she caught the sound of whistling, and several varieties of singing, together with the splash and splutter of noisy ablutions, and as she passed the building, she realised that these sounds all emanated from the row of shower cubicles. She was relieved to note that whereas yesterday the showers had been open for all to see, pieces of sacking had now been nailed roughly to the bottom half of each cubicle, secured by hooks of fencing wire, so that the lower portion of the ablutionist's anatomy was effectively screened.

Even so, Lindsay went scarlet with embarrassment as, too late, she realised that she had walked right into the men's bathing session. Head down, she scuttled along the row, obtaining, as she ran, a cineramic impression of flailing arms, dripping heads, muscular shoulders, grunts, splutters, whistles.

A sidelong glimpse of a freckled back and thatch of red hair that could only belong to Bluey—Mickie's face grinning cheekily over the hessian—Herb's toothless mouth agape as she scudded past—Artie's baritone from the final cubicle—

'I been chasin' sheilas for more than half me life, but seldom have I found one I'd ask ter be me wife,' Artie was rumbling enthusiastically as she flew past.

'*Don't* you try ter leave me, *don't* you try ter run——'

The united chorus of the refrain reached Lindsey's ears as she panted round the far corner. The occupants of all the cubicles had joined in for that bit, and the subsequent laughter followed her as she plunged her hand into her skirt-pocket and brought out the key of the store.

Inside, she slammed the door and stood for a moment, slightly shaken by her experience, then, after recovering her breath, she began to check over all the things that were in the room.

Lindsay had no idea what some of the articles were. After gazing around with a certain amount of self-exasperation at her own ignorance, she decided that the only system she could adopt which would make for sensible handling would be to regroup all the supplies which she did know along one lot of shelves, and place all the ones which were unfamiliar at the other end of the place. She would then be able surreptitiously to enlist the aid of one of the men, and by the time Rod Bennett turned up, she would be *au fait* with her domain. There was a hope in Lindsay's mind that he never *would* turn up! After all, that was what he hired a book-keeper for, wasn't it? Maybe he would just leave her to do things in her own way, and with the men's help she would manage to bungle along somehow. Lindsay found herself

78

praying fervently that this was the way it would be!

She had piled the heaps of khaki clothing together in a corner, sorted blankets and bolts of bright cotton materials, and was in the process of dragging a couple of rolled leather machinery-belts across the floor—they were surprisingly heavy, and covered with a grease preservative which added to their slippery state—when the door opened and a shadow darkened the entrance. Lindsay straightened, turned to face the bow-legged, lounging figure that now sauntered inside.

Artie's grin was faintly self-conscious. He cleared his throat noisily.

'G'day, Lindsay. A beaut mornin', eh?'

'Er—good morning. Artie, isn't it? I'm just beginning to put the right names to the right faces, I think.'

'Bang on, this time, then. Artie's me monicker, true enough. Williams is the other bit. Artie Williams.'

Lindsay paused uncertainly. She had not been properly introduced to any of the men yet, and now that one of them was actually here, announcing himself, perhaps she should shake hands. *Did* one shake hands out here in the Outback, or didn't one? They all seemed such casual, friendly people that Lindsay could not be sure. It was better not to take chances, anyway—better not to risk offending.

She wiped her hand down the side of her denim skirt, leaving a disastrous trail of belt-grease, and held it out in Artie's direction.

'How do you do,' said Lindsay formally.

Artie blinked, but only for a moment, before he gripped her hand in a crushing grasp and shook it vigorously.

'Reckon I'm O.K.,' he told her on a note of surprise that this slender, rather lost-looking sheila could possibly be concerned as to his present state of health. 'How about you?' he added, with commendable presence of mind.

'I'm O.K. too.'

Lindsay smiled, and Art smiled, and then they both laughed, quite uproariously.

'That's that, then,' observed Artie with some relief. 'Yer gone and got grease on yer skirt now, Lindsay.' He poked a gnarled finger in the direction of the smear.

'Oh dear, so I have!' she wailed. 'It's my only skirt, too.'

'Reckon there's somethink 'ere for that, though. There's somethink 'ere for *everythink*, supposed to be.' The station-hand began to go through the assortment of bottles on the shelf. 'Yep, 'ere we are—Kum-Kleen—I reckon that'll shift it.'

He handed her a stoppered bottle with a red and white label.

'Yer shouldn't of 'ad it *there*, though, Lindsay. Not right beside that belly-ache mixture. And look where yer've got the strychnine for them dingo baits! Good Gawd Almighty! If Rod sees any of them things mixed up with the stummick stuff, 'e'll 'ave yer hide, I'm tellin' yer! 'E can't afford fer folk ter be swallerin' the wrong stuff away out 'ere, yer know, Lindsay. The Flyin' Doctor ain't a ruddy miracle man, quick though 'e is when we need 'im.'

'*I* didn't put them there,' Lindsay hastened to point out in self-defence. 'I was just beginning to sort things out, Artie, and I haven't touched the bottles yet.'

'Well, they ought ter be locked up, and clocked in on that chart, see. It must've been that Lowney feller then—the last bloke. 'E was on the booze somethink awful this last while.'

'Oh, I see.' Lindsay had wondered about the previous book-keeper. 'Was he—er—dismissed?'

Artie shook his head.

' 'E would of been,' he asserted darkly, 'only 'e ran off with a well-sinker's wife first. Kind of took Rod on the 'op.'

'Oh.' Fancy anyone managing to take the psychic Rod Bennett on the hop! Lindsay was aware of a tiny thrust of respect for her predecessor, booze and all. 'Surely he must have been very upset—the well-sinker, I mean?'

' 'E was flamin' crazy at first'—Art spoke with retrospective relish—'but 'e soon got sort of used to it. 'E's got 'is sights set on a little filly out at Peperina since then. 'Ere, give me that cloth and I'll rub it for yer.'

Before she could reply, Artie had taken the cleaning fluid from her, splashed it liberally on to some wadding, and rubbed clumsily at her skirt with blunt-fingered, awkward hands. He appeared absorbed in his task, completely unabashed at his necessary proximity.

'There y'are! That's fixed it.' He handed back the Kum-Kleen, dropped the wadding in the rubbish tin, and grinned engagingly. Lindsay smiled back, then retreated quickly to the other side of the counter at the answering gleam in his eye. It was the self-same gleam that had been present in all those eyes that morning—was it only two mornings ago?—when she had alighted from the plane. All eyes but one pair, that is.

'Er—thank you, Artie. I'm very grateful,' she said from her place of instinctive sanctuary. 'Now, is there something I can do for you? Something you came in to get?'

Lindsay's direct question produced quite an astounding effect upon Art. The gleam in his eye faded instantly, to be replaced by a look of acute embarrassment. Colour gathered slowly under his rugged tan, deepening to such a rich plum shade that Lindsay wondered, in quick alarm, if the man was sickening for some sort of physical fit. He took off his wide, battered felt hat, wiped his forehead with a rough palm, scratched his ear uncomfortably, shifted his feet in their heavy boots, slammed the hat on again, and turned to her with a sudden show of iron determination.

'I reckon I never came for somethink in the store, Lindsay,' he muttered doggedly.

'For what, then, Artie?' Lindsay asked, intrigued.

'I came to get a kiss, that's what.'

The admission was delivered in such a strangled, choking, but determined tone that Lindsay was asking herself if she could possibly have heard aright.

'Did you say—you did say—a *kiss*?' she repeated, half startled, half incredulous.

'Yeah—a kiss,' Artie reiterated with a slight indication of returning courage.

'Yes, that's what I th-thought you said.' Lindsay's voice was weak. She sat down heavily on the pile of blankets.

There was silence for a moment, broken only by the sound of Art's still-restricted breathing processes.

'Well—will yer?' he asked, diffidently.

'I—I don't think—no, Artie, I'm afraid not,' returned

Lindsay firmly.

'*Please*, Lindsay. Just one.'

'No, Artie, not one. Couldn't you go over to—to Peperina, maybe? Like the—er—the well-sinker?' she suggested helpfully, touched by the man's air of defeat.

Artie shook his head dejectedly.

'It ain't the same,' he said dismally. 'Yer see, Lindsay'—he gave her a direct, pleading look—'it's gotter be *you*. Nobody else will do.'

'Me?' Her eyes rounded. 'But why *me*?'

Artie scuffed self-consciously at the floor-boards with the toe of his boot.

' 'Cos we're bettin' on it, see, Lindsay.'

Lindsay's eyes, round before, were now like saucers.

'*Betting* on it! Do you mean, betting on—er—on *me*?'

'Yeah, that's right.'

'Good gracious!' Her mind was racing, implications jostling with one another for pride of place.

'First bloke home collects the kitty,' Artie explained now, earnestly. 'I reckoned this was me chance, Lindsay, when I seen yer comin' in 'ere. I didn't mean ter startle yer, honest. I wasn't goin' ter *pounce* on yer, or anythink like that. Even now, if yer won't do it, well, yer won't, and that's me out. I'd most certainly 'ave liked ter collect, all the same.' His deep voice was wistful.

'And if it isn't you, will one of the others try?'

'You bet yer, Lindsay, they'll try. I don't know how or when or where, but they'll *try*—Herb and Mickie and Blue and Shorty.'

'And if *you* get a kiss, then they'll stop trying?' Lindsay was assembling her thoughts.

'That's it.'

'If *you* get a kiss, that will be the end of it?'

'That'll be the end of it.'

'Once and for ever?'

'Once an' fer all, Lindsay—you can bet on that!'

'I don't think so, Artie. I think there's enough betting going on around here without me starting,' Lindsay was driven to point out smilingly.

Artie grinned, unabashed. 'Gee, Lindsay, you're a little beaut! Does that mean you'll do it?'

'I'll do it, Artie. I don't think I have much choice.'

'Except who *with*,' he elucidated with some humility.

'I'd like you to be the one,' said Lindsay gently.

Artie scratched his ear, caught once more in a transfixing agony of embarrassment.

'I ain't much of a hand,' he mumbled apologetically.

'Never mind,' comforted Lindsay. 'I'll do all I can to help. But how will the others know? Will they just take your word for it?'

'Not them. That's the other thing. That's why I reckoned on this bein' a good time ter take the bull by the 'orns,' Artie was explaining. 'Cook's gettin' breakfast, and they're all out there waitin' around fer the tucker-bell, so if we was ter go outside——'

'I see. Let's get it over, then, Artie, shall we?'

Lindsay got off the bale of blankets and walked to the door with resolution in her step.

'I'll go yer splits, Lindsay, if yer like? How about that?'

'No, thank you, Art,' she declined with dignity. 'I don't wish to make off the deal, only to end it. It's as much for my sake as yours.'

'You're a beaut, a little beaut.' He pulled the door shut behind him, locked it, passed her the key. 'Not a word, though, eh, Lindsay? Not to Mannie, or to Rod? Rod, most of all. 'E'd skin us alive if 'e knew.'

'Not a word to anyone,' Lindsay found herself promising with due solemnity and a sense of complete unreality, as she and Artie walked together over the bare, smooth ground in the warm, early hush of that Outback dawn, until they were within sight and range of the clinking sounds of the hut-cook's breakfast pans, and in full view of the men who were hanging about waiting to eat that breakfast.

Lindsay and Artie stopped and faced each other.

'I ain't much,' warned Artie once more. He was very red indeed.

'If it's only for a bet, it doesn't matter, does it,' Lindsay reminded him encouragingly, 'just as long as it's a kiss.'

Strange that she should not mind! Strange that she should be the one to impart confidence and consolation to this big, awkward, inarticulate bushman! But then perhaps it was because she could sense in Artie a fundamental kindness, a basic decency, a hesitant humility and honesty that were oddly endearing qualities in a work-roughened, tough-living 'outbacker', that she didn't mind him being the *one*. Artie was nice, and Artie was on the level. If Lindsay hadn't agreed, he'd have been willing to leave it at that.

She sent him a warm smile.

'You're a decent kid, Lindsay.'

He put his hands on her shoulders, and gave her a quick peck on the cheek, and Lindsay, suddenly afraid that the gesture had not even been noticed by the men lounging around near the cook-house, found herself putting her arms right around Art's sun-seamed neck and squeezing hard.

They might as well do the thing properly, she told herself. It was better to leave no doubt at all in those other men's minds that a kiss had been exchanged, because she did not want to be pestered any more over this wretched bet! She wanted it settled, once and for all, as Artie had promised it would be, and that was why she hugged Art just as hard as she could, and even gave him a return kiss near the side of his stubbled chin.

That should do it! she told herself, noting with a sense of satisfaction that the men outside the cook-house were now standing immobile in their tracks, as though turned to stone by the unexpected scene they had witnessed. The conversation had ceased. The silence was so complete that it seemed to Lindsay as though the very birds had ceased to sing. Even the cook, who had stopped clattering his tin plates and pannikins about inside the cook-house and had come to stand in the doorway, suddenly stopped wiping his hands on the front of his butcher's apron and left his fingers dangling stupidly in mid-air.

Yes, thought Lindsay with gratification, *that* should finish the whole silly affair! The effect on the bystanders had been dramatic indeed.

She opened her mouth to say something light-hearted to

84

Artie—she *felt* light-hearted, as though she had successfully disposed of a potentially unpleasant business—and then she closed her lips again, because Artie's eyes weren't looking at her at all. They were centred on something right behind her, a little to her left, and they held an oddly riveted expression, every bit as dramatic in its intensity as the silent tableau down beside the cook-house.

Lindsay turned to see what could possibly have captured Artie's attention so completely, and stiffened as visibly as though she had been Lot's wife turning into a pillar of salt.

Rod Bennett was standing not far away, his feet in their heeled stockman's boots planted a little apart on the dusty ground, his brown hands linked casually into the plaited hide belt that held up his moleskins. That was the *only* casual thing about him, that stance!

Lindsay felt the impact of his shrewd grey gaze rake her with a force that was almost physical. She took an involuntary step backwards, bumped into the transfixed Artie, who seemed to recover his senses at the contact and shambled off towards the cook-house as fast as he could.

Rod Bennett ground his heel in the dust with a curious sort of savagery, turned without a word, and went the other way. Lindsay, still encased in her own immobility, stared after him until he was out of sight. Then she forced her tottering limbs in the direction of the homestead.

Breakfast tasted like sawdust that morning! Lindsay chewed her way through chop and egg with wooden concentration, aware of the relish with which her employer, to her right, disposed of his own much larger helping. She swallowed hot tea automatically, folded her napkin thankfully when the meal was at an end.

She might have known, of course, that a man like Rod Bennett would not allow such a facile escape!

'I wish to see you in my office, please, Miss Dutten,' he announced firmly when they finally left the table.

'Certainly, Mr. Bennett.' Lindsay tried to match his calmness, but failed miserably. She actually felt sick with dread. She could see her dismissal looming up to meet her, and felt powerless to prevent it.

If only she could explain! If only he could be made to understand what a light-hearted, meaningless, *silly* little act it had all been. Like a schoolgirl dare, almost. But Rod Bennett didn't look the sort who would have any patience with schoolgirls or their dares, just as he hadn't with his own men's inveterate inclination to gamble on any and every incident that presented itself. 'He'd skin us alive,' Artie had said, and Lindsay had promised not to tell. If she told, she would maybe be able to make Rod Bennett understand the harmlessness of that one little kiss, but in doing so she would forfeit her friendship with all the men, and in her capacity as store-keeper she would be coming into contact with them a good deal more than with the aloof and unfriendly Mr. Bennett.

No, to tell would be unthinkable. And yet *not* to tell meant the permanent banishment of all those things for which Lindsay found herself wistfully longing—the warmth of a grey-eyed welcome, the fond glance of respect, the caressing comfort of a true affection that was reserved exclusively for Mannie. Lindsay longed for the contribution she intended to make to Gundooee to be recognised in the same way. She wanted to be *wanted*, longed to be able to call Gundooee her home, the way Mannie could. Lindsay knew, as she followed the big, loping figure in the direction of his office, that this man was capable of all those endearing qualities that so attracted her, because he gave them all, unstintingly, to Mannie. How nice to bask in the sunshine of his approval, the way the old lady did, thought Lindsay enviously. If she, Lindsay, could just enjoy that approval, too, she would not ask for more. After all, she wasn't one of those lovely, sophisticated Brisbane Belles, with pretty clothes and loads of poise and a fund of amusing repartee. She was only simple Lindsay Dutten, longing for a home and a welcome, and that was as much as one could expect when one had flyaway hair, gangling limbs, an uncertain manner, and a skirt that still reeked of Artie's Kum-Kleen!

The interview only took a few minutes. Just a few, measly minutes, Lindsay told herself as she reeled down the passage and out on to the veranda. A few measly minutes to condemn you out of hand and shred your hopes into little pieces.

'I have no intention of discussing in detail the unsavoury scene I witnessed earlier, Miss Dutten. It did not come as any great surprise to me, however.' A jaded sigh. 'Like women in the shearing-sheds, I knew you added up to a packet of trouble the minute you stepped off that plane. And yet I hoped—I thought——' He was pacing angrily, visibly put out.

'*What* did you think, hope, Mr. Bennett?' Lindsay had asked humbly. There was something faintly encouraging in that slight hesitation in a man who was obviously not given to hesitations of any sort.

'Never mind what I thought,' he growled deeply. 'It seems I was wrong, anyway. But'—a disgusted glance—'on your *second* day—so short a time——'

'It wasn't like that, Mr. Bennett, truly it wasn't!' How awful to have to suffer like this, not even to be able to *say*, to have to go on letting him think—oh!

'I saw with my own eyes how it was, thank you, Miss Dutten. Explanations would be futile, in the circumstances.' How cold those grey eyes, how chilly that disdainful mouth! It seemed an effort for him even to speak to her, as though the sight of her was unbearably distasteful. He forced himself to proceed. 'Obviously, there is one thing, and one thing only, which as an employer I must ascertain. You were an agreeable party, Miss Dutten? A willing and agreeable party?'

Lindsay could only stare, mesmerised. Inside, she was hollow, unable to think.

'Come now, Miss Dutten, you can surely see that this is something I have to know? If you were coerced, compromised in any way, then it's up to me to discipline my men.'

'I was willing, Mr. Bennett.' Lindsay heard her own voice dully, echoing in a vacuum of despair.

'Yes, I thought so. That's how it appeared to me, too.' For some reason, his broad shoulders appeared to slump. Just for a moment, his eyes were a different sort of grey—wounded, vulnerable almost. And then the chill, the self-discipline, were back.

He doesn't like being wrong, thought Lindsay shrewdly to herself. He doesn't like to be wrong about anything, and his pride is hurt, and that's why he looked sort of *defeated* a moment ago.

'In that case I shall of course leave the matter where it is. But as for *you*—I shall have to have your categoric assurance that such a thing will not occur again. If it does, you'll go!'

'Oh, it won't, it *won't*, Mr. Bennett, honestly. It was only once—I mean—I wish I could explain——'

'Useless, in any case, when I have the evidence of my own eyes,' he reminded her quellingly. 'You may go, Miss Dutten.'

'Yes, Mr. Bennett. I'd just like to say——'

'You may *go*, Miss Dutten,' he repeated impatiently. 'I don't intend to waste more time talking about it. Just see that you keep out of the men's way as much as possible—and mine, too,' he added forcibly. 'It's as bad as having women in the sheds, damn it!' He was still muttering gruffly to himself as she scuttled for the door.

Lindsay saw little of him, indeed, after that. Certainly he was courteous when he came in for meals, but there was that way he had of being distantly polite that told Lindsay she was stateless, unaccepted, still very much of an intruder, who had brought with her nothing but unwelcome complications in his eyes.

Rod Bennett always made breakfast as brief an affair as possible. Hair still wet from his morning swim, brown throat exposed in his open-necked khaki shirt, he would favour Mannie with his warm, grey, affectionate regard, help her into her chair with a tanned, capable hand that could be curiously gentle, and give her that slow, endearing smile. Then he would turn to Lindsay, and the warm light would fade from his eyes, leaving them cold and, somehow, *careful*.

'Good morning, Miss Dutten,' was what she always got, accompanied by the merest curl of the mouth, a grimace that couldn't even be called a half smile.

With the other men, things were different. They were instantly and openly friendly, beguiling in their rough, outspoken way. She liked them for their cheerful, casual grins that lit their weathered faces whenever she appeared; their teasing, and their fun.

They reorganised the store for her; showed her how to work the transceiver; how to make a fly-veil with bobbing corks to keep those buzzing little pests at bay while she worked; how to tell when it might rain because the birds were flying low, or what the morrow would be like by the sunset. They taught her about the wild life around her, the bush mice, the marsupials, the eagles nesting in the mulga, the rabbits in their sandy, many-holed burrows, the honey-eaters seeking out the scrub blossoms, the path of the wild bees.

She learned that Sibbie and Bella had husbands, down there at the creek. They were the two aboriginal stockmen who had been at the plane the day she arrived, and their names were Jimmy and Tommo. Down at the gunyahs, she befriended the merry little children who ran about, fat-tummied and skinny-limbed, laughing widely whenever she appeared. They wore wispy rags, sometimes not even those, and the smell of dogs and goanna fat hung about them as they played down by the creek baiting yabbies, or dug for grubs under the bark of the trees, or simply ran about, pelting each other with quandongs, skipping with an old rope in the shade of a spotted gum, or throwing their home-made bubberas, warming the boomerangs first with all the earnestness and concentration of their forebears.

When their parents yelled 'All-about, quickfella, youse lot!' they would drop their playthings and run to get their tucker—civilised, station tucker, with plentiful meat and damper and johnny-cakes made with the white man's flour, now an accepted part of their life, just as were the fragments of white man's clothing which they wore, and the much-prized cheap ornamental combs which they stuck in their oiled hair.

Lindsay discovered that perfume of any sort was a very quick way to these simple people's hearts, and that their spending money—or 'finger' money as they sometimes called it—was often spent on hair-oil, highly scented shaving lotions (which Lindsay suspected found its way to their heads also!), and the ubiquitous combs and beads. Josie, one of the young teenage girls who sometimes came to help her mother in the house, had shown Lindsay a whole dillybag full of such treasures and trinkets. Laying them reverently on the ground between them, she had uncorked the stoppers on the small bottles of oils and lotions, sniffing with a properly ceremonial dignity, and explaining to Lindsay that this was the way to keep him 'smellum plenty strongfella, eh!', whereas the scent would soon 'go walkabout' if used in the traditional manner. Reeling from the heady, concentrated reek that assailed her nostrils, Lindsay conceded the point, and could only conclude that the cheap perfume had undergone some sort of horrid chemical metamorphosis through Josie's frequent exposures to the air and heat—or perhaps through sheer old age!

As stockmen, Jimmy and Tommo were a valued part of the Gundooee work-out, and their superb native horsemanship was evident even to Lindsay's unknowledgeable eye as they cut out steers at the dusty yards to which Mickie had obligingly driven her in the station jeep, expressly to watch the show. She marvelled at the control they displayed, both of the cattle and of their own mounts, because they made such exceedingly careless pictures in the saddle. Their bodies seemed to sag nervelessly in their faded shirts and felted trousers, battered hats crammed down on black glistening foreheads, Jimmy's broad nose and grizzled beard jutting beneath the brim, Tommo, with his filthy but ever-present pipe clenched unlit in his teeth. Even when the stock-horses whirled without warning in the wake of a scrubber, their bodies remained limp and uncaring, but tenaciously glued to that saddle, as though they and the horses were acting through the medium of a single mind.

'They make it look so *easy*,' breathed Lindsay, who had not ridden a horse since the podgy Taffy of her tender years.

'Well, it's not,' Mickie assured her laughingly. 'This is my third year here as a jackaroo—Shorty's, too—and they can still run rings around us, and most of the other men. Rod's the only one on the place who can rival them at that game—not surprising, really, since Jimmy's own father taught him all his horsemanship almost as soon as he could walk.'

'Jimmy's father? I hadn't realised that Jimmy had been here all his life. I thought, from what Mannie has told me, that the aborigines came and went on walkabouts, and never stayed as long as a whole generation in one place.'

'It's difficult to generalise, Lindsay, because there are so many different types among them, and a great many these days are of mixed blood, and adopt varying genetic attributes of both sides of such assimilations. Jimmy's great-grand-father was supposed to be an Afghan, one of the camel-drivers from further out, in the days before the Bitumen and the railway. He married a full-blooded aboriginal girl, and Jimmy's father, in his turn, married the half-caste daughter of a local storeman, so there was a bit of a mix-up all round.'

'And so they put down roots? No more wanderlust?'

Mickie nodded. 'You could say that I suppose. As development spread, and the seasonal ebb and flow of nature's bounty is counteracted by regular supplies of food and clothing from the stations' stores, there isn't the same need to go chasing off on a survival course from time to time, either.'

'No, I see what you mean. Which reminds me, talking of stores, tomorrow must be mail-day again, isn't it?'

'That's right.' Mickie slid off the tail-board of the jeep where he had been perching to drink a pannikin of tea, threw the dregs in the dust, and tucked his own mug, along with Lindsay's, into a corner among the assortment of junk that littered the back of the vehicle. He grinned, hitched his trousers, and jerked a thumb in the direction of the drafting-out operations. 'Smoko is over, then, Lindsay. Shorty will take you back, the lucky blighter. Rod said I was to take his place, and send him home with you. O.K.?'

'Yes, of course. And thanks for arranging it, Mickie. I *have* enjoyed watching!'

'Don't thank me, thank Rod. It was his idea, after all,' returned her escort surprisingly. 'Said he didn't suppose you'd had much chance to see cattle being cut out, where you came from.'

Yes, she could her him saying that, all right, thought Lindsay. She could imagine the ironic look in his eye, the sarcastic lift to his mouth. Batlow, he'd been thinking. *Batlow!*

Remembering the derision with which he'd referred to her beloved Utopian childhood home, Lindsay felt her first instinctive flame of gratitude to Rod for his thoughtfulness flicker, and then snuff out. It hadn't really been for her that he'd arranged this outing. He had merely wanted Mickie to change places with Shorty, that was all.

'Don't look so gloomy, Lindsay. What's there to be gloomy about in a mail-day? Unless, of course, you've been expecting a letter that didn't come? A *love*-letter, maybe?'

'Don't be a dope, Mickie,' Lindsay laughed, dragging her thoughts back unwillingly to what her young escort was saying.

'No love-letter, then?'

'Of course not.'

'No bloke down there in the Big Smoke, wilting away for lack of his Lindsay?' Mickie's blue eyes were teasing.

'No. No bloke.'

'No bloke *anywhere*?'

'Not anywhere.' She jumped down from the jeep, bare brown limbs flying as she leapt, a girlish figure in the white shirt, faded blue skirt and sandshoes which had seen her through her final schooldays.

'There's hope for me yet, then, eh!' Mickie gave her a playful chuck under the chin. 'I'm glad you aren't expecting a letter on that mail-plane, Lindsay girl.'

He gave her a two-fingered salute, jammed his hat down more firmly on his perspiring brow, and sauntered off in the direction of the dust-cloud of pounding hooves and wheeling horses.

Lindsay settled the fly-veil down over her own hat again. Then she took a sugar-bag from the back of the jeep and sat down in the small patch of shade on its off-side to await the appearance of Shorty.

No bloke anywhere. Not *anywhere*. That's what she'd said

92

to Mickie, and of course it was true. There was no man in Lindsay's life, there never had been, and there wasn't likely to be. No man whose letters she breathlessly awaited off that mail-plane with a fond yearning of the heart; no man to put his arms around her and tell her not to worry about all the things she didn't know; no man to kiss away the confused doubts that tortured her about her future here and all its uncertainties; no man whose broad frame she could lean on, whose shoulder she could cry on, whose love could make a little 'ugly duckling' believe herself, almost, to be a beautiful, sophisticated, needed, *wanted* swan.

No, there was no bloke in her life, no one at all.

But sitting there on that dusty sugar-bag in the small square of shade with the flies buzzing in a small, persistent cloud, and the grunts and shouts of stockmen and beasts undulating towards her on the swimming waves of heat, Lindsay knew that, if there *had* been such a bloke, she could picture almost exactly how she would like that bloke to be.

He would be tall and sunburnt, with lean, tanned cheeks, and an endearing sort of groove that ran from nose to mouth. The mouth would be firm, a strong but flexible sort of mouth that kept you guessing between tenderness and severity. His hair would be a crisp, blacky-brown, springing away from a wide, intelligent forehead with a tiny white sun-strip at the top where his wide hat protected it, and maybe there would be one or two little grey hairs glinting just near the ear, because this bloke wasn't exactly a youth, like Mickie and Shorty, he was experienced and responsible, inclined very often to be grave and serious and—sometimes—censorious. But he wouldn't be like that to Lindsay, of course. For Lindsay, he would smile, with the slow, careful smile that showed the uneven whiteness of his teeth against the brownness of his face; a sweet, reluctant sort of smile that lit his keen grey eyes with a warmth and kindness that came right into his deep, stern voice, too, whenever he said things like, 'Good morning, Mannie,' and 'Thank you, Mannie.'

Oh, *Lindsay*! Whatever are you *thinking*? Lindsay, shaking with the horror of self-discovery, got tremblingly to her feet, and walked slowly around to the passenger side of the

CHAPTER 6

A LETTER on mail-day?

Lindsay had not been expecting one, but she received one all the same. From Carleen. She recognised the slanted, forceful capitals just as soon as she saw them.

It was Lindsay's task to sort out the letters, taking Rod's to his desk, and collecting the outgoing ones he had left there to be put in the returning mail-bag. This she could do at leisure, since the pilot usually spent the best part of an hour drinking his tea and chatting to Mannie about 'local' happenings that took place maybe a hundred miles away. While she was dealing with the post, Herb and Artie carried her supplies up to the store for her.

Today Lindsay put her own letter carefully to one side, and took it to her bedroom. What on earth had caused Carleen to write?

She was soon to find out!

'Mummy was pleased to hear that you had arrived safely at Gundooee, and that you have settled in. It sounds a terribly out-of-the-way place, but my dear, you must surely have realised by now just who Rod Bennett is? It's incredible, Lindsay, it really is, that you haven't heard of him. I mean, he's one of *the* Bennetts, you silly child, not just a manager on a property. As well as Gundooee, they own a whole string of other places, *and* he's an international swimmer, into the bargain. I can forgive you for not knowing that, as you'd have been too young when he represented Australia, but the rest——! Poor sweet, it's that dull little life you've always persisted in carving out for yourself that's responsible for your sublime ignorance, no doubt, but he's the *toast* of Brisbane society, that man, and as yet he seems to have eluded marriage, *don't* ask me

95

how! Actually, I'm not working at the moment. John has just finished the promised series with Sarino, and a great success, very exhausting, though, and I've said I'll only consider some more later if he agrees to do things my way. He's beginning to bore me, actually—I think we've got to know each other too well, no mystery left, that sort of thing, and it occurs to me that you might invite me up to stay at Gundooee for a while. I've missed you, Lindsay, I truly have, and I've felt awful about some of the things I said. I didn't mean them, pet—*you* know *me*. Fix it with your employer, will you? Just say that you've a cousin who is worried about you away out there, and who wants to come and see for herself that you're all right. I know he has oodles of Queensland girls to stay at Races time, and anyway, when he sees me he won't mind a bit that you did it. Write by return, will you, and let me know when to come. Yours ever, Carleen.'

Lindsay sank down on the bed in a confusion of surprise and bewilderment. One of *the* Bennetts! Lindsay had no idea who *the* Bennetts were, but if he was one of them, she supposed that that must account for his air of undisputed authority and the frequent trips to other properties in that graceful red-and-silver plane of his.

As for the swimming—well, she shouldn't be surprised at that, either. Recalling the grace, speed, and power of the dawn performer whom she still secretly watched sometimes she could only think what an inappropriate exercising pool for a swimmer of international calibre was that muddy, high-banked ground tank, with its brackish water and makeshift springboard. Lindsay couldn't remember *any* names in that connection. Not being good at sport herself, she had had only a minimal interest in its various spheres, and it would have been a few years ago, anyway, because from all she had read about the big-time, one retired early from that particular level of competition. Why, by about twenty-six years of age one was almost regarded as passé! She'd have been a mere schoolgirl when Rod Bennett was at the peak in his field!

Not that she had reason to doubt anything which Carleen had said. Even that bit about Rod's being the toast of Brisbane society was synonymous with what Mannie had already told her.

But Carleen *here*? Something inside Lindsay went cold at the mere thought. She had found herself a haven of peace on this great, lonely station. Away from the hateful hurly-burly of the city, she could feel her cramped personality slowly emerging like a butterfly from a chrysalis. Tentatively at first, more securely now, Lindsay was beginning to regard herself as a part of Gundooee. Her relationship with the men was a warming one, full of fun and joking. Forthright criticisms, outspoken comments, gruff compliments were meted out to her in turn, all part and parcel of these big, spare-talking, easy-going station-hands, who had taken this particular 'blinkin' *lost*-lookin' little sheila' to their hearts, showing her the ropes, and protecting her from Rod's possible ire when the need arose. They cunningly cushioned her mistakes, concealed her ignorance to the best of their not inconsiderable, and sometimes downright ingenious ability.

Carleen *here*? Oh, no, she couldn't possibly. It would all be spoilt, the whole precariously satisfactory situation!

Lindsay got up off the bed, sat down instead at her dressing-table, and wrote quickly, with determination.

'Dear Carleen, Thank you for you letter. I'm so glad that your modelling series with Sarino was such a success. Congratulations! You must have worked very hard to deserve that result from such a demanding creature! I'm afraid you would find life very dull out here. There is really nothing exciting to do, as I'm busy most of the time (I have to do a lot of other things besides the actual keeping of the books, as it turns out!) I wouldn't be able to be with you very much at all. In any case, I feel my employer would regard it as something of an impertinence and an imposition to ask one of my relatives to stay, when I've been here such a very short space of time myself. I'm sure you'll understand. Please give my love to Aunt and Uncle.

  As always, Lindsay.'

She sealed the envelope, addressed and stamped it, and took the mail-bag back to the pilot in the kitchen.

' 'Day, Lindsay.' It was the same man who had brought her here from Emmadanda all those weeks ago. 'How's tricks?'

'Not too bad, Mac, thank you. And you?'

'Mannie and I are catching up on all the gossip, you might say.' He sipped cautiously at his steaming mug of tea, twinkled from the old woman to the young girl. 'I was just telling her you can expect company tomorrow, probably. Margie Lockwith from over at Dinewan was telling me she might drop in tomorrow to see Rod.'

'Who is Margie Lockwith?'

'The Dinewan Lockwiths. My last call before here. A real nice kid, Margie. You'll like her. A lot of people reckon that she and Rod might make a go of it yet.'

'Now, Mac!' Mannie's voice was reproving. 'That's idle gossip, and you know it!'

'Maybe. But where there's smoke there's often fire. Anyway, he couldn't get anyone more suitable, could he, Mannie, you'll have to admit that? There's nothing that Margie can't do—rides like a native, swims like a fish, sews, paints. You name it, Margie does it! To my mind, she'd make the ideal wife for some lucky cove, and with Rod around, no other blighter gets a look-in. As for her cooking—wow!'

'She's a capable lass,' conceded Mannie, 'and a very nice person, too.'

'That's what I mean. That's what I'm *saying*.' Mac stood up, slung the mail-bag over his shoulder. 'She's a real nice girl. She'll make a good friend for Lindsay here, too. That's all I mean. You don't mind, but I told her all about Lindsay being here, just a pint-sizer, I said, and all on her own. You'll like Margie, Lindsay.'

And when Margie arrived, Lindsay found that she did like her, just as the mail-pilot had predicted.

Margie dropped in, next day, quite literally. It seemed that as well as all those other wonderful things she was able to do, she could also fly a plane. She brought it down with a show of feminine skill on the station airstrip, and came to meet Lindsay, who had run out of the store at the unexpected droning noise low overhead.

A small, neat girl, she was, and therefore something of a shock to Lindsay, who had visualised a frighteningly capable-looking creature of Amazonian proportions. She had flaxen hair, bleached into oddly attractive streaks by the sun, a complexion as smooth and gold as a ripening peach, lazy blue eyes, and a good-natured mouth. When she smiled, Lindsay thought she had never seen such beautiful, white, even, pearly teeth as Margie's. They were perhaps her best feature, and as she smiled very often, one was constantly reminded of their particular fascination.

Instead of shaking hands, Margie put both of her own hands on Lindsay's shoulders, and gave the other girl something between a shake and a hug. The general message this greeting conveyed was one of open and unaffected friendliness, and Lindsay found herself instantly drawn to this pretty young woman who had flown in on that aeroplane as though it were the easiest thing in the world, and who still twirled a large pair of glare-goggles on one finger.

'Hullo! You must be Lindsay. I knew the moment I saw you! Mac has told me all about you, you see.'

Lindsay smiled. 'I heard you were coming,' she confessed. 'But I never dreamed you'd come down right out of the sky like that!'

Margie laughed, shrugged. 'Why not? It's the quickest way, after all. It takes ages to go round by Peperina, and the roads are practically non-existent. I wouldn't see nearly so many people if I hadn't learned to get myself around that way—not the ones I *want* to see, anyway!'

'Does that apply to me, by any chance, along with all those other lucky ones?' Rod Bennett's deep chuckle startled Lindsay. He was right behind her, but she had been unaware of his approach.

'You *know* it does! That's why I came on Sunday, to make sure I'd find you about the homestead somewhere. How are you, Rod?'

Lindsay saw him gather the other girl against him with a muscular brown arm, hug her in a casual, almost brotherly manner, and let her go, grinning lazily.

Pretty fit, thanks. It's good see you, Margie. Have you met—er—Miss Dutten?'

Margie raised a shapely eyebrow in surprise.

'*Miss* Dutten? Good gracious, Rod, what a horrid, unfriendly sound that has! I suppose you must mean Lindsay?' She was teasing him.

'That's right.'

'Then why call her by that other fearsome title? It sounds too formal for words! Don't tell me that he *always* says it that way, does he, Lindsay?'

'Well——' Lindsay was scarlet.

'Rod, I think that's unkind! He *can* be, when he wants to, you know, Lindsay. The old lord-and-master routine. He's probably still mad at you for being a girl, when he was expecting a man to replace that awful Bob Lowney. We heard all about it on the galah next day. Are you, Rod? Still mad?'

Rod Bennett linked Margie's arm in his, and turned her towards the house. He didn't seem angry or perturbed, merely amused.

'Just leave me to run my own station in my own way, will you, Margie? My little meddlesome Margie?' There was genuine affection in the look he bent on the girl now walking at his side—a patient, caressing, indulgent sort of look, Lindsay couldn't help noticing.

Margie smiled up at him, engagingly, because of those beautiful pearly teeth. There was laughter in her own eyes, persuasion, too.

'Well, I'm not coming ten steps further until you promise to say Lindsay, like the rest of us. Poor girl, what will she think of us? You told me when you engaged him—her, I mean—that the new book-keeper had had a good deal of experience of Outback life, and I'll bet this is the first Outback property she's ever been on where she was called *Miss* Dutten.'

'I'm prepared to bet on *that*, too!' Rod's deep voice was dry. He lifted a satiric eyebrow tellingly at Lindsay to let her know just what he meant. Then he seemed to take pity on her guilt-ridden expression, and capitulated with sudden, quite devastating charm. It appeared that he would do a lot

100

for Margie! 'Very well, then—Lindsay. Leave your work at the cottage just now, and come up to the house with us, will you? It will be an opportunity for you to get to know another of your own sex in this wilderness of men you've landed among. There have no doubt been times since your arrival when you may have longed for the company of a girl of your own age. I'm sure Margie will be delighted to oblige.'

Margie giggled. 'Said with all the superiority of his thirty years! Come on, then, Lindsay. Let's conduct this tottering ancient up to his homestead, shall we?'

The conversation at the table was animated that day. Margie kept up a non-stop flow, and although it was mostly about people whom Lindsay had never met, it was nevertheless entertaining and amusing. Rod Bennett smiled a lot more than he usually did when there were just Mannie and herself present, Lindsay couldn't help noticing, and when he did, it was in that slow, endearing way that lifted his mouth at the corners and spread a warm light into his eyes. There was no doubt at all that he was uncharacteristically well-disposed towards the enchanting, gentle Margie!

When she was leaving, she kissed Rod, then Mannie, then Lindsay, one after the other, without favour. It was a heart-warming gesture that brought Lindsay into the circle. She found herself beaming with pleasure, but if Rod had even noticed, his expression remained unreadable.

'We must introduce Lindsay around, Rod. Maybe I could bring some of the others over to play tennis, if the court is in working order.'

'That would be nice for Lindsay, Margie. I don't think the court has been rolled or marked for some time, but I'm sure Mickie and Shortie will be delighted to oblige if it means the chance of a game with some other young folk.'

'*And* you? You'll play?' Margie looked expectant, cajoling.

Rod grimaced.

'Probably not, I think, Margie. Not this time. I've rather a lot on hand just now.'

It's because of me, thought Lindsay miserably. He usually plays, but not this time, not when I'm included. He's never

101

going to approve of me being here, never, *never*.

Margie remained cheerfully unconvinced.

'We'll see,' she temporised. 'But you tell them to get the court ready, anyway, will you, Lindsay, and I'll round up a few of the folk one day. If we don't make our own entertainment out here, nothing ever happens in the social line, and I know there are heaps of people dying to meet you—especially after all the speculation that's been going on over the galah!'

'You women and your galah,' Rod chided, grinning suddenly. 'Get going now, Margie, before the light beats you. And give your parents my regards.'

'I will, and they sent theirs, of course. 'Bye, Mannie. 'Bye, Lindsay. I'll be seeing you.'

Lindsay watched the man and the girl walking companionably together back to the airstrip. She was bending over her files in the cottage when the little plane took off again, and from the window she could see Rod Bennett waving his hat as it banked once around the homestead and then soared off out of sight.

Several times during the following week, Lindsay found herself thinking about Margie's visit—wondering, too, about Carleen, and how she would take the news that her proposal had been turned down. Knowing well how much her cousin liked to get her own way without dispute, Lindsay could only feel thankful that she would not be present when Carleen opened her note. She could well imagine the sulky pout on that pretty mouth, the thwarted snapping of those lovely eyes!

It was towards the end of the week that Herb sidled up to the veranda next to Rod's office. Lindsay was busy checking over the numbered bottles in the station medical box, which was kept on a wall-fixture on the veranda, she supposed because it was a readily accessible place for all and sundry in an emergency, although only she, Rod, and Mannie were in possession of a key.

Shorty had cut his arm rather badly only two days before, and Lindsay had had her first experience of applying first-aid on the directions of the Flying Doctor over the transceiver. It was a nasty wound, and both she and Shorty had been several shades paler by the time she had finished cleaning and binding the arm and dispensing antibiotic tablets from one of the numbered containers. She felt that she had acquitted herself not too badly for a beginner, and had had an unexpected reward in Rod's quiet 'Well done, Lindsay,' when he heard about it that evening. Artie, who had shepherded the injured Shorty to the homestead and had been present at the performance, cancelled that out by exclaiming,

'Well *done*, boss? Crikey, yer should've *been* there! She was shakin' like a rakin' jelly! I near bust me sides at the look on Shorty's face—Nursie here was that white around the gills we reckoned she might cough up any time!'

'Artie!'

'That'll do, Art.' Rod's voice held reproof, but there was a smile lurking in his eye. 'Maybe she did even better than I thought,' he added kindly, and Lindsay felt quick colour coming into her cheeks at such unexpected praise.

She had dressed the arm successfully each day since then, and had boiled and re-rolled the used bandages. She laid them in their place now, and turned at Herb's approach.

'Hullo, Herb.'

'G'day, Lindsay. Are yer busy?'

'Not too busy to help if I can. What's up?'

Herb took off his hat, and twirled it self-consciously between his fingers. Then he put it on the small wicker table and pulled a crumpled piece of paper from his pocket. It was soiled and thumbed, as though it had been folded and unfolded a good many times by Herb's own leathery hands.

He coughed apologetically.

'I was thinkin', Lindsay. It's like this, see. I been tryin' ter write a letter fer about six years now, and I sort of reckoned —well, now that *you're* here—that maybe between us we could 'ave a go. That's if you ain't too busy?'

'Not at all, Herb. I'll help if I can,' she reiterated.

Herb gave a grunt.

'That's great! I reckoned yer might. It takes a feller a long time on 'is own, yer know,' he confessed candidly. 'I s'pose that's 'ow I ain't never got round ter doin' it fer a year or two. I thought I'd better make the most of you while we got

103

yer, Lindsay. Yer see, we all know Rod don't 'old with wimmen book-keepers, so I reckon yer won't be 'ere for *ever*. Not that *we* don't want yer!' he added hastily, as if he sensed the surge of distress in his listener. 'We'll cover up for yer just as long as we can, yer can bet on that! But—well, *you* know Rod.'

I'm beginning to, thought Lindsay sadly. That's the whole trouble. I'm beginning to, and I don't *want* to go away.

'Would you like me to write it for you, Herb, and you can sign it? Or I could type it out for you, down at the cottage?'

'Maybe if we was ter get it wrote first——' Herb dithered. 'It's ter me wife, actually.'

'Your wife?' Lindsay tried to conceal her surprise. 'I didn't know you were married, Herb.'

'I done it years ago, Lindsay,' Herb responded glumly. 'But I didn't go much on it, not fer long. I reckon I was as blind as a coot at the time. Shearin' out on the Barwon, we was. We was laid off a while between sheds, and the beer was runnin' a ruddy banker that night. There was this dame, see, and—well, I got in tow with 'er, somehow, and between 'er and this binge I was on, when I come ter me senses, blimey if she 'adn't got the parson, and the weddin' bells was ringin' and the lot! Nell, 'er name was.'

He sighed reminiscently, opened up the paper, and spread it out beside his hat on the little cane table.

'This is what I've wrote so far, Lindsay. Dear Nell, I 'ope you are well.' A gruff chuckle. 'That's poetry, ain't it? *Nell* and *well*. Reckon she never knew she'd married a blinkin' 'Enry Lawson! 'Ave yer got any ideas, Lindsay, as ter what we can put now?'

'It's difficult when you haven't—er—seen her for a while,' Lindsay replied tactfully. 'How long is it, Herb?'

'Must be about ten or twelve years, I reckon. She's livin' at Toowoomba, see. 'Er ma's got a café there, but I ain't been ter see 'er for years, see. There ain't been nothink ter take me over Toowoomba way, 'as there?' reasoned Herb mildly. 'What I mean is, why should *I* want ter to go to a place like Toowoomba?'

'Yes, quite,' murmured Lindsay delicately.

104

Oh dear! Poor Herb! And poor Lindsay. This was obviously one of the more challenging assignments that came the way of the Gundooee book-keeper!

Lindsay did her best. Between them they concocted quite the strangest epistle it had ever been her privilege to witness, mainly because of Herb's readiness to take instant offence if she did not adopt his own somewhat couthy suggestions. Ah well. He knew the distant Nell much better than Lindsay did herself, so who was she to argue?

She typed out the resulting letter, watched Herb scrawl his name painstakingly at the bottom, and addressed the envelope. By the time it was all done, and Herb had bidden her a satisfied goodnight, she felt quite limp and exhausted, as though all her natural creativeness had been drained out of her.

It was something, at least, that Herb was so pleased! He had dusted off his hat with the triumphant air of one who has achieved a difficult goal, and had gone sauntering off into the night whistling breathily through his naked gums.

Lindsay found that she was smiling to herself as she included Herb's letter in the out-going bundle on mail-day, wondering idly what Nell's reaction would be when she got it. There had been no suggestion on her husband's part that he missed her to any great extent! Indeed, apart from one or two meaty reminiscences unblushingly recounted by the prosaic Herb, the letter was innocuous in the extreme, and not by any stretch of imagination could it have been termed a passionate document. Lindsay could only hope that Nell, whose bridal bliss had been so short-lived, would not be disappointed!

The mail-bag contained a second letter from Carleen. What a week for letters, one way and another, thought Lindsay, slitting it open forthwith. She took the single sheet of paper from its tissue-lined envelope, and found herself beginning to tremble so violently that she had to sit down quite quickly.

Her face felt drained of colour and her breath came in funny little shallow gasps.

Disbelievingly, she read it again.

'How typical of you, Lindsay, to refuse me even a tiny little favour after all Mummy and Daddy have done for you. It would have been so easy for you to invite a relative out there for a while, but that was too much to hope for, wasn't it? Or did you start getting silly ideas of your own when I told you who Rod Bennett is? I hope not, because, my dear, you wouldn't stand a chance, and you know it. But that's no reason to be a dog-in-the-manger about him, is it. Anyway, it doesn't really matter, and in the end perhaps it's even to the good that he doesn't know we're even distantly related. I mean, with you on the payroll there, I prefer to have a separate identity altogether, so I have got Matt Standley, who is a friend of the Bennetts, to get me an invitation to Gundooee, and will be arriving shortly. As I shall be a guest, while you are in the category of an employee, I don't think our paths will cross much at all. Should you be tempted to let it be known that we're related, or in fact have ever seen each other before, then my advice is, *don't do it*, Lindsay. It would be too bad if Rod Bennett got to find out that you came there under false pretences, wouldn't it, pretending that you didn't know the post was for a man, when you and I both know you did? I gather he's the sort who'd hate to be made a fool of by any woman, least of all a minor employee. Matt tells me that he was quite furious about the mix-up over some woman book-keeper at the time, and that you're only there on sufferance because you didn't seem to have anywhere to go, so I shouldn't think you'd last a minute if he knew how you'd bluffed him. Well, Lindsay, all the best, and I shall look forward to seeing you soon—as a *complete* stranger, of course. Yours in haste, Carleen.'

Lindsay crumpled up the note and put it in the wastepaper basket, as if by simply throwing it away she could dispense with the whole problem.

It was not as easy as that, though! When Carleen set her mind on something, she always got it. Always! She had made up her mind to come to Gundooee, and so she was coming, with or without her cousin's connivance. Lindsay's imagination baulked at the reason behind Carleen's decision. It was too dreadful, too blatant, even to think about!

How had she managed it, though? How did Carleen ever manage to do all the things she wanted to do? By twisting the truth just the teeniest bit, Lindsay surmised. By a little artful pretence, a few well-chosen prevarications, a pathetic smile, a calculated and well-timed sigh.

But how, *this* time? How?

Lindsay knew that she would have to wait, and even then, perhaps she might never know. She was not in a position to mention Carleen's name, or the fact that she had heard from her, or had forewarning of her coming. She had no idea when, or how, Carleen intended to come. All she had said was that it would be 'soon'. She wasn't the kind to procrastinate, once her mind was made up, so Lindsay could only suppose that 'soon' might even mean next week!

Only a few more days, perhaps, and then—Carleen. The thought was almost unbearable, but Lindsay knew that the reality itself would be worse! Gone the peace, the tranquillity, the fun with the jackaroos and station-hands. Even the status quo of her relationship with Rod Bennett would be bound to change. Just now, there was a state of truce, precarious, *precious*. A word of praise could bring a glow to Lindsay's heart, a slow smile could transform her day. It was dangerous to become so—so—*fond* of someone, that the mere fact of being noticed by him could turn a mundane moment into a memorable one. Dangerous, and stupid. Lindsay, in her deepest self, knew that she was guilty of just such folly! She couldn't help herself, although she knew it was a hopeless situation, a quite fruitless expenditure of this soul-searing emotion, made even more impossible by the mere fact that Rod was who he was.

All this was hard enough to contend with, and now— Carleen!

Lindsay found herself talking to the pilot and Mannie with strangely wooden effort. Even her smile felt stiff and strained, as though her cheeks would crack, and it was difficult to concentrate on what they were saying.

'Margie was telling me she met you, Lindsay. She was full

of plans about brightening things up for you here.'

They'd soon be brightened up all right, thought Lindsay bitterly, but not by Margie!

'She's nice, Mac. She was really sweet and friendly, just like you said. She's going to bring some others over one day, and we're going to play tennis, it seems.'

'That's Margie! Always on for a bit of action. She can handle that plane O.K., too. She'll be trying to rope Rod in for a game, I expect.'

'He's busy these days.' Mannie spoke from her position behind the tea-pot. 'But he'll be glad of some company for Lindsay. We do worry a little bit about you, dear. I'm not as young as I was, or I'd do more to make life exciting, and Rod has been convinced from the beginning that this was no post for a girl. Too lonely.'

'But I love it, Mannie. I love it. The peace, the plains. I've got into the way of loving it all, just the way it is.'

I don't *want* it to change. I don't *want* it to be different, she wailed silently inside herself. But it will be, very soon. It's bound to be different, with Carleen.

Mannie did not appear to know anything at all about Carleen coming. If she had, Lindsay was certain that she would have mentioned it then, right there in the kitchen in front of the pilot. That was the way Mannie was—gentle, but forthright, in the candid Outback tradition. There was no pretence in Mannie, no hypocrisy, although of course she possessed a certain tact which was entirely lacking in the blunt-spoken, casual station-hands. Lindsay was now more amused than hurt by their frank criticisms, to which she had at first been much too sensitive. Their motives were ones of true kindness, and the inclination to help along a 'new chum' engendered most of their forthright offers of advice. Once one fully understood that fact, one could be grateful for the basic honesty of their approach. One always knew how one stood with them, and in a more subtle way, one did with Mannie also.

No, if Mannie had heard anything at all about a visitor coming—especially a female visitor—she would have been sure to mention it just now. That meant that Rod had not

108

told her about it, yet. He had not told anyone.

Lindsey was aware of her own tense expectancy each time there was a pause in the conversation after that. During even the most momentary silence, she would find her eyes fastened anxiously upon Rod's stern, deeply tanned face, waiting, waiting, for that announcement. It was like waiting for the judge to don the black cap, thought Lindsay to herself, with a grim attempt at a humour she was far from feeling.

When he finally imparted the information, he did it, as Rod always did everything, unpredictably—in his own time, in his own fashion, and at his own pace.

He didn't just work it into the conversation. He came specially out of his office to where Mannie and Lindsay were sitting comfortably in semi-darkness, and he came, she supposed, for that express purpose. They always sat there, she and Mannie, in the deck-chairs, looking out through the gauze to where the garden outlines were merging so rapidly into the night, chatting idly when they had something to say, lapsing into companionable silence when they hadn't. Rod generally retired to his study, working, reading, until the rest of the household had gone to bed.

Tonight, he was the one with something to say. Lindsay watched him switch off his office light, close the door, and come towards them along the veranda, a tall broad figure in pale drill trousers, a dazzlingly white shirt with uprolled sleeves, and the tie he always put on when he changed in the evening knotted neatly at his throat. His hair was damp from the shower, still smatted down tidily against his forehead, and as he drew up a third chair and took his place quite near, Lindsay could smell the faint, masculine aroma of cigarettes and shave-lotion.

Rod sat there for some moments, then stretched his legs out more comfortably in front of him and reached into his pocket for the makings. In the dimness his bare forearms were mahogany-coloured against the whiteness of his shirt. Lindsay caught the whiff of tobacco, knew that he was rubbing it around between his palms. A rustle of paper, the rasp of a match. Then smoke rising above his head—a tranquil plume that drifted peacefully away along the veranda.

When he had drawn on his cigarette in silence for a minute or two, he announced pleasantly,

'I have a surprise up my sleeve for you, Mannie—for you and Lindsay.'

'Yes, Rod?' That was Mannie, immediately interested.

'Yes. We're going to have a visitor.'

'Are we?' The old lady showed no surprise. After all, Rod often had visitors at Gundooee, so why should she?

'We are. I thought it would be a good thing for Lindsay, a little company about her own age, or at least, very little older. Another *girl*, at any rate.' He stressed his point delicately.

'Oh, that *will* be nice!' Mannie was enthusiastic now. 'Who is it, Rod? Someone who's been before?'

'No, she hasn't been before, Mannie. In fact, I don't even know her myself yet. She's a friend of Matt Standley's, and a very nice girl, he says. She's been working too hard, it seems, and has had a particularly nasty bout of bronchitis—she's prone to it, apparently. Did you say something, Lindsay?'

What Lindsay had actually said was 'Piffle!'—under her breath, of course, but she *had* made a tiny sound unintentionally.

'No, nothing, Rod.'

'I beg your pardon, I thought you did. Well, anyway, her doctor has advised a dry inland climate for a while, plus peace and rest, and when Matt asked me to have her, I was naturally very glad to agree—for Lindsay's sake. *Did* you say something, Lindsay?'

'No, nothing at all. I thought I'd swallowed a mosquito, just for a moment. I'm sure there's one buzzing about, and my throat suddenly went all tickly.'

'One rarely *swallows* a mosquito,' Rod pointed out, leaning towards her in the gloom, and treating her to a suspiciously probing inspection. 'Anyway, as I was saying, Matt said she's been under considerable stress lately, and the combination of dry heat, rest and a bit of peace and quiet immediately made him think of Gundooee. I'm very glad he did, and it will be very nice for you to have another girl around, Lindsay. I often think you're out with those men far more than is strictly necessary. It doesn't seem right. This

110

way, there will at least be two of you, and I'm sure you'll become good friends in a very short time. I've said that she's to stay just as long as she pleases. She's a model, apparently, and has no more assignments in the immediate offing. Very wisely she deferred them until she's quite well again, so I hope she may even stay for some months. I think the east room, don't you, Mannie? It's the coolest.'

'Sibbie will make up the bed tomorrow. When is she coming, Rod, and how?'

'On Thursday, in the early afternoon, I think. She's chartering a flight direct from Sydney.'

She would! Trust Carleen to miss out on those interminable hours of train-ride, toiling through desolate wastes, and changing at a junction which should have been Emmadanda, only Emmadanda was a whole forty minutes further on, and then finding out that Emmadanda wasn't a pretty little jacaranda-lined town but a one-horse outpost with two dogs and some crows and a rusty bucket shower, and waiting in grilling sunshine all alone for a plane you had been warned curtly *not* to miss, and coming down at Gundooee to find you weren't as welcome as you had hoped because you happened to be a girl, and that you were, in fact, downright *unwelcome* in one person's eyes, and that was the most dreadful thing of all, because they happened to be nice, expressive grey eyes, too, the sort you really wanted to have a welcome in. Trust Carleen to miss out on *that*!

A charter flight, direct from Sydney. And when she arrived, they'd know she was going to be a girl, because that's what Rod had arranged for, and that's what Rod would be expecting. A girl, both welcome and wanted.

'Her name, by the way, is Carleen Vincent.'

Oh, Rod! I could have told you that! thought Lindsay sadly.

'It's a pretty name, Carleen,' said Rod.

111

CHAPTER 7

WHEN Carleen arrived she stepped daintily down from the aircraft, taking Rod's extended hand to help her to the ground.

People always extended their hand to help Carleen—especially men! There was something about her fragile build, willowy slenderness and elegantly languid movements that called for such gestures. She had come to regard them as her prerogative, and was seldom disappointed.

Not today, anyway. You could tell by the way she peeped coyly up into Rod Bennett's tough, brown face, and the way her mouth curved into a tiny, oblique smile, that Carleen was anything but disappointed. And you'd have said, by the way Rod's lip curled faintly at the corner and his grey eyes kindled with surprised admiration, that *he* wasn't disappointed, either.

Of course, Carleen, looking as she did today, would have merited such a glance from even a confirmed misogynist, and Rod Bennett certainly was not that. He *liked* girls, Mannie had stressed that often. Especially tall, sophisticated, pretty girls who vamped him with an openly flirtatious eye, invited him with the pursing of their soft, rouged mouths, who kept hold of his hand for just that extra, lingering moment, as Carleen was doing now.

'Mr. Bennett?' Rod?' Her voice was attractively husky, with just the right degree of shy hesitation. 'Oh, I'm so glad to be here! Matt has told me all about you, and I just knew that Gundooee was the very place to help me recover my strength and get quite well again. And this is Mannie—I've heard about you, too. And I suppose you must be Lindsay, the little book-keeper?' Carleen's eye sought Lindsay's coolly. 'How odd to find a woman occupying a post of that sort, isn't it? Away out here one just naturally assumes that a

112

man would be infinitely more suitable, somehow.'

'Lindsay is making a surprisingly successful attempt at it'—Rod was watching Lindsay herself as he spoke, smiling quite kindly—'although it certainly isn't a usual position for a girl to find herself in. As you say, Carleen—I may call you that?—we do normally confine the position to the masculine field.'

'I would have thought so, naturally, although I expect as a temporary measure, that it works well enough. Would you mind carrying these for me, Lindsay? You can go ahead with them to my room if you like. I suppose you must know where it is?'

'Yes—er—of course.'

Lindsay stepped forward quickly, took the vanity-case and handbag which were being held out imperiously.

Carleen smiled up at Rod with faint apology.

'I still get a little bit tired, I'm afraid,' Lindsay heard her telling him sweetly as she left them, 'but I know I'm going to pick up very quickly now that I'm here. Do you have many other servants, Rod, to help you in the house? It looks quite enormous from here.'

His deep-toned reply was lost to Lindsay, who found that her teeth were clenched so firmly together that her jaw positively ached, and her fingers gripped the handles of Carleen's bags so tightly that her knuckles showed white under the pressure.

She dumped the bags unceremoniously on a chair in the east bedroom, and turned to discover Carleen coming through the doorway with Rod just behind her.

'I say, do be careful of that case, will you, Lindsay, and don't go hurling it around like that? I'm not accustomed to having others treat my possessions so carelessly. I trust you aren't so lackadaisical about *everything*, my dear?' She put her hand to her forehead. Her beautifully-kept and manicured fingers were spread out in a touchingly weary gesture. 'My goodness, it *is* warm, isn't it, out here? Or perhaps it's just that I'm still not quite myself.' An apologetic smile in Rod's direction. 'I'm perfectly strong, *really*, but you must forgive me if I don't appear so just now. It's all very frustrat-

113

ing when one is unaccustomed to having been ill.'

'Not at all, Carleen,' Rod's voice held a concern that must have gratified the girl who had sunk on to the bed with a gracefulness calculated to show those long, shapely legs and curvaceous hips to their best advantage. 'You must take care, and only do just as much or as little as you feel able to. It's much hotter here than in Sydney, of course, but once you're acclimatized, you'll probably find the dry heat easier to withstand than the humidity of the coast. Perhaps you should rest just now.'

'I think I will, if you don't mind. There's cologne in my cosmetic case there, Lindsay. Perhaps you would be kind enough to fix me a nice cold pad—you *do* have iced water, I'm sure?—and I shall put it on my forehead and close my eyes for a while.'

'Yes, do that. I'll leave you to Lindsay's ministrations, then, Carleen. Just remember that you're very welcome here, and make yourself at home.'

'You are sweet, Rod. So considerate. And I don't wonder that Matt immediately thought of Gundooee as the very place for my convalescence. What a charming and delightfully modern homestead it is! I've always adored the country, and I know already that I'm going to love it here. You've given me such a warm welcome already.'

He had, too! thought Lindsay grimly to herself, as Rod's heavy step faded away through the hall. No salt tablets thrown carelessly at her with a kitchen mug half full of water—not for Carleen! Oh no! For Carleen there had been a kind concern, a gentle indulgence, a lingeringly warm regard, tinged with admiration and considerateness—a very male, protective sort of look, it had been.

When the sound of those heeled stockman's boots had quite gone, Carleen opened her eyes again and looked straight at Lindsay.

'You can get the iced water if you like. Some in a bowl, and a jug for drinking would be nice. I wasn't pretending when I said just now that my head is aching. They gave me a whale of a send-off party at the Club last night. You'd have thought I was going to the Never-Never, the way they went

114

on.' She looked about her. 'It almost is, actually, isn't it?'

'Is what?'

'The Never-Never. What a ghastly stretch of country to fly over! All that peculiar tufty desert, and those stones thrown around all over the place. I must say it's a relief to find such an attractively civilised human being at the end of it. He's even more handsome than I'd remembered from his photos.' She gazed at Lindsay's flushed, indignant expression with malicious curiosity. 'Do you find him handsome, I wonder, Lindsay?'

'Who?'

'Rod, of course—who else?'

'I haven't really thought about it,' Lindsay replied coldly.

'Then don't begin to, darling, will you, and it will be much much pleasanter all round. Tell me, are there many other women on the scene at the moment? Any since you've been here? Ones of *consequence*, I mean.'

'I really couldn't say.'

'Come, darling, you must know. You're only human, after all, and you can't fool me, either. I can see that you're alive to Rod Bennett's attractions as a man. I saw the way you looked at him just now—a sort of awareness that you never had in Sydney—and in certain aspects I can also see that you've matured quite surprisingly since I saw you last. However, it's not *you* I'm talking about at the moment. Has he had any other members of the fair sex coasting around lately?'

Lindsay gave her cousin a look of unconcealed disdain.

'What a ruthless, calculating creature you are, aren't you, Carleen, to even ask such a thing when you've only just arrived.'

The other shrugged, laughed huskily and without shame.

'Well, one does like to know the military strength of one's opponents, darling, after all. If you want to be cagey and uncooperative, go ahead by all means. It won't worry me! I shall ask that old governess or whatever she is. What's her name? Mannie? I shall ask Mannie, and she'll tell me all I want to know without even guessing she's been catechised. I can be quite subtle when necessary, you know, Lindsay.'

115

'Carleen, if you expect me to stand by while you cold-bloodedly——'

'Wait!' Carleen interrupted, waving an imperious hand for silence. Then she leaned up on one elbow off the pillow and looked Lindsay over with eyes that glittered oddly. There was something a little bit frightening in the pale, menacing measure of that look. 'Let's just be clear on one point, Lindsay, shall we—although I thought I'd made the position clear in my letter, actually. The only thing I expect of *you* is silence, do you understand? I'm not asking you to do anything, or say anything. Your role is simply one of abstention, and that should be right up your negative little street, shouldn't it? But don't you dare presume to moralise, or to judge, will you, Lindsay? That would be presumptuous of you, my dear, and I should make you very, very sorry if you did. Do you understand?'

'I've always *understood* you, Carleen.'

'Good. Then there's no need to underline the situation any further, is there? Go and get that iced water for me now, will you, Lindsay? Oh, and by the way——'

'Yes?' Lindsay paused woodenly in the doorway.

'Now that we've discussed things'—Carleen smiled sweetly and appeasingly—'there's no need to refer to them again. There's always the possibility that we might be overheard, and in any case, I don't intend to fraternise with the employees at Gundooee to the extent of long, intimate dicussions closeted in my bedroom. From now on, just remember your own position here, and the fact that I'm a guest in your employer's household, and I'm sure we shall get along perfectly, Lindsay.'

'Yes, Carleen.' Lindsay felt the words clotting in her throat. In fact, it was all she could do to speak at all just then, so overwhelmed was she by disgust and misery.

At tea that night it was almost worse! To have to sit there, watching it all, and saying nothing, took all the strength of will that Lindsay could muster. She had left it too late now, in any case, to do a thing about it. Carleen was here, an ever-present threat to Lindsay's own security, and Carleen was enjoying the situation enormously. She had spent the afternoon resting on her bed with the veranda-blinds pulled down outside to screen off the glare and heat. Lindsay had heard the shower running in the bathroom she shared with Carleen at just about the same time as she heard Rod turning on the spray in his own private shower-recess off his own room. After Carleen came out, the whole hall was pervaded by the tantalising scent of her expensive eau de toilette. If Rod had by any chance forgotten that they now had a new, and very feminine, addition to the household, he must most certainly have been reminded of the fact by that enchanting, pervasive perfume.

Tonight Carleen was wearing a filmy dress of printed chiffon, with long transparent sleeves and a softly pleated skirt that did wonderful things for her beautiful legs. Encased in clover-pink nylons, they seemed incredibly long and shapely. Her shoes were of a deeper, toning shade, with delicate silvered heels and matching silver buckles. She had swept her long golden tresses into an elaborate coil on top of her head, to reveal the pretty set of her small, neat ears and the gentle curve of her neck above the frilled throat of her frock. The effect was at once as tender as a petunia, as dramatic as an orchid.

Lindsay was very much aware of the contrast they must make. She had put on the skirt of her linen suit, and her 'other' white blouse, and was even now regretting her bare brown legs and the old-fashioned shoes which she had successfully renovated with an application of honey-toned colour before she came to Gundooee. Up till this moment, she had been satisfied enough with these things, but tonight, her few possessions seemed duller, more inadequate, than ever before. In her bedroom she had taken extra care with her make-up, feathering her brows into pretty arches, adding a touch of mascara to her long, curling lashes, brushing her hair until it shone in a nut-brown obedient curtain.

Lindsay had then gazed at herself in the mirror, staring critically back at the wide green innocence of those eyes in the glass with a feeling of self-reproach. Why was she going to this extra trouble tonight? Because of Carleen? Because of Rod? Or just because she felt so miserably overburdened by

117

the present untenable situation into which she had been precipitated?

Lindsay couldn't answer any of those questions honestly. Not tonight. Her mind was a welter of confused ideas, chaotic thinking and muddled emotions. All she *did* know, as she surveyed her girlishly simple reflection in the mirror, was that fine feathers *did* make fine birds—or, at any rate, they certainly helped! And Lindsay didn't possess any feathers at all, only a white 'other blouse', just slightly better than her everyday cotton shirt, and a skirt that was admittedly an improvement on her faded denim one, and a pair of shoes which looked just a little nicer in their present sand colour than they had in their previous scuffed white shabbiness.

Carleen was being put into her chair, quite tenderly, by Rod. As he bent a little to push the chair into place, his head, behind the girl's own fair one, appeared darkly swarthy, almost saturnine. In his crisply laundered shirt and narrow trousers, he looked carelessly, urbanely handsome.

When Carleen put her head back and smiled her acknowledgement of his thoughtful gesture, his white teeth glinted momentarily, and his eyes darkened inexplicably. Like that, they were almost black, unfathomable, tantalisingly unreadable.

'You're feeling better, Carleen? You certainly *look* very decorative and charming, I can assure you, but outward appearances can be misleading, and of course you did have an unpleasantly tiring trip to get here, I'm afraid.'

Tiring? Huh! And what about poor Lindsay's own unpleasantly tiring trip? There had been no sympathetic enquiries for her, no tender, darkening glances. Just a brief injunction *not* to miss Mac's plane, and when she got here, a reproving glare when she dared to comment on the heat, a couple of salt tablets, and a scarifying lecture on the importance of stating one's sex when one applied for the post of book-keeper on Gundooee Station.

'Oh, *so* much better, thank you, Rod! In fact, I'm feeling quite refreshed—my old self, almost. I'm longing to take part in all your country activities again.' She leaned towards him.

'I've brought my riding clothes, of course,' she confided eagerly. 'I suppose you have some good horses here—hacks, I mean—as well as those funny nondescript stock-horses. I really appreciate good horseflesh, you know!'

'Do you, indeed? I'm sure we can supply you with a suitable mount, in that case. I've a very sweet little mare, part Arab, that should be the very thing, I think. In fact'—a flattering appraisal of Carleen's deliciously appealing profile —'I should think that you and Chalita will make a very well-matched pair.'

'May I ride with *you*? What I mean is'—Carleen hesitated delicately—'all those *men*——'

'Yes, of course. I shall take you whenever I can, if you really like that sort of thing—whenever it is suitable, that is,' Rod promised agreeably.

'Such a pity that you won't be able to accompany us, too, Lindsay. You *did* tell me you couldn't ride, I think?'

Lindsay hadn't told her anything of the sort! She hadn't needed to, because Carleen already knew it. She knew perfectly well that the functional boarding-school to which her younger relation had been sent had not provided extra frills in the form of expensive riding lessons, as her own school had done.

'We gotter *do* somethink about it,' muttered Artie indignantly, some two weeks later. 'Ain't we, Mick? We gotter *do* somethink. She's in fer the knockout stakes, that dame is, Lindsay—any mutt can see that. She's makin' rings around yer, that's what! She's been out with Rod on them perishin' 'orses every day this week, givin' 'erself airs, preenin' them fine feathers, and never missin' a single trick in the knockout stakes.'

'What are they, Art? The—er—knockout stakes?' Lindsay felt moved to enquire. Artie's indignation was of a quite ferocious nature.

'Never *you* mind what they are, Lindsay. You don't know dames like we know dames,' he told her darkly. 'That's not surprisin', either, 'cos you ain't a dame yourself—not like '*er*. You're just a decent little slip of a dinkum little sheila, that's what you are, and that's what she's not. She ain't dinkum, she ain't on the level, she's just a *dame*, and me and the other blokes ain't goin' ter let a dame run rings around our Lindsay, are we, see? We ain't goin' ter stand by and let a spoofer like 'er get one-up on you in the knockout stakes. What'll we do, though, Mick, eh?'

Mickie grinned. 'We could teach her to ride, for a start.'

'Stone the blinkin' crows, so we could! Why didn't I think of that before? We teach 'er ter ride, and then she can go out with 'em, too. And that makes three of 'em, don't it, instead of just them two.' Artie chuckled exultantly. 'By crikey, that'll shift the odds a bit, eh!'

Lindsay smiled innocently from one man to the other, touched at their concern. It was nice to be a dinkum little sheila, and not just a dame! It made you feel warm and soft inside, and it made you not mind quite so much about the handsome couple Rod and Carleen made, riding off together on those lovely horses.

It was true, what Artie had said. They had been out together every single day this week, at one end of the day or the other. Carleen looked superb in her tailored riding pants, polished boots and open-necked shirt of deepest blue silk. The part-Arab mare, Chalita, was a delicate-stepping creature, the prettiest dappled grey, and, as Rod had predicted, the horse and rider were perfectly matched in elegance, style, and beauty of movement. His own mount was the bay stallion he always used, an intelligent, rather mettlesome animal that he rode on a curb and martingale. Looking after them enviously as they went off across the plain, Lindsay could not stop herself thinking how wonderful it must be to ride at Rod's side like that, in close companionship—just you and Rod and the horses and the plain.

'Would yer *like* ter ride, Lindsay girl?' asked Artie now. 'Would yer like if we learned yer?'

'I'd love it, Artie,' she replied promptly, with enthusiasm. If she could ride, then perhaps Rod might ask her, some time, to ride with him over the plain, the way he was doing now with Carleen. She would leave the competition stuff to them, if they wished to enter for some races, which was what these stakes must be. She would not aspire to those heights, but if she could attain a certain proficiency, why then, some day he might ask Lindsay herself to go with him—perhaps when Carleen had gone back to Sydney.

'I'd just love it!' she repeated breathlessly, her eyes shining.

Shorty looked her over critically.

'You can't wear that skirt, though, Lindsay. That won't do.'

'I have my shorts.'

'Shorts ain't no use,' Artie told her bluntly. 'The stirrup leathers'll pinch yer legs, see. Ain't yer got any strides?'

'Strides?'

'You know. Duds.'

'No jeans, or anything?' suggested Mickie.

Lindsay thought of Carleen's beautifully cut jodhpurs. She had noticed two pairs in Carleen's room when she had been making the bed one day.

'No. No jeans,' she admitted forlornly.

'Why not use some of them khaki duds in the store?' Herb said. 'There's 'eaps of 'em there, ain't there, an' if the bookkeeper can't lay 'er 'ands on 'em, then I don't know who can!'

Herb's idea was unanimously adopted in lieu of any better one being proposed, and that was how Lindsay began her riding lessons—clad in a pair of khaki trousers which were the smallest size she could find in the pile. As they happened to have a thirty-two-inch waist measurement, it was necessary to wear a belt (happily the store could provide that, too!), beneath which the khaki cloth bulged in uneasy lumps and folds right down to the place where she had rolled the turn-ups over an extra couple of times to enable her shabby sandshoes to peep out the bottom.

They brought in a horse called Dusty on which to teach her. Dusty was an angular beast, all drooping limbs and bony protuberances. He had a large, deceptively unintelligent head, a sleepy eye, and a tendency to help his rider into the saddle by dint of a well-aimed nip. Lindsay was terrified of him.

'He's so—*tall*,' she said dubiously, eyeing the distance be-

121

tween the saddle and the ground with some misgiving.

'It ain't 'im that's tall, it's you that's small, see, Lindsay. It's a different thing altogether, that.'

'It amounts to the same thing, surely, Artie?'

'No, it don't! Where's yer spirit, eh? Come on, Lindsay, once we get you up there, yer'll be O.K,' he assured her bracingly. 'Up yer go, now!'

Willing hands pushed and lifted, and Lindsay felt herself borne through the air, willy-nilly. Then she was somehow in the saddle, fumbling for the reins with nervous fingers.

'Git yer feet in the stirrups first.' Artie.

'Don't hold the reins *and* that monkey-grip, Lindsay. He's not energetic enough to buck, anyway.' Mickie.

'Straighten out yer legs, Lindsay. The way you're crouchin' up there, yer'd think you was perchin' on a flamin' ant-hill.' Herb.

'Just relax, now, Lindsay, and give him a little kick.' Shorty.

'Gently does it!'

They all yelled advice. Dusty edged forward reluctantly. His limbs appeared to be quite rusty with disuse, and upon that encouraging supposition, she kicked a little harder and he walked gingerly around the saddling-yard. It was comforting to discover that Dusty was even less enthusiastic than she was herself!

The first lesson was pronounced a success by all who contributed, and after that, the procedure was repeated every evening just before sundown, when the men had ridden in, unsaddled, watered, and fed their own horses, with varying degrees of progress on the pupil's part.

'Yer better get good quick, Lindsay,' Artie urged her one day, watching the two specks that were Carleen and Rod coming through the shade trees along the creek on their horses. 'We want yer ter be real good, quick, Lindsay—quicker than wot you are, see.'

'I can't see any need to hurry, Artie,' she replied mildly. 'Surely it's better to be slow and steady, and learn thoroughly while I'm about it?'

'There ain't time for that,' retorted Artie obscurely, and it seemed that the others were in agreement with him.

'I think we'll take you for a longer ride tomorrow, Lindsay,' Shorty told her. 'Mickie and I will come back early. What you need is a longer spell in the saddle, to get the proper feel of it. This way, we're stopping and starting too much.'

'Very well, if you think it will help.'

Lindsay was amenable to any suggestion that might be of benefit. She was actually enjoying her riding lessons, and it was thrilling to be past that tedious stage of having to be led once she was outside the yard. She was certainly beginning to acquire more confidence, and was well content with her own advancement. However, the men had all been so kind, had put so much time and effort into her initiation, that she was willing to please them in any way she could.

She came back from that expedition so stiff and sore that she could hardly move when she finally slid from the saddle. Her nose was sunburnt because her hat had kept sliding back when Dusty trotted or cantered, and her face was scarlet with effort, beaded with a fine dew of perspiration, and smeared by several trails of grime where she had been swiping at the wayward flies which got under her veil.

She was going to be late for tea! Lindsay quickened her pace, awkwardly because of the stiffness of her limbs, the soreness of her racked muscles. She slammed the wicket gate in the white fence, and raced up the path, head down—smack into Rod Bennett.

'Hold on there!'

He gripped her arm, steadied her, and then stepped back a little. He was already changed, into a blue shirt tonight, with a cravat at his neck instead of a tie. The effect was one of rakish charm. As dark as the devil, thought Lindsay, and with the same dangerous fascination! Her heart was pounding, and a pulse beat in her throat. The breathlessness she was experiencing had little to do with the fact that she had been hurrying.

'Oh, I'm sorry. I just wasn't thinking where I was going, I'm afraid.'

She looked up to find Rod's eyes crinkling at the corners

as he inspected her state of dusty dishevelment. When his eyes reached her trousers, he had to grin, quite openly. His teeth glinted in the half light.

'I must say you're a ball of fashion, Lindsay. Have you been having some more riding lessons?'

'How did you know about my riding lessons?' she asked in surprise. He had never put in an appearance at them, and the only glimpses of him that she had caught were of a distant figure, usually in the company of another distant figure—Carleen, of course.

'It's my business to know what goes on on my own station, Lindsay,' he reminded her with a strangely quizzical expression. 'How are you coming on, by the way?'

'Not very fast, it appears,' she admitted humbly. '*I am* quite pleased with my progress, but the men don't seem to be. They say I'll never win the—er—knockout stakes at this rate.'

Rod's grey gaze sharpened. His eyes narrowed with a keenness that made her feel uncomfortably self-conscious all of a sudden.

'Do they, by George! So that's what they say, eh?' He stroked his chin with a brown, square-tipped finger. 'I've noticed them all there, putting you and Dusty through your paces every night, and I reckoned they must be up to something.'

'Yes, they've all been so kind. They want me to learn—and of course I want it, too. I had a pony once, long ago, at—er—at Batlow.' She paused uncertainly, wishing she hadn't said that. She waited for the quick frown that the mention of her childhood home usually brought, but surprisingly, it did not come. Rod was still stroking his chin. He appeared deep in thought.

'Did you, Lindsay?' was all he replied, abstractedly.

'Yes, a dear little coloured one, brown and white.' She hesitated, then—'What is it, Rod, this knockout stakes? Something to do with the Races at Peperina?'

'No, not at Peperina, Lindsay.'

'But a race?'

'I suppose you *could* call it that,' he murmured gravely. 'A

124

race, but with no set time or place for the finish.'

Lindsay wiped her palm over her moist forehead in a sudden, worried gesture, carrying the dusty smear near one eyebrow right across to her temple.

'Oh dear!' she exclaimed nervously, 'I do hope they aren't expecting me to enter for it. I'd never be good enough.'

Rod caught her hand on its way back from making the new dust-streak, and said sharply,

'Good God, Lindsay! What have you done here?'

He turned her palm upwards and inspected it more closely. Her hand in his looked strangely pale and small.

'They're blisters,' she told him simply. 'I went for a long, *long* ride today. I keep wanting to use both hands on the reins, but they all say I've got to learn to control the horse with just one hand, because of opening gates and carrying things. They say that everyone out here can ride with only one hand, so I did it the whole time today. That's why I've got blisters.'

'I see.' He released his grasp. 'You'd better put something on them. Are you feeling stiff?'

'A bit.'

'Have a good hot bath instead of a shower tonight, Lindsay. Take your time, and soak. It will help the stiffness to go away, and it doesn't matter if you're late for tea, just once.'

'I will, Rod. Thank you.'

'Lindsay.'

'Yes?'

He looked down at her, his sternness softening visibly.

'Don't worry about the knockout stakes too much,' he advised her kindly. 'If the men happen to mention them again, just say that Rod says there would be no point in you entering for them in any case. Have you got that? *Rod says.*'

She sighed relievedly.

'I'm glad. I won't worry any more, then, Rod.' She turned to go.

'That's right. There's no necessity to worry. And— Lindsay?'

'Yes?' She turned back.

'About not being *good* enough'—he put a hand beneath her chin, tilted her face gently, looked right into her eyes with a quite unfamiliar expression in his own steady grey ones—'I think that sometimes, Lindsay, you're inclined to underestimate yourself.'

A rustle sounded through the gauze near by. Then the veranda door swung open, and Carleen appeared.

'Oh, there you are, Rod! How nice of you to suggest a walk in the garden before tea. I'm sorry to have kept you waiting. Good gracious, Lindsay, you aren't even changed yet. You'll be late for tea if you don't hurry.'

'I'm—just going,' Lindsay whispered huskily.

'Take your time,' Rod reminded her as she went. 'It doesn't matter at all if tea is late tonight.'

Lindsay did not suppose that it did! Not tonight! With a heart that ached unbearably, she watched Carleen link her arm through Rod's and wander down the path at his side in a drift of French perfume. It obviously mattered to neither of them that supper might be late! Lindsay went stiffly to her room, peeled off her dusty clothes, and soaked. She felt curiously depressed—so much so, indeed, that she did not even bother to put on her 'best' skirt and blouse for the meal. Her faded blue one matched her own faded blue mood, and so on it went, along with several dabs of cold cream to the tip of her sunburnt nose and forehead. Her skin would probably peel, she realised gloomily, and peering into the mirror she could discern a thickening crop of freckles. *Freckles!* Lindsay powdered them despairingly, and made her way to the dining-room.

Rod appeared to be in an unusually benign mood tonight. He smiled a lot, and adopted a leisurely, bantering tone with Carleen, who as always centred the conversation upon herself as much as possible. When Rod was in one of these teasing moods of his, he suddenly seemed much younger—carefree— as if he had purposely shelved his many responsibilities for the evening with the express intention of enjoying himself. This was the way he had been with Margie, and now he was the same with Carleen. There was something about both of these young women that appealed to Rod, without a doubt.

126

With Lindsay, he was different.

Reserved? Inscrutable? Lindsay sought in her mind for the correct definition, failed to find it.

What else could she expect, in all honesty? She was simply the book-keeper—the unforgivably *female* book-keeper—and as such she received the somewhat distant consideration of a courteous employer who was indubitably a very busy man, with lots of more important things about which to think than his personal approach to the more sensitive among his employees.

Watching covertly as he engaged in a bout of diverting repartee with Carleen, his mouth curving in a cynically attractive manner, his eyes glinting appreciatively as she leaned towards him, Lindsay remembered that moment outside this evening with a curious little pang. Just for one second, as he gazed down at her in the gloaming with that darkening expression, it had seemed to Lindsay as though he was seeing her, for the very first time, in a human light. She could still feel the warmth and firmness of his hand as he took hers, the strength of his fingers, the kindness beneath his lazy amusement over her khaki store trousers with their bulging bottom and rolled-up cuffs.

Just for one second, out there in the garden, it had seemed to Lindsay as though some hidden, unbidden magic had drawn herself and Rod together in its spell. Something quite intangible had been happening, something that had set Lindsay's nerves deliciously aquiver.

And then the gauze door had creaked on its hinges. With Carleen's appearance, the magic moment had fled—probably for ever.

Lindsay could not imagine any girl being lucky enough to have a moment such as that one with Rod twice in any lifetime!

CHAPTER 8

THE following week Margie brought a party of young people over to play tennis.

Shorty and Mick, the two jackaroos, joined in, and together with Carleen and Lindsay, made up a party of eight. The boys worked hard for a couple of evenings beforehand, sprinkling the court with water, rolling it, and marking out new white lines with lime. Lindsay did all she could to help, carrying water, moving the strings that they had stretched out as a guide to straightness, and bringing them mugs of tea or beer at intervals. Carleen was conspicuous by her absence, although she did appear once or twice, simulating interest in their progress, but at the same time taking care not to linger sufficiently long to be given something to do.

The visitors who walked up from the plane with Margie all had on crisp white tennis clothes, and even Mickie and Shorty, when they came whistling up from their quarters, looked unfamiliarly smart in their white shorts and shirts, socks, and whitened tennis shoes, their muscular limbs appearing more brown and sinewy than ever in contrast.

Lindsay knew that her own shorts and shirt were, as always, a compromise, but she was proud of her sandshoes, which the boys had whitened for her when they were doing their own, and which had come up like new. She found herself looking forward to the afternoon enormously.

She played a passable game of tennis, and once she learned that Rod himself had opted out on the pretext of doing some work in his office, felt her self-consciousness slipping away. He would 'be around', he assured them, and would certainly attend the barbecue lunch on the lawn, and would come out from time to time to cheer them on and see who was winning. Even Carleen's own pleas could not persuade him to change his mind about playing, and when she discovered his intention not to take part, she immediately said that in that case, she wouldn't either. She was sure he could do with some company, and she'd promise not to distract him if his work was really as important as all that.

Only Margie's diplomatic intervention saved the numbers from being thrown out by having one girl too few. With an ungracious shrug, Carleen finally agreed to take part.

'Not the easiest of visitors to have around, I should imagine,' Margie murmured softly, looking after Carleen as she strolled away. 'How do you get on with her, Lindsay, I wonder?'

Lindsay, too, watched the elegant blonde girl as she stopped to chat to the people in Margie's party. She ignored Mick and Shorty, just as she ignored all the other employees on Gundooee, hardly deigning to pass the time of day with them. As for Sibbie and Bella and those other loyal and friendly aborigines from the gunyahs down on the creek, she avoided these with a noticeable fastidiousness that almost amounted to mysophobia.

Today Carleen had on a sleeveless tennis dress with a brief, pleated skirt that swung in a pretty, kilted effect about her long, slender legs. Her hair was tied back with a broad red ribbon that matched the little scarlet motif on her pocket. She was laughing in that familiarly husky, attractive way at something one of the men was saying to her, spinning her racket carelessly with one hand as she replied.

'I don't see very much of her, Margie,' Lindsay admitted, shrugging briefly. 'None of us do, really, except for Rod.'

'I see.' The other girl looked thoughtful, and just a little bit puzzled. 'Is she staying for very long, do you know, Lindsay?'

'Until she's quite better—I'm quoting Rod now. She's had—er—bronchitis, or something, I believe.' Lindsay was vague.

Margie raised an eyebrow, smiled openly, that pretty, candid smile that showed her pearly, even teeth.

'She looks as strong as an ox, if you ask me—disgustingly healthy, in fact. Oh well, come on, Lindsay. Shall we go and help Mannie and Rod start the barbecue?'

Following Margie over the lawn, Lindsay found herself hoping that Margie's own feelings had not been hurt by her revelation that Rod and Carleen were so frequently in each other's company. There had been such an odd look in her eye for a fleeting second, and Lindsay wondered if Margie, for all her gaiety and undiscriminating friendliness towards everyone, might not be vulnerable where Rod himself was concerned. That was what Mac had hinted in the kitchen one day, and it was all too possible that he could be right. People like Margie were better than most at concealing the depth of their emotions, and Lindsay hoped, quite fervently, that Carleen would not in some way inflict a hurt on this friendly girl whom she was beginning to like so much. Margie was worth ten of Carleen, she thought fiercely. How blind men could be, if they were dazzled by that lovely, shallow façade!

The barbecue was a success, by any standards. Large succulent steaks from the station's cold-room were grilled over the open fire, and accompanied by an assortment of salads and fruits prepared by Mannie and Lindsay. Rod was turning the steaks, doling out potatoes which he had buried in their jackets in the hot ashes to cook. He handled the operation with the dexterity born of many years of preparing meals in the great outdoors with a minimum of culinary equipment.

Margie and her crowd had brought cold desserts as their contribution to the lunch, and after that Rod boiled the billy, in the traditional country way, placing a small, sappy eucalypt bough carefully across the top to disperse the smoke, and tapping the blackened billy all round when he had brewed-up, to sink the tea-leaves to the bottom. They drank the tea scalding hot. It was a refreshing finish to what for Lindsay had been an excitingly unusual meal, although the others, even Carleen, were obviously well versed in the barbecue art.

Afterwards they all lay around for a while to recover, in the plots of shade on the lawn, talking idly, smoking, exchanging views and stories. Then the first doubles players tossed for service, and wandered over to the court, and Lindsay,

Margie, Shorty, and Mick began to clear up the remains of the picnic and carry things into the house, insisting that Mannie should leave everything to them, and go to lie down on her bed for her afternoon sleep, as she was accustomed to doing each day.

By the time they returned, Rod had dealt with the dying embers of his fire and had strolled across to watch the tennis in progress. When they approached he stood up, moved to one end of the long wooden garden seat to make room for them all, and then they all sat down again. Lindsay, at the other end of the bench, hoped that he would soon tire of looking on, and that he would have gone back to his office before her own turn came.

He didn't, of course. When Carleen and the others came off, he passed around the beer and iced fruit juice from the table just behind him, and chatted to his visitors.

'You play a very neat game, Carleen.' She heard his deep voice among the others. 'That's quite a backhand you have, and you obviously use that pretty little head in tennis, as in everything else. That lob of yours broke deadlock, and then you were home and dry.'

'How nice of you, Rod, to notice. I do wish *you* would play, too, though. Won't you change your mind?'

'Not today, I think. I might give you a game of singles some time, if you like, now that the boys have the court in order. I don't promise to spare you, though, just because you happen to look so delectably feminine. I'll be out to win, I assure you.'

She gave a small, secretive smile.

'Darling, you never do spare me, do you? I thrive on it, Rod, that masterful touch! And remember—*I* am out to win, too, so that should be interesting, shouldn't it?' she murmured.

Lindsay looked away. They were talking in riddles which she did not understand, but the smug, complacent expression on Carleen's face sent little shivers down her spine, for no particular reason.

Her eyes met Margie's, and what Margie did then surprised her. She closed one eye, and winked at Lindsay, quite

131

solemnly—and Lindsay knew that she, too, had heard that snippet of conversation.

Lindsay never made up her mind, afterwards, whether it was that upsetting morsel of conversation, or Rod's own presence on the sidelines, which was responsible for her lack of concentration, but whatever it was, Shorty must have cursed his inept partner soundly more than once under his breath. Apart from one or two miraculous recoveries, she had never played such appalling tennis in her life. She slammed, whacked, hooked, hesitated—all with disastrous consequences. And then a singing ball from Mick put an end to it all.

In other circumstances, Lindsay might have been grateful for such an abrupt finish when she was acquitting herself so badly, but just now it was difficult to feel gratitude, to feel anything, indeed, but that searing pain in her left eye, that peculiar knocking in her head, that distant woolliness in her legs.

She could only stand rooted to the spot, her racket at her feet, her hand clapped hard against the injured eye, while its companion watered in sympathy.

'Gosh, Lindsay, I'm *sorry*!' Mickie had hurdled the net and come quickly to her side. Voices gabbled all about her.

And then someone spoke a little louder. Lindsay recognised that tone of brusque authority even though she was unable to see its owner.

'All right, everyone, I'll take care of it. There's no need to break up the party, that game was a foregone conclusion anyway. You others have another set now, and I'll look after Lindsay.' She felt a firm grasp on her upper arm, leading her away. 'Come with me,' said the voice near her ear, in very much the same tone as it had done on her very first day— that forbearing, polite, no-nonsense tone that had bidden her, '*You* come with *me*.'

Lindsay permitted herself to be led into the house. Rod took her straight to the bathroom, pushed her gently but firmly into the cane chair there, and flicked on the overhead light. Then he pulled her fingers away from her streaming eye, and cupped her face in his hands.

'Let me see, Lindsay, please. Look up. Look down.'

He was completely impersonal in his efficient inspection. Finally he squeezed out a cloth in cold water, formed it into a neat, square pad, and placed it against her eye, putting her own fingers back over it.

'Just hold that there for a while, and I'll get some iced water from the kitchen for the next round.'

'W-will it be all right?'

Rod grinned.

'You're going to have a corker of a black eye, I should think, but in all other respects it's fortunately unharmed. You must have shut it instinctively as you turned to avoid the ball. One's reflexes can be surprisingly quick and effective under those circumstances.'

Lindsay derived cold comfort from his words.

'A *black* eye? Oh no! You mean, the kind that then goes purple and yellow by turns?' she asked in dismay.

'That's the kind I mean, exactly. A pity, I grant you—I prefer them green and soft, myself, just as you do. Green and soft, like a mist on a lily-pond.'

Rod was saying *that*, about *her* eyes? He couldn't be! She bit her lip in vexation that the lily-pond greenness, in one of them, at least, was evidently gone for some time if his diagnosis was to be trusted.

'Maybe a piece of steak——' she suggested timidly. 'I've heard that it sometimes works.'

He chuckled.

'Haven't you had enough steak for today?' he asked whimsically, then, shrugging, 'Very well, Lindsay, I'll get some. There was plenty left over from lunch—but I'm afraid your optimism will go unrewarded. *Nothing* is going to prevent that eye from turning black.'

When he returned, he took her out on to the veranda and adjusted one of the deck-chairs near his office door into a reclining position.

'Sit down there, Lindsay, and lean right back. You'll be more comfortable and cool here. Does your head ache at all?'

'Only a tiny bit. It's nothing.'

Rod drew up a chair close beside hers, and leaned over her,

putting the piece of steak he had brought gently in place. He was devastatingly near. Even the faintly nauseating odour of uncooked meat right next to her nose did little to inhibit the emotion that Lindsay felt go surging through her at his proximity.

'Close the other eye, too, Lindsay. I'll hold it in place for a while, and then I must do some work. I shall be very near in my office, though, so you must call me if you want me at all.'

Lindsay obediently shut both eyes. She was glad to, because she couldn't have gone on looking at Rod's square jaw-line, brown column of throat, and wide shoulders much longer, and since his chest across her line of vision rendered any other view virtually impossible, it seemed prudent to obey.

She sighed.

'I'm sorry I messed up the afternoon for everyone. I can't think how I did it.'

'Never mind about it now. These things happen; although' —she could detect the smile in his voice—'I must say you're a glutton for punishment, aren't you, little one?'

A light touch brushed over her brow—just the barest suggestion of a hand's caressing movement. Lindsay must have imagined it. She kept her eyes shut tightly because she did not want to discover that she had been wrong.

'So *there* you are! I've been searching for you everywhere!'

Lindsay opened her eyes abruptly, struggling to a sitting position and said; slightly breathlessly, because she had been startled by the other girl's silent approach, 'I—I'll take it now, Rod. There's no need for you to hold it, any more. Th-thank you for all you did.'

'How is she, anyway?' Carleen did not bother to address herself to Lindsay. 'We've had another set, and now the other three are having to play cut-throat.'

There was a waspishly accusing note in that statement that was not lost upon Lindsay, although it appeared to escape the man beside her.

He stood up, stretched in a leisurely fashion, and said

equably,

'She'll live, I think, Carleen. Did you have a good set? Who won this time—you and Barry?'

'Of course, darling. I always win—if it's at all possible.' A pretty, deprecating smile took the boastfulness out of her reply. 'I was just telling Lindsay that the other day, wasn't I, Lindsay? I suppose some of us are born to win, others to be defeated—it's probably all a matter of destiny. So far, I've been lucky.' She yawned complacently. 'I'd love a cool drink, Rod. Could I have one, do you think? And then we could carry some more out to the lawn for the others, couldn't we?'

'You may prefer to stay there and rest for a while, Lindsay,' Rod suggested kindly, as he turned to accompany Carleen along the veranda.

'I—yes—I think I shall, if you don't mind,' she mumbled confusedly. Anything to be spared the sight of that slender hand resting possessively on his bare brown forearm, those guileless eyes turned up to his, the inviting intimacy of that smile that effectively shut out the rest of the world, and left just two people—Rod and Carleen.

By evening Lindsay's eye was swollen and darkening, and when she got up next morning she saw that the entire area was puffy and discoloured. Alas! As Rod had forecast, no measures known to man could have prevented her from ending up with a black eye that would have made many a prize-fighter's battle scars look pale in comparison.

She was down in the store later on when Carleen approached, looking elegant and appropriately cool in a sleeveless turquoise tabard over matching shorts. She clucked sympathetically at the sight of Lindsay bent over her log book at the far end of the room.

'Hello,' she greeted her amicably. 'You appeared so miserable at breakfast this morning that I thought I'd come down and offer my services. Don't look so surprised, Lindsay. I really was sorry for you yesterday, but there didn't seem much point in not going on with the party. I'm sure you'd have only felt worse if we'd all stopped, anyway.'

'Oh, I would!' Lindsay assured her eagerly, warmed at this

135

unexpected *volte-face* on the other's part. 'I'd have felt dreadful if everyone had stopped playing just because of me. And Rod was really awfully kind.'

'*Wasn't* he! I thought so, too, I must say. With him there to administer first-aid and comfort, there was really no need for anyone else, was there?' Carleen surveyed the store with idle interest. 'What are you doing now, Lindsay? What are all these things, for goodness' sake?'

She picked up one of an assortment of unfamiliar objects from the pile on the counter and turned it between her fingers.

'Those are machinery spares—windmill ones there, and those are for the bores. This pile is mainly electrical, and that lot are for Rod's plane.'

'Goodness, aren't you clever, knowing which ones are which!' Carleen's voice held genuine admiration.

Lindsay flushed.

'I didn't at first,' she admitted humbly. 'I got into some awful muddles, but the men rallied round and helped, so that Rod wouldn't find out how ignorant I was. They taught me how to identify them, and there are some illustrated catalogues—look, these ones here, all numbered, you see—and I still refer to these any time I'm in doubt.'

'And after you tick them there? What then?'

'Then they go to the machinery shop or the blacksmith's shop, and the men just take them when they need them. All I'm doing here is checking them against the invoices to make sure that everything has arrived that was ordered.'

'Oh, I *see*.' Carleen ran her hand along the counter thoughtfully, inspected her fingers, and wrinkled her pretty nose at the dust she had gathered on them. 'Rather a depressing place, isn't it? And so is the whole homestead, if one never had a break, I should think. Of course, once Rod is married, I don't suppose for a moment he'd want to live away out here in the back-blocks—he'd probably just visit occasionally in his plane.' She bent down to inspect the shelves under the counter. 'Heavens, what stuff! And what's in those cupboards there? The locked ones?'

Lindsay showed her, explained that these were not drugs

in the medical sense, but simply potentially dangerous fluids, for which the men had to sign if they received them.

'And of course the people down at the creek aren't allowed them even if they *could* sign for them—which of course they can't.'

'You mean, the blacks?'

'Yes, the aborigines.'

'Why ever not? They could always put an identification mark in the book, surely? You know, a cross or something in the way of an individual squiggle.'

Lindsay shook her head.

'Rod says not. He says there's no reason for them to need any of those things anyway, not in the course of their particular work, he meant.'

Carleen folded her arms, smiling faintly.

'What an archaic set-up, isn't it!' She gazed out of the window, with which the saddling-yard was aligned. There were only two horses remaining, reins looped over the rail, heads dropped close together, as though they were exchanging whispered horse-talk in the heat while they waited. At this time of day the men were usually all away, but evidently there must still be a couple of them about the place, still to ride out. 'And do the blacks ever come and bother you to give them things?'

Lindsay ticked off an item in her book, and put it into its correct pile.

'No, never. At least, one did just once. He pointed to some bottle or other—I forget what—and said he wanted it to clean harness with. But when I said he couldn't have it, he just laughed and went away.'

'Here, let me do some of that with you.'

Carleen was in such a pleasantly friendly mood that Lindsay would have felt churlish had she refused.

Together they listed all the spares on the bench, Carleen reading them out and ticking off the quantities while Lindsay identified them and put them into the correct pile. It was a laborious business, and it was not difficult to guess that the transparent Carleen was very soon utterly bored by the monotony of it all. Her attention was inclined to wander,

137

but she resolutely struck to her post, and the two girls had actually completed the task, and were preparing to go back to the homestead, when the door opened and Artie and Tommo came in.

Artie appeared quite taken aback to discover that Lindsay was not alone, and even more surprised that her companion was none other than the stand-offish young woman whom he had disdainfully classified as a dame, and who up till now had been in the habit of treating him as if he didn't exist at all.

He touched his hat, and became very red.

'G'day,' he mumbled, his eyes shifting back to Lindsay as quickly as possible. 'I wonder if them galvanised staples 'ave come in yet, Lindsay, the ones we was waitin' for last week?'

'They'll be here somewhere, Artie.' She eyed the un-opened packages still to be checked. 'It will take me a while to find them, though, I'm afraid. Could you come back, maybe?'

Artie prodded the boards with the toe of his dusty boot, undecided.

'I'm supposed ter be out with 'Erb right now, mendin' a fence, see. 'E's goin' ter think I've lost me bloomin' way in the scrub, ain't 'e, I'm that late. I've got everythink else we're needin' ter take out except fer them rakin' staples.' He hesi- tated, brightened. 'Tell yer what, Lindsay. When you come across 'em, you leave 'em out on the counter, and Tommo 'ere'll bring 'em after me, see. 'E's ridin' that stretch anyway, this arvo, and I reckon maybe we'll 'ave enough ter keep us goin' till 'e comes. You leave 'em out and 'e'll get 'em. 'E can go down 'ome fer some grub in the meantime. O.K?'

Tommo rolled his eyes and nodded sagely to show that it was O.K. by him, too, and then he and Artie disappeared together, leaving Lindsay and Carleen to start sorting fran- tically through packages and parcels once more.

'Drat those men! I thought we'd finished.' Carleen's good humour had evidently been tried too far. She helped half- heartedly after that, impatient to be gone, and heaved a sigh of relief when at last the carton had been unearthed and put conspicuously on the bench-top above the shelves.

As they went out together, Lindsay reached up to the nail above the door and retrieved her bunch of keys.

'I never dare to leave them in my pocket,' she explained, 'in case they drop out when I'm bending down somewhere and I lose them. I've made a point of hanging them up when I come in, and the same in my own room up at the house. Funny how things get to be a habit. You soon find yourself doing them automatically.'

'Aren't you going to lock just now?'

'No, because Tommo will have to come back for those things. I'll just take the keys with me, though. It's only for an hour or so, in any case, while we have lunch.'

The two girls had their meal with Mannie—just the three of them. When Rod was out all day, there did not seem much point in preparing anything elaborate. Carleen was a light, selective eater in any event, always preoccupied with her figure, and Mannie had the elderly person's dislike of anything too heavy or substantial, so they usually settled for salad, or a simple snack of eggs.

After lunch was over, Carleen asked Lindsay to come to her own bedroom, and once there she stood for a moment, hesitating, before asking the younger girl, with a noticeable display of diffidence, if she could possibly do her a favour. The customary demanding note was quite absent from Carleen's voice just now, and as she made her request she smiled with unfamiliar warmth, and Lindsay found herself responding. What else could she do but comply, in view of Carleen's amiable overtures and her help in the store that morning?

'It's this, Lindsay. The hem of this frock. I must have caught it on something—look!—and I've ripped some of the stitching out. Quite a lot of it, I'm afraid.'

Lindsay inspected the garment. It was of fine lawn, a rather lovely tobacco brown print.

'I'll do it for you this evening, if you like.'

Carleen's lips pursed with disappointment.

'Oh dear, I'd hoped to *wear* it this evening,' she murmured plaintively. 'It's so hot today, and my other dresses all have sleeves. Couldn't you be a dear and do it now? How long would it take? I'd do it myself, but you know how hopeless I am with things like that, and it's such very fine material, I'd be certain to make a hash of it.'

Lindsay glanced from her watch to her cousin's hopeful countenance, and gave in.

'Sit in my window-seat, here, then, Lindsay, and I'll get Mannie's work-box for you. I saw some thread there exactly this colour the other day. The light will be at your back there.' She darted off eagerly, brought back the sewing kit and thanked Lindsay prettily once more.

'I'll leave you to it,' she said from the doorway. 'Just put it on the bed when you've finished, and I shall hang it up later.'

Carleen wore the dress that night. It had been a painstaking task to make all those tiny unseen stitches, but one would never have known that anything had been wrong with it at all. Indeed, its wearer had seldom looked lovelier, decided Lindsay impartially. There was a certain glow about Carleen this evening, a translucent beauty in her classic features, an unusual serenity in her sometimes discontented blue eyes.

Rod himself seemed aware of her in a different way tonight, too. Gone was the bantering, teasing tone he so often adopted, the sophisticated sparring and amused cynicism which he and Carleen so often employed in their verbal jousting. Tonight he was responding to this new, serene Carleen with a flatteringly serious and masculine interest which the recipient evidently found inordinately pleasing. Her thoughtfulness to Mannie, her inclusion of Lindsay in the conversation, reflected a mysterious but by no means unwelcome change in her attitude, and after dinner she even helped to carry out the dishes before joining Rod in his office for a cigarette.

Whether it was that Carleen's newly acquired good humour rubbed off on everyone else, or whether it was the fact that it induced an answering affability in Rod in particular, Lindsay could not have said. Whatever was responsible, there was a subtle alteration in the atmosphere at Gundooee homestead over the next couple of days, and Lindsay basked in the change. No undercurrents of uncertainty, jealousy, or sarcasm were there to disrupt the pleasant state of existing harmony. Carleen was noticeably kindly disposed to all and sundry, Rod was less watchful and critical, and Mannie almost purred with satisfaction that life was now as pleasantly peaceful as it had been when she and Rod were alone.

Indeed, if anything, it was even nicer now, she confided to Lindsay in the kitchen. It did Rod good to have the girls around. An old lady was no fit company for a young man of thirty, who should be thinking about marriage and a family of his own. Mannie had strong views on the subject, and did not hesitate to air them when she felt inclined.

'I wouldn't be surprised if those two have come to some sort of private understanding,' she observed when she and Lindsay were alone one day. 'I've never known Rod to be quite like he is just now, not even with Margie. He's more relaxed and happy, somehow, than ever before. As for Carleen—well, I must admit I've been quite wrong about her. I didn't take to her at first, but she's been so different lately, thoughtful and kind, I can only think that perhaps the poor child's recent illness made her narky, and that she's feeling better now. I know what it can be like, trying to appear normal, and be pleasant, when you aren't feeling too well. It's all a bit of a bother, but one has to pretend, to save a fuss.'

A knife had twisted in Lindsay's heart, a knife that caused a pain of bitterness to flood through her whole being.

Carleen, who had come with blatant calculation to annex Rod Bennett for herself, looked like succeeding, if Mannie's observations were accurate. And as for Rod, he had never seemed happier, as if he had suddenly found something for which he had been searching for a very long time. Lindsay had herself sensed the very thing that Mannie had put into words!

You were supposed to be *glad* when a person you loved found happiness, Lindsay reminded herself fiercely. You were supposed to be glad in an unselfish, basic sort of way. Easier said than done, that, but she'd have to try! And she'd have to be glad for Carleen too. It really did appear that

Carleen had fallen properly in love with Rod—with Rod as a person, and not just as a wealthy, athletic, eligible symbol whom she had come intentionally to pursue. What else but love could account for such a devastating change in someone's nature, could bring about that amiability and softness which had previously not existed?

Lindsay put these thoughts firmly to the back of her mind, and concentrated on Mannie's last sentence. It was, to Lindsay, a revealing one, although she was certain that Mannie was totally unaware of that fact. It confirmed something of what Lindsay had actually suspected for some time now, and that was that the old lady was far from well. Just lately, Lindsay couldn't help noticing that Mannie spent much more time resting in her room, and when she reappeared, she did not seem refreshed. Often, too, when she rose from her chair on the veranda, she would stand quite still for a while, as if the effort of getting up had been almost too much for her, as if she had to give herself a minute or two to readjust.

Observing these signs, Lindsay had taken over some of Mannie's tasks in the house as unobtrusively as possible—so unobtrusively, indeed, that the old woman seemed hardly aware of it—and lately she had made a point of coming up from the book-keeper's cottage or the store in plenty of time to help Mannie prepare the evening meal. In the mornings, too, it was as often as not Lindsay herself who cut thick hunks of cold meat and sandwiched them with pickles and butter between bread-slices for Rod's saddle-bag, and who turned out a tray of puffy golden scones to cool in time to accompany those sandwiches.

Mannie had perhaps noticed, but if she did, she made no comment. Maybe she was too weary and languid to bother remarking on the fact, but more than likely she refrained because, as she had said just now, one did not welcome a fuss.

On that realisation, Lindsay closed her lips upon what she had been about to say. She would respect Mannie's wish for privacy, but the sight of those tiredly circled eyes and the lines of suffering about the old lady's mouth did nothing to make her decision to keep silence an easier one.

It was the one discordant note in a presently idyllic world, that secret which Lindsay was convinced that she shared without Mannie's knowledge.

Before dinner-time came round that evening, Lindsay was able to display the lemon pie she had made while Mannie was having her rest, and the casserole already cooking slowly in the oven. Sibbie and Bella had peeled and prepared all manner of vegetables for her to put in it, and it smelt unbelievably appetising as Lindsay lifted the lid and showed Mannie what she had done. Her reward, if she had sought one at all, was in the gentle glow of appreciation in Mannie's tired eyes as she had thanked her.

After dinner, she and Mannie drew up their deck-chairs and talked desultorily. Further along the veranda, from Rod's study, came the soft buzz of voices in conversation— Carleen's light, fluted tone, and Rod's own deep one. Lindsay steeled herself not to listen to the muffled sounds of that intimate, after-dinner chat.

The air tonight was laden with perfume. It came from the border of stocks just outside the gauze screen in front of the place where they sat, and from the bed of geraniums in the centre of the lawn. Beyond, the trees were ghostly shapes, lifting a tangle of silvered branches to the moon that floated timelessly above it in its sea of stars.

Lindsay lay back, contemplating the peaceful scene, loth to disturb the soothing silence by speech or any other means, when it was rudely broken by the sound of running feet. They thudded over the hard, bare moon-bathed ground— nearer, nearer. Then the wicket-gate slammed at the bottom of the garden, and Jimmy pounded along the path, up the steps, through the swing-door.

'Boss! Boss!' he was yelling urgently. 'You come quick-fella, Boss, allasame that cheekyfella water burn-up, burn-up, in bingie belonga Tommo!' Rod was out of his study in a flash, flicking on the veranda light.

'What did you say, Jimmy?' he asked sternly. 'Better you talk clear, eh—not gabble-gabble allasame nobody savvy. Clear, Jimmy. Slow, eh? Now, what is it?'

Jimmy's dark, glistening chest was heaving. All he had on was a pair of khaki trousers. His feet were bare, and it was the first time that Lindsay had ever seen him without the beloved pipe which was usually clenched in his strong white teeth.

'That proper badfella water Tommo drink out of that bottle, Boss. Him get plurry mad, bin chase them lubras and piccaninnies—pokem! pokem!—alonga that big stick——' Jimmy's wiry black arms jabbed out savagely in all directions to illustrate his point.

'Where is he now?' Rod asked abruptly.

'Him bin lie on ground now, Boss. Them others hold 'im down while I get Boss, plenty quickfella, see.'

The others had gathered around Rod and Jimmy.

'Wh-what does he mean, Rod? What's he saying?' Carleen put an anxious hand on Rod's arm.

'It sounds as though he's drunk,' was the terse reply.

'Drunk! But where could he get drink, away out *here*? And what could he possibly get drunk *on*?'

'The only place he could get it'—Rod sought and held Lindsay's eye—'would be the store. As for what it *is*, that I intend to find out.'

His eyes were dark with anger. Lindsay's own were fastened on his face, as though mesmerised with foreboding. All the colour had left her cheeks, so that the bruised place around her eye stood out in liverish relief.

'You come, Boss, eh? That proper cheekyfella water, make Tommo crawl oneside alonga that ground allasame him plurry carpet-snake with 'is back broke, see. That badfella stuff *killum* Tommo, Boss!'

'Oh no!' The words escaped Lindsay's numbed lips in an agonised protest. She swayed on her feet.

Rod's hand steadied her. In fact, his fingers bit brutally into her soft flesh as he shook her slightly and said with grim emphasis,

'Not *kill*, you little idiot. He means *hurt*. By the sound of things, he's a long way from dead!'

Without another word he followed Jimmy through the gauze door and down the steps. Seconds later, the little gate

144

clicked back into place, and the two figures disappeared in the night.

'Goodness, what a thing to happen!' Carleen sounded shocked.

Lindsay sank down into the nearest chair. She dared not think, could not *let* herself think, how such a thing could have come about. The only certainy was that it *had*!

Down at the gunyahs came the shrill barking of dogs, the almost hysterical crying of children, and at one point a blood-curdling yell.

'I think I shall go to bed.' Mannie got up stiffly, gave Lindsay's arm a tiny, comforting squeeze, under cover of the semi-darkness, and tactfully withdrew.

A match rasped as Carleen lit a cigarette and stretched her legs.

'I'll stay with you, if you like,' she volunteered. 'I doubt if I could get to sleep with all that racket going on, in any event.'

Lindsay swallowed, unable to trust herself to speak. A strange fear had her in its grip, a sort of guilt that *wasn't* guilt. How could it be, when she knew perfectly well that she had always been so careful of all those fluids and poisons at the store, ever since Artie had warned her on her very first day? Rod will have your hide, he'd said. Remembering, Lindsay shivered. It was a shiver of shock, of dread, of this guilt that wasn't, of an odd, instinctive hopelessness.

It seemed an interminable time before things were quiet once more down at the settlement. One by one the noises abated, until, with the last plaintive whimper of the last dog, there was finally silence.

Shortly after that, Rod came back. He came treading purposefully along the veranda with a curiously set face, hitched around a chair with the toe of his shoe, sat down, and commenced to roll himself a smoke. The fact that he hadn't uttered a single word unnerved Lindsay completely. Anything would seem preferable to this ominous silence!

Carleen spoke first. 'Is he all right, Rod?' she asked, half fearfully.

'He'll do,' Rod replied shortly. He took a long pull on the

cigarette between his fingers, and exhaled as though he were expelling a weary sigh at the same time.

'Was it—was he drunk?'

'Yes, Carleen, I'm afraid he was drunk. Very drunk. And what he was drunk *on*'—a significant pause—'was methylated spirits.'

'Did he tell you that that's what it was?'

'He didn't have to tell me,' Rod pointed out tersely. 'The poor beggar was stinking with it.'

'Oh.' Carleen pursed her lips in concern. 'How awful for you!'

'But worse for him,' he observed tritely. 'He'll have a blinder of a hangover in the morning, and probably won't be fit for days.' Another pause. 'He got the meths from the store, by all accounts. I won't say *stole* it—these people aren't strong on the moral issues.' Rod turned to Lindsay, addressed himself to her exclusively, holding her in a direct penetrating regard. 'If you have an explanation, Lindsay, I'd certainly like to hear it,' he said quietly, although he didn't sound as if he'd really *like* to hear anything she might have to say, at all!

Lindsay licked her lips.

'I'm terribly sorry, Rod, truly I am, but I honestly can't see how I could be to blame. I mean, I've always been so careful, ever since you said. I—I always keep the store locked, and I just don't see how he could have got it.'

'Always? Without fail?'

'Yes, always. *Truly.*'

Carleen's dress rustled as she uncrossed her legs, reached forward to stub out her cigarette.

'Not *quite* always, Lindsay.' She seemed reluctant to speak. 'I mean, do forgive me, my dear, for pointing it out, but you didn't the other day, for instance, did you? That day at lunch-time, remember? You said it wouldn't matter for an hour or two.' She waved a manicured hand apologetically. 'I don't want to interfere, of course. I'm not *meaning* anything, but just in the cause of accuracy——' Her voice tailed off uncertainly.

'*Did* you leave it unlocked one day over the lunch period,

Lindsay?' Rod's voice had a depth of grimness that made her flinch.

'Yes, but——'

'And yet you've just told me that you always lock up, without fail?'

'Yes, well, I do.' She floundered unhappily. 'I mean, there was a reason, that day. The men had staples to collect. I left them on the counter for them. But everything else was locked. I swear it was!'

'You mean you *think* it was,' he corrected her mercilessly.

'No, truly. All the cupboards were locked, every one of them, although the main door was open.'

'It was from the cupboard that he got the stuff, Lindsay. The second on the right.' Rod's voice was oddly bleak. 'Far from being locked, that cupboard door wasn't even shut. It was wide open, so he just took it.'

'Rod, you *must* believe me. Please?' Lindsay was begging him in her distress.

'Why should I believe you, Lindsay—much as I would like to? You have already made one false statement. Why not another?'

Lindsay could only gaze at him in nightmarish disbelief at what he was saying. Through a mist of horror she heard Carleen's voice saying silkily,

'Darling, you're only *human*, I mean, aren't we *all*? Anyone can make a mistake.'

Rod Bennett got to his feet, looked down to where Lindsay sat, nursing her knees in hunched-up misery.

'Some mistakes are redeemable, others are not,' he said harshly. 'I find it very difficult to forgive a mistake that is caused by arrant carelessness and not an error of judgement. I'm deeply disappointed in you, Lindsay. That's all I'll trust myself to say on the matter tonight.'

Without waiting for a further reply, he went into his office and shut the door.

Carleen stirred in her canvas chair.

'Poor Lindsay,' she said sympathetically into the darkness. 'It does look as though you may have cooked your goose, doesn't it?'

CHAPTER 9

FOR Lindsay, the days that followed were unbearably lonely. She could confide her thoughts and fears to no one, so she was forced to exist in this awful vacuum of solitariness, just Lindsay and her suspicions. They were uneasy thoughts to live with. It was bad enough to even think such things, but to be unable to unburden herself to anybody made the situation even more unpleasant.

Whom, after all, could she tell? Not Rod, with this new barrier of reserve and aloofness between them. He was absolutely unapproachable these days!

Mannie? Yes, perhaps, if she hadn't known that Mannie already had enough with which to concern herself, in her fight against failing health.

Carleen? No, most of all, not Carleen!

Lindsay shied from the thought of a direct confrontation with anyone who could be capable of the dastardly deed of which she suspected her distant cousin. Carleen had demonstrated to Lindsay that she would stop at very little to gain her ends! She had shown that she could be completely and utterly ruthless—clever, too. She had somehow managed to unlock that cupboard at the store, had actually left the door ajar in order to tempt poor old Tommo beyond endurance, and—cleverest of all—had succeeded in locking it again and returning Lindsay's keys to her room without coming under the slightest suspicion from anybody.

When could she have done it?

Lindsay, tossing and turning in sleepless torment, could only suppose that it must have been that day at lunch-time, when they had been together at the store. Carleen would have had time to run back with the keys and unlock the cupboard while Lindsay had been helping Mannie with the lunch. And? After lunch? Lindsay hated herself for thinking this way, but the whole thing added up, didn't it?

Carleen had prevailed upon her to do that hem before going back to the store. She had seen to it that Lindsay sat in her window-seat, from which the route to the store was invisible, and she had taken the keys from Lindsay's own bedroom and relocked the cupboard. That peculiar serenity—smugness, Lindsay could call it now, in the light of what she knew!—had stemmed from the fact that Carleen realised, almost immediately, that her plan had half succeeded already. Doubtless she had inspected the contents of that cupboard to make sure there was nothing really lethal in it when she opened it, and when she returned, had noted the disappearance of the large purple flagon.

It only remained to be patient, to wait. In time, her action was almost certain to rebound in the only possible quarter where blame could logically be laid—upon Lindsay herself!

When morning came, Lindsay was thankful. She crawled out of bed, walked softly out on to the veranda—a wistful, unhappy figure in her thin cotton pyjamas.

From the tank came a splash in the half light, and the birds rose screeching and chittering from its banks and settled in the garden trees, shuffling their wings resentfully. Rod was having his morning bathe. Lindsay watched the dark head moving in the water through eyes that were suddenly misted over, so that the outline of the swimmer became blurred and wavy. They were out of sympathy now, she and that swimmer. They were poles apart in every way. Carleen had successfully seen to that!

Lindsay returned to her room, pulled on her clothes, and went to breakfast, helped Mannie to clear the table, made her own and Carleen's beds—Carleen refused to allow Sibbie and Bella into her room—and then took down her keys and started off for the cottage.

Before she came around the corner near the blacksmith's shop, Lindsay could hear the animated conversation that was taking place. As there was a certain amount of intermittent hammering and clanking going on as well, the talk almost amounted to a forthright exchange of shouts, so that Lindsay could not possibly have failed to hear it, even had she wished. And as she took in what was being said, she *did* wish—very much indeed! Artie and Mickie were the participants, and she didn't like the gist of that conversation at all!

'I'm tellin' yer, Mick, it won't do. *She's* goin' around like a cat wot's got all the cream, and our little kitten ain't even got scraps!'

'You're right, Artie, so help me, you are. But what can we do about it?'

'Well, you ain't done much ter shorten them odds, and that's a dinkum fact. What in ruddy 'ell you was at, near doin' 'er in altogether with a rakin' tennis-ball in the eye, I can't think. Why can't yer play tennis more gentle, for Pete's sake?'

'It was purely a case of rotten luck, Artie, that's all.' Mick's voice was conciliatory. 'She just didn't seem to see the ball, and wham! I must say, she wasn't playing all that well, in any case.'

'I 'eard as much from Shorty. I wouldn't put me money on 'er against a blinkin' mosquito, with a tennis racquet. But this other—well, I reckon we 'ad a good chance, Mickie, until this latest flummoxer. I got me own ideas about *that*, too,' Artie added mysteriously.

'There's not much hope at the moment, Art, I grant you, but maybe we can do something to tip the scales a bit. You leave it with me.'

'Well, if yer don't do better than yer did on the tennis-court, 'eaven 'elp us! Our Lindsay's goin' around lookin' about as fetchin' as a flippin' pirate, with that yeller patch all round 'er eye!'

'You leave it with me,' shouted Mickie again above the hammering. 'I'll think of something. Oh, hullo, Lindsay. A beaut morning, isn't it?'

He grinned at her from his post at the head of the restive horse which his companion was busy shoeing.

Artie looked up, too, rather sheepishly. He had a home-rolled cigarette and two shoeing nails stuck moistly between his lips, and the horse's near front hoof between his legs. To Lindsay it was miraculous that he had been able to speak at all in his present state of occupation, let alone speak so loudly.

'Hullo,' she replied, with a friendly smile. 'A nice day, yes.'

'We was just talkin' about yer, wasn't we, Mick?' Artie informed her now, quite unnecessarily.

'About me, Art?'

'Yeah, Lindsay, that's right. Tell me, 'ow's yer blinker comin' on?'

'If you mean my eye, you can see for yourself,' returned Lindsay unhelpfully.

Artie did. He placed the horse's forefoot carefully back on the ground, returned his bent back to an upright position, and inspected her critically.

'Jeez!' he gloomed. 'If you arst me, it was nicer purple. It's gone a kind of a mustard yeller, ain't it?'

'That means it's getting better. It will go on fading all the time now, and it's not a bit sore any more, so that's a relief. Soon it will be back to normal, I'm sure.'

Back to its lily-pond green—only Rod never noticed any more, not these days.

'Maybe not soon enough,' Artie sighed almost under his breath.

'Soon enough for *what*?'

Better have this out here and now, Lindsay decided. In view of that disquieting exchange she had just heard, there was no time like the present to bring things out into the open. Whatever the men were up to—and it was obvious that they were up to something—Lindsay had no desire to be involved in any way. She was in enough trouble without them engineering any more!

'For what?' she insisted, determinedly.

Artie scratched his ear bewilderedly, while Mickie stroked the velvet nose of the animal he was holding.

'Aw, nothin', really, Lindsay. Skip it.'

'No, Artie, I won't skip it—not this time.'

'It ain't nothin', honest,' he assured her with a gaze as blank and innocent as a lamb's.

Lindsay hesitated. He certainly appeared convincingly

truthful, but——

'Look here, you two,' she said firmly, 'I'm not going to ask if you don't want to tell me, but there's just one thing I think you should know. If it's anything to do with the—er—the knockout stakes, you can forget about it. As a matter of fact, I mentioned it to Rod, and——'

'You *what*?' Mickie's hand jerked the horse's head unintentionally.

'Slit me gizzard! Yer *never*?' exclaimed Artie in disbelief. 'What did 'e say?'

'He said'—Lindsay told them very clearly and slowly— 'that there was absolutely no use in my even thinking of competing in it. *That's* what he said.'

She marched off, leaving the men staring at each other in consternation.

'Maybe 'e's bluffin', of course, Mick. I reckon it's still worth a try.'

Artie's considered comment, which just reached her ears as she disappeared, dispelled any satisfaction Lindsay was feeling that she had at last put a stop to their undisclosed machinations.

She was finding out, the hard way, that there is no one so obstinate, determined, persistent, *conniving*, as a big, tough, casual, stubble-chinned outback station-hand with something to lose! She only wished she knew what Artie was conniving at. You'd think he and Mickie could see for themselves that, even with the aid of those riding lessons they had given her, she would never be good enough on a horse to enter an actual race.

And the knockout stakes! It sounded like a very fast and very professional elimination race, that—not at all the sort of thing that Lindsay, who could do little more than cling precariously to Dusty's long, bony back when he chose to trot, might ever win. Not *ever*!

'My progress seems to be at a standstill, somehow,' she confessed to Mick that evening. Like everything else in life at the moment, she could have added forlornly, but of course she didn't. That was something one had to suffer in silence, just as one had to accept Rod's distant courtesy, Carleen's

152

smug air of triumph, and the kindly, unspoken sympathy of the station-hands themselves, which in itself was enough to tell her that even they believed that she had been careless about that cupboard, and were sorry for her because she had incurred the Boss's wrath.

'Never mind, Lindsay,' the young jackaroo replied comfortingly. 'If you can just hang on for a couple of weeks, till we get the Dinewan block mustered, we'll give you a really intensive course when we come back. That's all you're needing, you know—practice.'

'Dinewan? Isn't that Margie's home? The Lockwith property?'

'That's correct. It's right next their boundary, which is why it's called that. It isn't the furthest outcamp on the place by any means, but it's the least accessible, in rougher country, with a river-bed between us and it. That's why Margie finds it easier to pop over in her little plane.'

'I see. And do you *all* go?'

It would be almost a relief to be without Rod for a while, thought Lindsay mournfully. The old Rod was gone, and in his place was a tense-jawed, curt-tongued, bleak-eyed stranger whom Lindsay could well do without. If only Rod was going, the interval would give Lindsay time to condition herself, as best she could, to these new circumstances that prevailed here at the homestead. When he came back, he might even have forgotten about the lapse for which he believed her responsible, or, if not forgotten, at least forgiven!

'Yes, we'll all be out.' She heard Mick's answer with unmitigated relief. 'It usually takes us a week or ten days out there, the rounding-up and branding. It's scrubby, difficult country to work. Oh, hello there, Carleen, I was looking for you, as it happens. That's what I came up to the house for.'

Carleen raised an indifferent eyebrow, posed herself carefully in her chair to make the most of her lovely figure in the emerald shift she wore tonight.

'Were you?' she said with noticeable lack of enthusiasm, crossing her legs daintily and plucking a cigarette from her monogrammed gold case.

'Yes. I'll tell you what it is.' Mick did not allow himself to be put off by her disinterest. 'Tomorrow we're going to be dropping dingo-baits from the air, and I wondered if you'd like to come too? It's an exhilarating experience, one I'm sure you'd enjoy.'

'Oh!' Lindsay leaned forward eagerly. 'Could I come too, Mick, do you think? I'd be so interested to see what you do.'

'Sorry, Lindsay,' he told her regretfully, 'but there wouldn't be room for you both. I'll be handing the baits, and'—a pause—'Rod himself will be the pilot, as always. It calls for quite skilled flying, you know.'

'If Carleen isn't keen——' Lindsay glanced hopefully to where the other girl lounged back in her chair, smoking.

'Who said I wasn't keen?' Carleen smiled rather snubbingly. 'Of course I'd love to go. Rod's been promising to take me for a ride in his plane for ages.'

'It will be around ten o'clock, then. You come down to the strip.'

'I'll be there,' she promised airily, and even waved a friendly hand as Mick took his departure. 'Perhaps, next time, you will get a turn, Lindsay,' she said patronisingly, and as always, when Carleen looked like that, Lindsay found her fingers clenching tight against her palms in sheer irritation.

The Carleen who stepped out on to the airstrip that morning was an elegant Carleen in beautiful separates of matching rose shantung. The open-necked shirt, the divided culotte-skirt into which it was tucked, the wide belt cinching her tiny waist, were appropriately casual and sporty—just the thing in which to do a stint of aerial dingo-baiting.

The Carleen who returned was a different Carleen altogether. This Carleen was an abject Carleen, a depleted Carleen, a very sick Carleen, and judging by the glitter in her baleful blue eye as Mickie led her tenderly up the path, an angry Carleen, too, although at the moment she didn't appear to have the energy with which to show it. She leaned heavily on Mickie's arm as she wobbled along at his side. Her cheeks were verging on what could only be described as chartreuse, her forehead moist and streaked with perspiration, her hair lank and unattractive, her pretty shantung outfit all limp and crushed and stained.

'How *dared* you!' Lindsay, standing speechlessly behind the gauze, heard Carleen almost spit the words out, albeit weakly. 'To make a fool of me like that in front of Rod—oh! —how *dare* you?'

'I'm sorry, Carleen.' There was solicitude in Mick's tone as he supported her along the path. 'But how was I to know you wouldn't be an exactly happy passenger?'

'*Happy?* Ugh! *You* knew.'

'Of course I didn't, or I wouldn't have dreamed of asking you, would I? I was very sorry for you up there, believe me, especially when Rod got so angry. You mustn't take his impatience too much to heart, though. As I said, low flying like that calls for a great deal of skill and judgement, and a chap has to give it all his concentration for every single second— even when someone's being sick right there beside him, and begging him to stop.' Mickie looked down at the wilting figure pityingly. 'If only you hadn't kept clutching at his sleeve, he wouldn't have got so furious,' he pointed out reasonably.

'Well, *you* did nothing to help, I must say,' she replied, with pure loathing in her voice.

'I couldn't very well, could I? I mean, I was so busy putting those baits down the shute on each run. It's the low flying, you know, in this climate, that sometimes makes it just a little bit bumpy. The heat comes up off the ground to meet the aircraft—boom, boom, boom. That's why one has to go fast when it gets rocky——'

'Will you *stop* it?'

'I'm sorry, Carleen. I was only explaining why the—are you going to be sick again?'

'My room—hurry!'

'The east one, isn't it? We'll go in the other door, then. It's quicker. Never mind, Carleen, you'll soon feel better. And don't be too upset about Rod. It's difficult for any man to pilot a small plane successfully at such a low altitude with a hysterical female clutching at him all the time, as I've already said. And then to be sick in the *cockpit*——'

Mickie's reproachful voice disappeared around the corner with Carleen. A few moments later, he passed by again, and Lindsay saw him cram his wide felt hat on his head at a triumphant angle and step jauntily down the path. On his face was much the same smug, self-satisfied, victorious sort of smirk that Carleen herself sometimes wore when—oh!

Lindsay stared after Mickie with widening eyes and open mouth. Then she walked quietly to Carleen's room.

'Can I do anything for you?' she asked timidly, in genuine sympathy.

'Oh, go *away*.' The muffled reply was so discouraging that Lindsay obeyed it—and went.

She and Mannie had lunch alone that day. Carleen's door was shut, and the blinds on the French window that gave on to the veranda were pulled down, too. Lindsay knocked gently, but receiving no reply, she and the old lady decided that it would be best to leave things as they were.

Lindsay had gone back to her office in the little pink weatherboard cottage, and was adding up bank accounts for the aboriginal employees' trusts, when a plane droned overhead and banked around the homestead before coming down. She had supposed it to be Rod, coming in from another expedition, but then she remembered that he hadn't been about for lunch, so it couldn't be Rod after all.

It was Margie. Even as she came walking up from the strip, tugging off her goggles, Lindsay was aware of something different about her—a certain suppressed excitement, an aura of sunshine and happiness that was a reflection of the shine in her calm, blue eyes, the gleam in her pearly smile, the bloom on her peach-soft cheeks.

'Oh, *Lindsay*!' She hugged the other girl as if she were attempting thereby to transmit some of her own special secret, blissful wonder. 'Oh, *Lindsay*. I just had to come and tell you—share it with someone! I just couldn't wait! Lindsay, *look*. Isn't it the most beautiful, gorgeous, dreamy thing you ever saw?'

She held out her small, capable, sun-browned hand for her companion to inspect the band of three winking diamonds— a big one in the middle and smaller sisters on either side.

So that was it! Lindsay should have guessed. What else could have given Margie this extra special glow? What but betrothal to the man she loved and longed for gave *any* girl that extra special glow, come to that? And Rod—that's why he had not come in for lunch. He hadn't gone dropping dingo-baits or riding the run or any of those things at all— not *this* afternoon.

This afternoon he had gone over to Dinewan. He was probably there, even now, waiting impatiently for Margie to come back again.

'Margie!' Lindsay's voice was husky with feeling, and her eyes were a little bit sort of moist—just with surprise, she told herself, even though she had really been expecting it!— but the hug she gave Margie in return was warm-hearted and generous and sincere.

'I'm so very happy for you, Margie, and as for Rod—well, I've always thought he deserved the very b-best, and he could not have chosen a nicer, more wonderful person than you. I hope you'll be marvellously happy.'

Margie stared.

'Rod?' She giggled. 'Whatever has Rod got to do with it? Lindsay, are you all right?' she added anxiously.

Lindsay ran a hand across her brow as though it hurt.

'I—don't know,' she said stupidly. 'I—am I mixed up, or something?'

The other girl laughed merrily.

'Or something? I should just think so! My dear, that ring on my finger was put there by Mac, *not* Rod. Isn't it the prettiest little ring?' She twirled her hand for the sun to catch the stones.

Lindsay swallowed.

'*Mac?* But I thought—I mean—we all thought——'

'I know.' Margie nodded serenely. 'Even Mac thought it, too, the idiot, although I did my level best to show him where my feelings lay. Short of knocking him on the head and dragging him to the altar, I couldn't have done much more in the way of chasing that man without losing my self-respect altogether. Heavens, even the reason I took my first flying lessons was because of Mac—you know, a shared experience, a bond in common. But it all went right over his head!' She shook her own head in mock despair.

'It's wonderful news you've brought, Margie,' Mannie enthused over the tea-pot in the great, long kitchen, which was somehow the spot where all the gossipy conclaves at Gundooee homestead always seemed to take place. 'Where will you live, my dear? Mac's people are from further north, aren't they?'

'Yes, his brother runs the family place, and he's been looking around for something suitable for ages. He took on this contract for the mail-run to fill in time until he found exactly what he wanted. It gave him a marvellous opportunity to see all sorts of properties, and with the kitchen cuppa and the gossip thrown in along the route, to hear of anything that might be coming on the market. Now he's bought the Emerton place on the other side of Peperina, so I'll be very near home, really. It's all so wonderful!' Her eyes were shining with merriment. 'I had to hint like anything when he told me he'd bought the property,' she continued in a spate which simply couldn't stop. 'You know, I kept saying how marvellous, and would he be going to live there very soon, and how I supposed he'd be thinking of getting married, and—oh, the shameless things I had to *say* before the penny dropped! And then the silly darling duffer just suddenly looked at me in the queerest way and said, look here, Margie, you can't possibly mean, and I said that's just what I *do* mean and do I have to spell it out in words of one syllable, and then he just sort of sighed and grabbed me and nearly squashed the life out of me. Do you know this, he hadn't ever even kissed me before, not once, and—oh, Mannie, I'm in the seventh heaven! Isn't that really the most gorgeous little ring you ever did see? Do look.'

'It's sweet, Margie. And how nice of you to fly straight over and tell us before it gets out over the galah! Once that happens, the whole of Australia will know! I'm sure Rod will be enormously happy for you, too, just as we are.'

In the hall on her way out again, Margie stopped and put her hand on Lindsay's arm to detain her. Her eyes, now, were oddly serious—not alive with dancing excitement as they had been in the kitchen, but soberly sincere.

'It's true, Lindsay,' she assured her softly, 'what Mannie said just now. About Rod, I mean. He *will* be pleased for me.' She paused again, then—'Lindsay, there's just one thing I'd like you to know, about all this. Rod has never, ever, thought about me in the way you may have supposed, nor I about him. He's always been to me like the older brother I never had, and I—well, you could say he's regarded me as a sister, that's all—sometimes even a little nuisance of a sister, I dare say! I've always recognised that fact, never expected or wanted anything different. I suppose that's the reason why we've always got on so well together, and had such fun. He's one of three brothers, you see. There are no girls in Rod's family at all.'

Lindsay's eyes were exploring Margie's earnest face.

'Margie, why are you telling me this?' she asked slowly.

She couldn't stop herself asking that. It was something she felt compelled to know.

Margie gave her a direct look. It was a look of extraordinary understanding and kindness.

'Because,' she replied simply, 'you're in love with him, aren't you? I just felt I wanted you to know.'

Lindsay's eyes were full of tears which she utterly refused to shed. She turned her head away, gazed blankly at the picture on the wall beside her, not really seeing anything at all.

'It—doesn't really matter, Margie,' she told the other girl in a choked voice. 'It won't make any difference—none at all. But it was nice of you, anyway. Thanks.'

Margie gave her hand a sympathetic squeeze.

'Where is she today, anyhow?'

Lindsay did not have to ask to whom Margie referred. They both knew *that*!

'She's asleep in her room, I think. She—er—isn't very well today.'

'Lindsay, I'm *sorry*,' Margie said, before she left her there in the dimness of the hall and went back alone to her little plane—and Lindsay knew, from the compassion in Margie's gentle blue eyes as she spoke those words, that this time they

159

did not refer to Carleen!

She did not see Carleen again until tea-time that night. She was still pale and heavy-eyed, but in a way even more feminine because of it, in an appealing sort of way.

Rod seemed to think so, anyway! As he brought her a brandy and lemonade from the drinks cabinet in the sitting-room and leaned over her in her chair, he was more solicitous than Lindsay had ever seen him before.

'Drink it, Carleen, please. It will do you good, I think.' He smiled with charming persuasiveness.

Carleen put back her head and gazed up at him, her lustrous eyes eloquent with apology. She laid that ever-possessive hand on his arm, and said softly, 'Rod, darling, I'm *so* sorry about this morning. What fools we girls can be sometimes, can't we! We're so—so weak, and you men are so strong—you really do show us up to our great discredit sometimes, you know. It isn't kind.'

Rod passed her the glass he held, regarded her with a certain grave deference.

'My dear, it's I who should apologise. I behaved like a boorish brute, and to a guest in my own house, at that. It was unforgivable of me, I know, but perhaps you'll be generous and try to forget, hm?'

The way she was gazing at him, she'd have forgiven him if he'd chopped off her head, thought Lindsay to herself with uncharacteristic waspishness.

'But of *course*! I've done that already, where you're concerned. After all, it wasn't you who invited me on such a ghastly expedition, and I must admit, looking back, that you *did* look a little surprised and put-out when I insisted on coming.' She smiled appealingly. 'I was so terrified, but do you know, I've learned something, too, Rod, from the experience. I've learned that we women aren't designed for such tough and frightening assignments at all. We're too delicate and easily alarmed—at least, I know *I* am. In future, I shall know my place as a member of the weaker sex, and leave those things to men. To *you*, Rod.'

'I'm glad to hear it, Carleen.' He patted her shoulder comfortingly with a large brown hand. 'You're much too fragile and lovely to enjoy such things as that this morning, especially when you've been ill lately, too. I dare say Mickie only meant to be kind, but I'm sure most men would agree with me that your role in their world should be in the nature of a decorative one.'

'Why, Rod! How gallant of you!'

Carleen sipped her brandy, obviously mollified.

Later, when Rod invited her to come for a ride with him on the following afternoon, she appeared keener than usual, but her eyelids drooped suddenly and her pretty mouth took on a slightly petulant pout when he added, carelessly,

'Perhaps you'd like to join us, too, this time, Lindsay—you and Dusty?'

Lindsay flushed.

'Oh, I don't think—I mean——'

He glanced at her, took in her dubious expression, and his jaw tightened.

'It's an order, if you prefer things that way,' he said more firmly. 'I want to make sure that you're safe on the horse my men have allotted you, and also to check your progress. Presumably, after all those tedious lessons, you must have learned a little, surely?'

She pressed her lips together.

'Very well,' she answered, somewhat ungraciously, aware of the superior gleam in Carleen's eye. 'If you insist.'

'I do insist.' Rod was adamant. 'After tomorrow, I and the rest of the men will be away for possibly more than a week, and you three women will be here at the homestead alone. I have no qualms whatever about Carleen's own superb horsemanship, but I certainly don't want *you* tinkering around in my absence on some animal which you have possibly little or no idea how to control. I shall see for myself tomorrow, so please be ready to accompany us.'

'Very well, Rod.'

She refused to look Carleen's way this time, but she knew that the other girl, well aware of her shortcomings on horseback, was secretly amused at the prospect of the morrow's ride.

Lindsay arrived at the saddling yard punctually next day

to find Dusty tied to the sliprail, waiting for her. Carleen was already mounted on the daintily prancing Chalita, and she was immediately aware of just how wide a margin there was between both the proficiency and the sartorial appearance of Rod's two equestrienne companions! Lindsay looked down ruefully at her bagging khaki trousers, whose excessive width had pleated itself neatly out over the belt around her middle like a frill around a leg of ham. Oh well—— She shrugged resignedly, observing Rod's striding figure approaching from the region of the near-by power-house. It was too late, now, to do anything about those trousers even had there been an alternative. It was too late to do anything about anything!

Rod helped her into the saddle, handed her the reins, and let down the sliprail before mounting his own snorting stallion and following her out of the yard.

For Lindsay, that ride represented a gruelling experience that she would never care to repeat. Mostly it was because Dusty's stubborn gait was somehow unmatched to that of his more active equine mates, she decided regretfully, as she jogged along behind the others in an uncomfortably bumpy trot.

It seemed to Lindsay that she trotted for miles that afternoon, without respite. Miles and miles. The other horses ambled along at a fast, lively walk, ears up, eyes alert, necks straining to be given their heads, while, in the rear, Dusty trotted and trotted, urged on by the thud of Lindsay's sandshoes digging ineffectively into his foaming flanks.

Lindsay slowed down to a walk, savouring the brief moment of respite, but as the distance between herself and the others appeared to be widening at an alarming rate, she was soon forced to urge him into that monotonous trot once more.

Carleen seemed to have purposely set out to capture Rod's entire attention on that ride. She talked animatedly, every now and then gesturing with graceful eloquence to illustrate a point she was making. There wasn't a doubt that Rod was being entertained to the fullest of Carleen's not inconsiderable ability, and all the time Lindsay trotted and trotted a little to the rear.

162

The miles went by—or, at least, Lindsay found herself hoping that they were going by. You could hardly go on trotting at this maddeningly frustrating pace without some distance being covered, could you? The only trouble was, there was distance everywhere, out here. So much distance. Flat, brown, plains sort of distance. Muted, hazy, *distant* distance. Outback, relentless, *interminable* distance.

It seemed to Lindsay, as Dusty followed those others at this tireless jog of his, that he and she were trotting along on an actual treadmill of distance!

When the stitch that had developed in her side became almost unbearable, she managed to release a furtive groan under cover of Carleen's tinkling laugh, and when, presently, a sound started up deep in the region of Dusty's sagging middle, she thought that perhaps he had developed a stitch in sympathy. The sound inside him was like a heavy boot stepping on a creaking board, and it came with montonous regularity, every time his bony carcase vibrated to his own trot.

Rod must have heard it, too, the creaking board sound. He stopped, came back, took in her set face and twisted mouth with instant concern.

'What is it? A stitch? Can't you spur this old nag on a bit, Lindsay?' He smiled kindly. 'I remember what it can be like—as a boy, jogging along on a pony behind the men's horses, having trouble keeping up. Won't Dusty go a little faster for you?'

She shook her head. 'I'm sorry, Rod. I can't get him to go faster, or even slower, unless he walks—and he takes his time about that, too. He just has a mind of his own, that's all. I suppose, at his age, one does! If we can only stand still a minute, the pain in my side will go.' There was pleading in her voice. It was wonderful to be standing here, and not trot-trotting on into the distance.

Rod pushed back his hat, considered her thoughtfully for a moment, and then said apologetically,

'I'm sorry, Lindsay. I thought you were handling him quite well, actually. I'll tell you what we'll do. You take Chalita for a little while. Carleen has ridden most of the steam out of her anyway. Carleen can easily cope with Martian, and I'll relieve you of old Dusty for a while. He'll perhaps go better for me. Some of these old horses can be sinfully cunning when it suits them. They need a firm hand, and a rider who's up to their tricks. Do you mind, Carleen?'

'Of course not.'

Carleen looked pleased at the idea of riding Martian. She mounted him with ease, laughing as he sidled around with arching neck and rolling eye, disapproving openly of his unfamiliar rider. It was a challenge, and she handled it beautifully.

There was admiration still lurking in Rod's eye as he turned now to Lindsay and held Chalita firmly while she clambered awkwardly into the saddle.

Straight away, things seemed to go wrong. The little mare shied suddenly away, jerking the reins from Rod's grasp before Lindsay had secured them properly in her nervous fingers. She leaned forward frantically, missed the reins altogether, flung her arms instead around Chalita's dappled neck, and the animal promptly went mad. She plunged and reared away over the ground, and Lindsay didn't quite know what happened next.

There was a distinct curse as Rod threw himself on to the surprised Dusty and dug in a brutal heel in hot pursuit. Pounding hooves sounded deafeningly close to Lindsay's ears, and then as Rod came alongside, Chalita propped on all four feet, as if mischievously aware that the game was up. Lindsay, by this time too confused to know what she was doing or why, went sailing through the air in a neat arc and landed with a resounding thud in the dust not far away.

It only seemed a matter of seconds after she hit the ground before she was being scooped up into a pair of powerful arms and crushed against a khaki-shirted chest.

'Lindsay! Lindsay? Thank God——' as she opened her eyes she saw his set face above her, pale with remorse, tense with anxiety.

Lindsay smiled, rather sleepily. She still couldn't quite think how she had got here, close against Rod's broad chest, cushioned in his muscular hold.

'I'm all right,' she assured him, almost happily.

'Thank heaven for that!' His deep voice was oddly harsh in its relief. 'I should never have tried it, Lindsay. It was all my fault. You aren't quite ready for Chalita, I'm afraid. Can you walk? Sure? Let me see you do it. I'm sorry, Lindsay, but there seems no alternative to Dusty, after all, does there?' He gave her the ghost of a grin, still pale beneath his heavy tan.

'We'll *all* walk, this time—very slowly,' said Rod quite tenderly, as he put her into Dusty's saddle once more. 'If necessary, I'll lead him.'

And that was how they returned to the homestead, with Carleen on Chalita prancing skittishly in front, and Rod on his impatient stallion, pulling a recalcitrant and by now extremely weary Dusty behind him.

'Gawd'l'mighty! Look at that!' Herb poked Artie sharply in the ribs and indicated the approaching trio. 'What d'yer make of that, now, Art?'

His companion screwed up his eyes against the setting sun, and squinted with critical interest at the horses and riders. Then he cupped his hands over his wrinkled forehead to make quite sure he was seeing right before replying gloomily,

'Nothink very good, by the look of it, 'Erb. That's *'er* in the lead, I reckon, as natty as yer please. Cor, she can ride, that dame! And there's Lindsay comin' up be'ind, only why's Rod leadin' 'er, for Pete's sake? We learned 'er 'ow ter ride, didn't we? Why d'yer suppose 'e's leadin' 'er?'

Lindsay saw the two figures drift tactfully out of view behind the tankstand, but she was too weary and worn to even wonder who they were or why they were there.

Rod seemed aware of her exhaustion, too.

'You go up to the house, Lindsay. Carleen and I will turn the horses out for the night.'

Carleen and I.

It was dismissal, but Lindsay was past feeling hurt or rebuffed. Three's a crowd, she reminded herself dismally, especially when the third one can't even ride properly!

'Pst! 'Ere! Lindsay?'

She had passed the tankstand now, to be confronted by Herb and Artie. They were idling casually in her path with their hands in their pockets. Herb coughed.

''Ullo, Lindsay!' he greeted her, on a note of surprised discovery, as if she was the very last person he expected to see passing behind this tankstand, albeit it was right on the recognised route to the homestead from the yard. ''Ave yer been out fer a ride, then, eh? With Rod and *'er*, was it? 'Ow did yer get on, Lindsay?'

Not even Herb's sublime approach could hide the anxiety behind his question. Artie, too, was standing waiting for her reply with bow-legged curiosity.

'I didn't get on. I got off.' She attempted a smile that was somehow not very successful.

'*Stone* the crows! Yer mean—yer don't mean yer fell off?' Art shook his grizzled head incredulously.

'I didn't fall off. I was thrown off.' She felt her tender places gingerly. 'I was *hurled* off,' she confessed, with a fleeting, urchin grin, but just the slightest tremor in her voice all the same.

Lindsay pushed past them, making for the house. She was not in a mood for further conversation right then.

'Well, I'll be danged!' Herb looked after her, and Artie, too, knocked back his hat and gazed after that small, hurrying figure. His angular bow-legged body had slumped into a curiously dejected arc.

'It don't seem too good, I must admit.' Artie cleared his throat noisily, and looked his mate squarely in the eye. 'I reckon the knockout stakes might soon be over, 'Erb, an' it'll be Bluey and Cook collectin', worst luck—not us.'

'Maybe not, Art, old cobber.' A spark of returning optimism gleamed in Herb's beady eye. 'We could win out yet if we play things right, yer know, Artie. Maybe Mick'll 'ave another of them bright ideas.'

'Bright ideas? Jeeze!' Artie spat neatly to one side to register his disgust. 'Them brain-waves of Mick's is about as subtle as a man-eatin' crocodile sittin' on a mudbank.'

'Ah well,' Herb said on a sigh, 'while there's life there's

'ope, Artie. Ain't that what they say? While there's life there's 'ope.'

But you could tell, from the way he said it, that not even Herb believed it, really. Not now.

CHAPTER 10

THE men rode out next morning.

Lindsay pressed her nose to the gauze and watched them until they were out of sight. Blue and Shorty and Cook had gone ahead earlier, and now the others followed, Rod riding in front with Jimmy and Tommo. Artie, Herb, and Mickie bringing up the rear. They all rode the same way, these men, legs thrust out long in the stirrups, wide hat pulled down, body angled in a carelessly relaxed position in a saddle that was cluttered with saddle-bag, water-bag, ropes, pint-pot, and various other impedimenta to fulfil their present needs. A couple of horses without anyone on their backs loped along beside Herb, but there were other spares, too, already out at the Dinewan Block. Hughes, a boundary rider, lived in a hut out that way and could provide extra mounts, as could his mate Jenison from the Billabong outcamp.

Lindsay had only seen these men to nod to on mail-days, and even then they did not always bother to come in to the homestead. She knew approximately where they lived, though, and others like them at the other huts and outposts. Each place was identified on the wall-map in Rod's study by a neat cross. Beside the crosses were names like Billabong, Goofgap, Rainbow, Loophole, Force Eight, Blue Lady, Dog-leg Plains, or simply, in one particular instance, Fawcett's Place.

That cross with 'Fawcett's Place' printed beside it was the most outlying one of all, and Fawcett himself had never been in for a single mail-day since Lindsay's arrival.

When she mentioned this phenomenon to Artie, he had laughed and replied,

' 'E's a kind of 'ermit, see, Lindsay. Old Fawcett don't take ter company. Yer'd be lucky ter see 'im as often as yer see

Santa Claus 'imself, and that's the truth. Sometimes 'e don't come in fer a whole year, and then it's only because 'is rakin' beard's beginning' ter trip 'is feet up and 'is shears is blunt.'

Lindsay didn't quite believe Artie, but all the same, whenever she looked at that far-away little cross that was Fawcett's Place, she envisaged a bearded recluse, an independent, fierce yet lonely old man, a mysterious and strangely poignant figure.

The knot of riders that she watched until they were a mere dust-ball in the distance weren't going anywhere near Fawcett's Place today. They were heading west and then tracking along the dry creek-bed until they got to the Dinewan Block's camp. Rod had shown her on the map when she asked him to, a brow raised briefly in surprise that she should evince an interest. The truth was that Lindsay's imagination was captured by the immensity of space represented on that map—the spread of 'the Bush', as she privately called it. She had had to learn, very quickly, that 'the Bush' meant not only the pretty, lush area where she herself had been born and spent those first six Utopian years, but many other things as well. 'The Bush' had hundreds of different forms— endless mutations, depending upon which part of it you happened to be in! And now Mickie had told her that 'the Bush' where they were now going to muster was a different Bush again from the homestead and its environs.

The idea held a peculiar fascination for Lindsay, and so she pressed her nose to the gauze and viewed their departure with as much awe as if they had been John the Baptist departing for the Wilderness.

When there was not even a dust-ball left, she gave a little sigh, and went to find Mannie. The old lady was in the kitchen, sorting through some articles for Sibbie and Bella to wash. She had delayed the laundry this week until Rod had left, so that she could include his things at the last minute.

Lindsay noted her pallor and the blueness around her mouth with misgiving.

'Let me do that for you, Mannie dear,' she said quickly, hiding the rush of sympathy she couldn't help feeling, 'and I'll do the lunch, too, today. Why don't you go and lie down

169

for a while? We might as well make the most of the men's absence, don't you think, and we can eat very lightly while Rod's away, can't we?'

Mannie smiled wearily.

'Perhaps I will. Thank you, Lindsay.'

She was more than usually quiescent—a disquieting sign, Lindsay could not help feeling, with a strange sense of foreboding, but Carleen, in whom she later confided, merely shrugged and pointed out,

'She's old, Lindsay, isn't she? I mean, what do you expect, at her age, out here in this wretched climate? It's a wonder to me that Rod bothers to keep her on. An old people's home would be more suitable, and she'd be comfortable there, with no responsibilities. He's probably just putting it off until he gets married. In my opinion, there certainly would not be room for both that old woman *and* a wife here at Gundooee, and I shan't hesitate to say so when the moment is right.'

Lindsay could only stare, quite horrified at Carleen's callousness. What was more, the way she had spoken, it seemed as if Mannie had been right about that private understanding. 'I shan't hesitate'— 'when the moment is right'.

A chill shiver ran through Lindsay. Carleen had spoken as if she was almost the mistress of Gundooee homestead already.

'It's always a mistake,' continued Carleen reflectively, as if completely unaware of the effect her casual words were having upon her listener. 'It's been proved time and again that two women in the same house can be a fatal mistake.'

'But surely an old lady, a dear, elderly person like Mannie could hardly make any difference, and when Rod is so—so fond——'

'Too fond. Such sentimentality can cause friction, just as much as could the presence of a younger woman.' Her eyes narrowed suddenly upon Lindsay, as she amended, softly, 'Even younger women employees. Book-keepers, for instance.'

'Carleen, please don't talk like that to Mannie, will you, not yet—even if you're thinking and feeling that way. If you could just help me to persuade her to take things a little easier, I'll fill in for her. That's all I want. I—I shan't expect *you* to have to do anything extra.'

'It would be presumptuous of you if you did, darling. Just remember that I'm here as a visitor,' Carleen pointed out silkily.

In the end, persuasion was not required to induce Mannie to ease up a little. Fate took a hand instead, in the form of a collapse from which it was quite difficult to bring the old lady round. Carleen helped to carry her into her room and lay her on her bed, but it was Lindsay who later assisted her to undress, comforted her, and brought her a reviving cup of warm, sweet tea.

'I think I should call up the doctor, Mannie,' she suggested worriedly.

'No, please don't do that, Lindsay—not while Rod's off. I'll be all right if I rest. That's all I need, my dear—a good rest in bed.'

'But just to *ask* him?'

'No, Lindsay, please don't do that. I'd hate all the fuss.'

Lindsay hesitated, but finally allowed herself to be dissuaded.

The next few days were dreary ones. Lindsay missed Mannie's company about the house, and soon came to realise that she had somehow acted as a buffer between herself and Carleen, who were beginning to get on each other's nerves. Lindsay was normally able to conceal, or at least control, the irritation which Carleen's behaviour frequently induced. Often, when she felt her fingers clenching into her palms with hurt or annoyance, she had simply walked away to see what Mannie might be doing. And Mannie, like as not, would start to tell her something, to talk about some entirely different topic, and Lindsay's ire would begin to fade.

Now she could not do that. There was no escape from Carleen's baiting, and you would almost have said that the other girl was aware of that fact, perhaps even trading on it. She was not in a pleasant mood at all these days. Lindsay supposed it could only mean that she missed Rod's company and masculine attentions.

When, at the beginning of the next week, the rain started, the situation deteriorated even further. The dark, low-hanging clouds were a reflection of Carleen's black mood, and the rain that drenched and drizzled by turns kept time with Lindsay's own fits of depression and malaise. She took care to stay out of Carleen's way as much as she possibly could, and derived a curious sense of comfort from going to Rod's study, and looking at the wall map which hung there.

It was comforting to be able to put one's finger on the exact spot where those men were, comforting to know that their work must be almost done, out there at that little cross that was the Dinewan Block camp, comforting to think that they would soon be back at the homestead, and then this miserable phase would be over. Soon Carleen's overbearing presence would be diluted once more by the banter and teasing of the jackaroos and station-hands, even if, at the same time, she must also witness the strengthening of the other girl's association with Rod himself.

'I wonder why you do it, Lindsay?'

Carleen's voice, cool and composed, made her jump.

'D-do what?'

'I wonder why you come in here—into Rod's own office—and stand there looking at his map all the time? What do you get out of it, Lindsay?' There was a sarcastic glitter in her eye.

'Why, nothing. I mean, I only come to look. Just to see where they are, sort of thing.'

'You mean where Rod is, don't you?'

'I—didn't say that.' She tried to pass, but Carleen put a hand across the doorway and blocked her path with a deliberate movement. 'Please let me go, Carleen. I have to get the breakfast.'

'No, *you* didn't say it, Lindsay'—Carleen ignored her request—'It's *I* who am saying it. You haven't the guts to say it, have you? You'd rather just sneak in here and look at his things, at that map.' She smiled nastily. 'Tell me, Lindsay, what else do you do?' she asked with cynical curiosity. 'Do you stroke his possessions and moon in his chair, as well as gaze at his map? Perhaps you even go to his bedroom, and worship there in silence.'

Lindsay stared.

'Well, do you?'

Lindsay felt the first faint quiver of alarm. She had never, ever, seen Carleen in quite this mood before. It was somehow rather frightening. It quite made one's blood congeal.

'Carleen, don't be stupid! You don't know what you're saying!'

There was a secretive smile hovering on those lovely lips, a smile quite without amusement.

'Oh yes, I do. I know more than you think, my dear Lindsay. I've watched you, the way you look at him and leap to do his bidding. I've seen you come mooning in here since he's been gone, too. I've even heard you confess that you're in love with him. You are, aren't you?'

'Carleen. *Please!*'

'Oh yes, you are. I heard with my own ears. You didn't deny it to Margie, did you, out there in the hall? You didn't deny it to her as you're doing to me.' Carleen's eyes were ice-pale. 'I've known ever since I overheard you talking that day. I only suspected before, but then I knew. And if I hadn't, the drooling way you looked into Rod's eyes when he picked you up the other day was enough to tell me. Enough to tell *him*, too.' She looked at Lindsay with naked dislike. 'I believe you fell off that horse on purpose. All that nonsense about a stitch in your side——'

'Carleen, you must be mad!' Lindsay's mouth was dry, her eyes wide with dismay.

Carleen gave a laugh that was oddly shrill and chilling.

'Mad? No. But I will be if things carry on like this much longer, you little snake in the grass! How *dare* you stand there pretending that butter wouldn't melt in your mouth, that you don't understand a word I'm saying, that *you* don't want him, too. Well'—a shrug—'you aren't going to have the chance, Lindsay. You're going, do you hear? Things were fine until you started all this "poor little girl" business—those blistered hands, your eye, that fall off Chalita. You can give up trying to draw attention to yourself all the time, and *go*.'

'Wh-where would I go?' Lindsay stammered, stupefied.

'I don't know and I don't care, but you'll leave here, that's the one sure thing! You'll *get out!* If you don't'—she passed a hand over her trembling mouth—'if you don't, I'll tell Rod what a deceitful little creature you are, and he'll *make* you go. Wouldn't you rather leave of your own free will than under a cloud?'

Lindsay squared her shoulders. Doormat! Doormat! chided a tiny voice inside her—and it seemed to be *that* voice which spoke just now, not her own one at all.

'I don't intend to leave, Carleen, of my own will or yours. If you tell Rod about my initial deception, I'll tell him that you unlocked that cupboard and let Tommo get at that stuff, on purpose.'

Carleen smirked.

'I thought you might say that,' she nodded calmly. 'You haven't the slightest hope of proving it, though, have you? It would simply be my word against yours, wouldn't it, and if you lied in order to get this job in the first place, you could soon lie again, couldn't you? As Rod said to you at that time, anyone who makes one false statement can always be expected to make another. Why should he believe you?'

Lindsay's shoulders sagged, but she would not admit defeat. She licked her lips.

'Carleen, I—I've no intention of letting you bully me any longer. You've done it all your life and got away with it, but not any more. And I can tell you this—*I* am going to speak to Rod when he comes back. I'm going to confess everything, as I should have long ago. I know he'll send me away, but not before he knows about you, too—how you schemed to get here, how you made me promise not to tell, and the reason why. He'll loathe the pair of us, and we deserve it.' She lifted her head, and looked the other girl soberly in the face. 'I'll admit to you now that I love Rod. I know he doesn't even see me, doesn't even know I exist, but I love him and I'm not ashamed of it. In fact, I'm proud of it! And because I do love him, I'm not going to stand by and see him go into marriage without his knowing the whole story, and then he can judge for himself. If I confess, you're going to be exposed, too! You don't love Rod, Carleen. You don't love anyone. You've never cared for anyone except yourself in your whole life. Just yourself.'

174

Carleen's face was aflame with temper. She almost looked as though she was going to hit Lindsay. Indeed she raised her hand, palm open, and Lindsay found herself cowering away.

'Shut up, will you. Shut up! I won't listen! You aren't going to spoil things for me, Lindsay, not now, not after going so far. I *will* have my way, I will, I will! I *hate* you, do you hear?'

Her voice had risen to a scream. The colour had drained from her face, leaving it parchment-white, contorted with pure fury into an ugly mask. Carleen put her hands up to her face with a frustrated little moan and flounced away.

Seconds later, from the living-room, there came a tinkling sound, the crash of breaking glass. Typically, Carleen must have taken out her rage and venom on some ornament! At almost the same moment, Lindsay heard a tiny noise from Mannie's bedroom—a strange, lingering little sigh that broke the sudden silence following that crash.

Still numbed and shaking from her confrontation with her cousin, she raced into the room, sick with dread, knowing instinctively that something was very far wrong. Then she stumbled back to the door, trying to rally her common sense for this new emergency.

'Carleen! Carleen, come quickly. *Please*. Mannie's ill, terribly ill. I think she—she may even be dying. Please come, Carleen—quickly!'

To her credit, Carleen came, the tears of rage still wet on her cheeks.

Together they lifted Mannie's unconscious form, covered her with blankets, noted the heavy breathing, that strange blueness in her face.

'We'll have to call up the doctor, won't we, Carleen? The Flying Doctor. We'll have to get him here as quickly as possible.'

She looked across to Carleen for support, for help, and was surprised to see the expression that came over her cousin's beautiful, classic features. An indescribable expression, it was, calm and bitter and desperate all at once.

And then Carleen shook her head. Kneeling there on the

other side of the bed, with her face all pale and pinched and strained, and the tears drying rapidly beneath her eyes, she simply looked back at Lindsay—back and *beyond* her—and shook her head.

'Lindsay, we can't,' she said in a curiously dead, shocked voice. 'We can't call up anyone. I've broken the transceiver.'

Lindsay's own heart seemed to stop for one terrifying, suffocating second.

'You've *what*?'

'I've broken it, Lindsay—the set. I didn't mean it—that alabaster vase, the big figurine, I was so furious—you know what my temper's like.' Carleen's voice was no more than a whisper, with a note of pleading and despair in it that Lindsay had never thought to hear. She was moved to instant compassion at the other's overwhelming air of shame and remorse.

'What shall we do?' she asked stupidly. Her brain seemed to have stopped functioning, events had crowded in so fast.

Carleen wiped her eyes.

'I didn't mean to,' she said hoarsely. 'You do believe that, Lindsay? I didn't aim on purpose, it just seemed to fly out of my hand, it's so heavy. And you haven't ordered batteries for the other one, have you—the set that needs recharging, down at the store?'

'I was going to. Next mail-day.' Lindsay's tone was bleak.

Between them, Mannie lay without moving. Still that laboured breathing, that dreadful blueness in her face.

'You'll have to go for help, Lindsay.' Carleen stood up, smoothed down her skirt with sudden decision.

'Help? How?'

'You'll have to go out and get Rod. You'll need to ride out.'

Lindsay looked askance.

'Ride? Away out there? I'd never manage to do that, I'd never make it. *You* could, though, Carleen. It's our only hope. If you could get to Rod and tell him, he could fly Mannie out to the Base hospital in his plane.'

Carleen shook her head. Her normal colour was returning—and so was her normal voice!

'Why should *I* go, for heaven's sake? It's not my place to do that, is it?'

Lindsay stared. 'But you can ride, and I can't. You *know* that! And anyway, it was you who broke the transceiver, the wretched thing.' Her patience was beginning to give way under the spell of the old, taunting look with which Carleen was favouring her.

'And *you* forgot to order spares for the battery-set in the store,' Carleen returned evenly. 'You admitted as much last mail-day. It's you who is the employee, after all, Lindsay, isn't it, and your duty is clear. I'm merely a guest in this house, remember. Anyway'—she lifted her shoulders somewhat fatalistically—'why should it really worry me whether Mannie lives or dies? She's old, after all, and she might not like that Old Folks' Home much, might she, in the end?'

'You—oh!'

'You hurry and put on your trousers, Lindsay, and I'll catch and saddle your horse for you.' As Lindsay turned blindly to the door, she heard Carleen add, 'You'll know where you're making for better than I, anyway. You've certainly studied that map often enough!'

Lindsay dragged on the baggy trousers she had borrowed from the store, crammed her hat with its bobbing fly-veil on her head. Then she filled one of the canvas water-bags that hung out on the veranda and ran down to the saddling yard —down through the deserted village of outbuildings that were all part of Gundooee homestead—past the little pink weatherboard cottage, past the store, enmeshed in a nightmare that this could really be happening to her.

'Where's Dusty?'

Carleen looked up from the strap she was tightening around Chalita's girth, and shrugged.

'Not in, it seems. This is the only horse that's handy.'

Lindsay was aghast.

'But I'll never get there on Chalita, Carleen. Wh-what if she bolts?'

'Just see to it that she bolts in the right direction, and you'll get there all the quicker, won't you?' Carleen retorted tartly. 'For goodness' sake, Lindsay, be realistic. Even if Dusty was around for me to catch, you'd never get there on *him*—not all that distance, when it's all you can do to even make him trot. Here, give me your water-bag.'

'Carleen, *wouldn't* you go?'

'You know the answer to that, so why ask?'

Lindsay pressed her lips together so that the wicked things she wanted to say just couldn't get out to turn into actual words. Then she crossed her fingers, muttered a brief and silent prayer.

'Hold her for me, won't you, Carleen?' she whispered fearfully. 'Don't let go too soon, like Rod did.'

Carleen gave her a searing look of scorn, but nevertheless she did hang on to the cheek-strap quite tightly until Lindsay was in the saddle, and waited until she saw the reins firmly in her grasp before letting go.

'Keep looking in case Mannie comes to, and frets, won't you, Carleen?'

'Don't saw her mouth like that, Lindsay—that's why she's tossing her head.'

'Look after Mannie.'

'I will—and good luck!' There was a curious twist to Carleen's mouth as she said that. Then she turned away towards the house, not even taking time to wave.

Perhaps that was as well, as it might have startled Chalita, who was behaving in a very fractious manner as it was!

Lindsay was secretly terrified. She had read somewhere that a horse has a built-in communications system that tells it when its rider is frightened, and she was doing her best to stifle her fear in case Chalita might discover it.

Several times during that lonely morning journey, Lindsay thought Chalita *had* found out. She had several isolated moments of sheer panic—once when the highly strung mare shied suddenly at a tiny snake that wriggled in the dust quite near her hoof, and once when for no apparent reason at all she reared up on her hind legs and snorted. Somehow, on both occasions, Lindsay managed to keep her seat, and to refrain from putting her arms around Chalita's neck again. Instead, she reached frantically for the monkey-grip on the pommel and clung to both it and the reins with almost hysterical strength.

These experiences appeared to unsettle Chalita as much as they did her rider. There was a faint quivering right through her body, a pricking of her ears, that told Lindsay her own fright had been communicated. Her palms were sweaty with it, her forehead beaded with it, and her shirt, too, clung to her back with the very stickiness of pure, uncontrollable fear.

By noon she had reached the point in the dingo fence where she knew she must leave its guiding ribbon and break away to the west. Lindsay was loth to leave that comforting landmark behind. Ahead of her was more rugged country, with stunted scrub that sometimes screened her way. The rain had stopped, but the ground was treacherously soft in places, and the horse blew through her nostrils in terror as her hooves sank in the ridges of sand which must be traversed.

Lindsay's mouth was parched. She would have liked to stop and have a drink from her water-bag, but Chalita seemed sensitive to even the slightest touch on her rump, and Lindsay was afraid that if she once got off she would never manage to mount again on her own. If she could only stay in the saddle, she must be getting near that camp, surely, judging by her watch and the position of the sun.

Now Chalita was pushing nervously through a belt of scrub. The sickly smell of gidyea was all about them, and in the distance was a disquieting and unidentifiable sound, a peculiar, sighing sort of sound that Lindsay found it impossible to place. Like grit rushing in the wind, if there had been a wind. The little mare did not seem too happy about that sound, either. Her fits of quivering started again, and she blew gently through dilated nostrils, rolled her eye, and walked sideways.

When they breasted the next ridge, Lindsay's eyes rolled too. They almost rolled right out of her head, and she thought she might be going to cry. With frustration. With disappointment.

After all, it was a terrible anticlimax to have endured what she already had, to have managed to stay aboard Chalita

179

through that long, hot, lonely morning, with the sun sucking back the moisture from the plain in a greedy steam, and her fear drying up her mouth, and not being able to get to that water-bag, and the gidyea exuding this nauseating smell, and her own perspiration running into her eyes, to find herself thwarted by a dried-up creek-bed that wasn't dry any longer.

Lindsay eyed the widespread stream of muddy water with a sinking frustration. The trees that represented the edges of the creek-bed were a depressingly long way out into the stream, even though the water only lapped their trunks at the base. Bubbling eddies of froth moved lazily away into the main current from where the slow-moving stream was disturbed by those trees in its midst. She could only survey the flood that stretched in front of her with an indecision that she knew was cowardly, while the mare shook beneath her.

Away on the other side of the water, a bell sounded distantly. A bell? Yes, there it was again, the faintest tinkle. To Lindsay, the tinkle was like an angel sound from heaven, beckoning her to come. Surely a bell must mean a human habitation. The camp?

She leaned forward, shivering every bit as uncontrollably as Chalita, and together they went into the water, slipping and splashing towards the other side.

Lindsay was more than half-way across when the water first touched her sandshoes, causing her to hunch her knees into a sort of jockey position. By the time her rolled-up trouser cuffs were soaking, Chalita had started to swim.

Lindsay's mouth went slack with horror when she realised what that rhythmic, floating sensation beneath her meant. She clung limpet-like to the saddle, but when the water broke over that, too, and eddied around her waist, she knew that she would have to swim as well. But how did you swim, in an outback, swollen, rushing creek, with all your clothes on and your hat with its bobbing-cork fly-veil sitting on your head?

The hat was tossed recklessly into the current, and Lindsay saw it bobbing away from her, corks and all. Her shirt, too? Oh, no! Not with all those men at the outcamp, away ahead where the bell had tinkled. Too late, now, anyway.

Chalita's gallant little head, thrusting forward, was all that remained above water.

Thoughts galloped through Lindsay's brain at alarming speed. What did you do? What did you *do*?

Well, first of all you had to keep contact with your horse, hadn't you? You got off carefully, and you kept hold of the saddle and you sort of swam along too. But did you get off on the upstream side or the downstream side? Upstream, you had the current to contend with, pushing you close against the horse, and that might not please Chalita. Downstream, you might be carried away altogether, to the Gulf of Carpentaria or Lake Eyre or wherever this particular creek was running to. Or you could get off backwards and hang on to the tail, couldn't you? Lindsay was sure she had read that somewhere in a book once, in the library at school. The Indians did it, in South America.

At least that was a middle course—the tail.

You just kicked your feet out of the stirrups, like this. No, like *this*! Try again, Lindsay—perhaps the Indians didn't use saddles. And then you worked your way backwards, slowly, because the current didn't want you to do that, and tried to snatch you away. And then you slid down over the rump and grabbed your horse's tail. Her tail? Her *tail*? Oh, there it was! Lindsay's fingers entwined themselves in its coarse, comforting, floating strands and hung on grimly right near the tip.

The water took all force out of the horse's flailing hind-feet, so that although they were quite near her they were powerless to harm. Discovering this, Lindsay's confidence returned. She kept her head above the water quite easily as they passed the second line of trees, and Chalita began to flounder into quieter waters.

And then a voice yelled from the approaching bank.

Lindsay was so surprised to hear a voice—a *human* voice, at a time like this!—that she almost forgot to listen to what it was saying. Even when she concentrated, the words made little sense.

'Leggo, missus! Leggo that tail, quickfella, missus, alla-same them hooves belonga Chalita proper killum you! Leggo quickfella, missus. They mebbe killum you *finish*!'

It was the way that raucous voice yelled *finish* that prompted Lindsay to let go. She was reluctant to part company with Chalita—this creek had forged an extra-ordinary bond between them—but when the word 'finish' was yelled at you in that sort of voice, it had a horribly final sound.

Her fingers slackened and the tail floated away. She heard Chalita's feet clattering through the shallows, but when her own feet sought for a hold, she banged her knee on a stone—floundered. Then the pull of the current was snatching her back, and her head went under.

Lindsay choked and struggled, with her mouth full of the swirling brown water. It sang in her ears, and twined itself around her limbs, so that her efforts became feeble and in-effectual. So feeble—just that singing in her head, blotting out thought.

When Tommo dragged her up the bank he flipped her over like a codfish, and pressed the water out of her lungs, and when she had recovered from her fit of coughing he turned her back the other way, helped her to a sitting position and grinned.

Lindsay didn't grin back. She didn't feel much like grinning.

'You nearly drowned me,' she accused him croakily.

'O.K., missus. All good-oh now, eh?'

'Not good-oh, Tommo,' she whispered plaintively. 'I've just been d-drowned.'

Tommo's white teeth flashed in an ear-splitting smile.

'You proper sillyfella missus, not get back alonga dat saddle quick. You wait till water bin shallow, dem cheeky-fella hoof they pokum you allasame they killum you, eh, missus? Maybe killum you finish! Kick you to glory!'

Lindsay stared silently into those laughing dark eyes.

'You want Tommo take you alonga that camp, missus? Two, mebbee three mile? Eh?'

'Yes, please, Tommo,' she begged. 'Take me to the camp.' And then she fainted.

Lindsay was thankful afterwards that she hadn't known

much about that ride to the camp. When she came to her senses, it was to find herself slung ignominiously across Tommo's saddle like an ailing sheep. Her head dangled and her legs dangled and her middle felt as though it was being sawn in two.

When Tommo clattered into the camp and unloaded her with a singular lack of ceremony into Rod's arms she passed out again, but this time, when she regained consciousness, she was surprisingly still in them, but wrapped in a blanket, wet clothes and all.

Lindsay looked up into Rod's anxious grey eyes and then she put her head against his shirt and cried. She couldn't seem to stop crying, even though he was holding her so comfortably and stroking the damp hair away from her eyes and saying over and over in a tender sort of voice, 'Don't cry, Lindsay, you're all right now, darling, don't cry, Lindsay,' and she began to think that so much crying must have made her delirious.

It was only when he said more severely, 'Why did you do it, Lindsay? Why have you come?' that she remembered, with a sudden shock that effectively banished her hysteria, just why she had set out in the first place. Through chattering teeth she told him about Mannie, about the transceiver being broken accidentally.

All the time she was speaking, Rod listened attentively in silence, grave-faced, patient. Only when she mentioned the transceiver did he interrupt.

'Couldn't you have used the other set, Lindsay? The one at the store?'

She shook her head miserably, began to shake uncontrollably.

'I c-couldn't. I meant to order b-batteries. I was g-*going* to, but I h-hadn't *done* it.'

'I see.'

He put her down gently, flat on the ground, and went away, and when he came back again, it was with neat spirits in a tin pannikin.

'Drink it, Lindsay.' He raised her up in his arms again, held the mug against her lips. 'Just drink it up. It won't matter if it makes you sick. Maybe you've still got some of that river water inside you.'

He gave the ghost of a grin as he tilted the contents carefully down her throat. Then he laid her back, stood up, and said from that incredible height,

'Now, don't worry, Lindsay. I'm going to contact Dinewan on my transmitter. It hasn't the range of the transceivers, you see, but the Lockwiths' place isn't far from here at all, and they can then contact Base for me.'

He went away again, and Lindsay closed her eyes, feeling the raw spirit coursing through her, bringing with it a warming glow. Her nausea was diminishing.

When he came back this time, Rod's face held a puzzled expression. He put a blanket-roll he had brought underneath her head, and looked at her strangely. When he had sat down beside her, he said, almost carelessly,

'Funny thing, that. When Margie got through, they said they'd received the Gundooee call over the morning session, and that Mannie has been taken in. She's safely at the hospital right now.'

Lindsay's gaze was blank. Even Rod's face swam a little out of focus.

'But—received a call? They couldn't have!' she protested weakly. 'The transceiver was broken, *smashed*. At least, Carleen said——' Her voice died away as realisation dawned.

'What did Carleen say?'

'She said—she said—I thought—— It doesn't matter really.'

Lindsay was feeling sick again.

'It matters to *me*.' Rod spoke with quiet emphasis. He was silent for a moment. 'I'll tell you what Carleen is saying now, and that may help you to remember.'

'Saying *now*?' she repeated, incredulous.

'Well, a few minutes ago, to be exact. When Margie contacted the homestead on the set that was working.' He paused, continued without expression. 'Carleen says now that you got completely hysterical when Mannie collapsed, and went haring off on horseback before she could stop you. I must say'—he looked at her critically—'you did seem

184

extraordinarily overwrought.'

Rod's face wavered again. It came and went in a kind of vacuum of weakness, a fantasy feeling that this couldn't possibly be happening.

'In fact, you're still overwrought, I think, Lindsay.'

He gathered her shaking frame in his arms again, but this time Lindsay clawed at his hands, pushed him from her even though a spasm of that dreadful weakness assailed her.

'Don't touch me, not if you don't believe. You—don't believe me, d-do you? You don't trust me, Rod.'

'Hush, darling.' He resisted her fumbling attempts to push him away, and held her firmly. 'Of course I believe you!'

Suddenly she went limp in his arms. What was real, what was false, in this swaying, reeling world? It must be the aftermath, the shock. You couldn't get almost drowned, and not suffer some sort of momentary ill effect.

'Well, you shouldn't,' she mumbled wearily against him. 'You shouldn't trust me, do you hear me, Rod? I've deceived you s-since the very beginning.'

'Shh! I know.'

'You c-can't know.' She moved her wet head irritably, closed her eyes. 'How can you know, when I'm only j-just telling you? I pretended.'

'Yes, I know, pet, I know.' His deep voice was humouring her, as if she were a petulant child. 'You pretended to be a man, or rather, you omitted to state that you were a girl. A woman.' His arms tightened about her. 'I've known it all along.'

Lindsay's eyes opened again.

'How could you know?'

'It's what's called passive deceit.' He smiled faintly. 'You didn't even put *Miss* Lindsay Dutten on the stamped and self-addressed envelope which you enclosed for a reply. I checked with Mannie afterwards, and as I suspected, you'd just put L. H. Dutten—most unusual, that. Even people who accidentally leave it out before a signature almost always remember to put it on an envelope.'

She gazed at him incredulously. 'You knew from the beginning?'

'From the beginning,' he agreed calmly.

'Then why didn't you send me away?' she asked suspiciously.

Rod's grey eyes twinkled with sudden amusement.

'Because of Clancy,' he replied with a solemnity that was belied by the laughter in his eyes.

'Clancy?'

'Yes, Clancy. Remember? Clancy of the Overflow? I didn't think he'd like it.'

'Like what?'

'I thought he'd be disappointed if, having come all that way, your bush friends didn't greet you with those kindly voices, the way you expected them to. It would have been letting old Clancy down a bit, if I'd sent you away.'

'Oh.' Her eyes fell before his. '*Your* voice wasn't very kind,' she mumbled, gazing at his middle shirt button.

He grinned. 'No, it wasn't, just at first, was it? I reckoned you were making plenty of bush friends for the time being, and hearing plenty of kindly voices without mine. Getting kisses, too.'

'Oh, Rod! You mean Artie?' She looked up again, dimpling. 'Rod, that was only for a bet.'

'Yes, I realised that—a good bit later.' A pause. 'Do you only give away kisses when a bet is involved?' he asked in an odd sort of voice, bringing his head down very near to catch her reply.

Colour washed over Lindsay's pale cheeks.

'No—yes—I mean—of course not!' she said weakly. His face was really terribly close, so close that it was difficult to think what she was saying. His grey eyes, smouldering darkly, were within inches of hers. And his mouth, that firm-lipped mouth—so close——

'Then we don't have to bet on it, do we,' he stated calmly, before he bent his head just that little bit more and covered her mouth with his.

Lindsay returned that kiss with a heady sensation of utter and unprecedented bliss. Half-way through she even managed to disentangle her damp arms from the blanket and put them around his neck, with the result that Rod seemed to go

186

on kissing, only this time with a mounting passion that left her breathless.

Finally, he held her away from him and said indistinctly,

'Dear heaven, Lindsay, how I've wanted to do that! When you're my wife, I'll kiss you just as often as I please,' he told her with a return to his normal, masterful tone.

'My—your——? What did you say? Just then, Rod?' She spoke rather feebly, because she was still recovering her breath.

'You heard me, Lindsay, my own sweet darling. I'm warning you of my intention to marry you, that's all.' He smiled down at her, the passion still blazing in his eyes at war with the gruff matter-of-factness in his voice.

'Oh, Rod!' Lindsay breathed his name ecstatically, flung her arms around his neck again, half laughing, half crying, with a mixture of delight and sheer physical weakness.

He kissed her gently, as if sensing that she was almost at the limit of her strength, and then he took her hands from behind his head.

'I'm only telling you now,' he told her with mischievous candour. 'I can choose a better time and place for *asking* you, Lindsay. The men will be in soon, and your shirt's still wet. You'll have to get out of those clothes, and I'll dry them by the fire here. I'll give you this blanket to wrap around you till you get them back, and I'll dry that blanket, too. Can you manage, do you think? Could a prospective husband help in any way?'

Her cheeks were aflame.

'I—I'll manage, thank you,' she said hastily.

Rod chuckled softly.

'Over by that tree, then.' He helped her to her feet, handed her the second blanket. 'Tonight we'll light a second fire, a little bit away, so that the sound of the ringers changing places won't disturb you. You'll hear the ringer out there in the darkness singing his cattle to soothe them and stop any other night noises from alarming the mob.' A smile crept into his voice. 'I'll make sure Artie's not one of them tonight. His singing is of a rather unrestful quality, and his repertoire of songs is pretty border-line, too. You can have my saddle for a pillow, and you should sleep all right. Tomorrow we'll ride back in together.'

Lindsay paused on her somewhat wobbly course to the tree.

'Goodness!' she exclaimed. 'I forgot all about Chalita! She ran off when I let go her tail. What shall I ride back on?'

'You mean Dusty, of course,' he said abruptly, striding after her and putting a hand on her forehead. 'You aren't still shocked, are you, Lindsay?' he added, with a sudden return of anxiety.

'Chalita,' she repeated firmly. 'Dusty wasn't around, so I came on Chalita, but she ran away when I—when I was in the w-water.'

The memory of that drowning sensation made her shiver.

'I see. Well, she'll come in during the night, probably,' he told her evenly. 'Don't worry about it, Lindsay. She'll hear the bells on the tailer's horses—she knows the sound well. She'll come sniffing around, and we'll catch her.'

Lindsay wriggled her way out of her wet clothes and came back wrapped in the second blanket, handed Rod her other things. She felt incredibly slack and weary, but wonderfully happy and content, too.

Rod accepted the clothes. The firelight was at his back in the rapidly descending dusk, so that she couldn't see his expression clearly, but when he spoke his voice was angry, heavy with control.

'*You* couldn't have caught Chalita, Lindsay, never in a million years. You couldn't have saddled her either. And when I think of you *riding* her——' He broke off, swallowed audibly. 'Both Chalita and Dusty were in when I rode out here, Lindsay—not in the saddling yard itself, but in the horse paddock, close at hand,' he informed her bleakly.

Then he waited.

It seemed to Lindsay, from the patient stance of those dusty, elastic-sided boots planted there in the dust, that Rod might be prepared to wait there for ever till he got a reply. There was a certain relentlessness about him that told her he was in one of his 'I expect and intend to get an answer' moods.

She rubbed her hand over her brow, looked up at him with misty green eyes that were hollow pools in her white face.

'Do we have to talk about it?' she asked, pleading.

'No, darling, we do not.' He patted her shoulder with unexpected kindness. 'We don't need to talk about it for a long, long time—not until it's just a memory. Just one little thing, though, Lindsay. Carleen knew about your own pretence from the beginning, didn't she?' His grey glance was probing.

Lindsay nodded dumbly.

'O.K.' Surprisingly, Rod smiled. It was that slow, caressing smile that just curled the corners of his mouth. 'I'll talk to her when we get back. There'll be absolutely no unpleasantness, but I don't think you'll see her much again. I'm sure she won't want to stay, in fact, once she hears we're getting married.'

Lindsay smiled tremulously. She couldn't voice her gratitude. Some day, she would tell Rod everything. Not just now, though. It didn't matter right now.

She went over and sat in her blanket beside the fire which Rod had got going for her, and watched the evening routine in the camp. When he came back with her dry clothes she put them on again, over by the same tree.

The men straggled in, in twos and threes, turning their horses loose with bell and hobbles to pick up what they could, carrying their saddles back to put them where Rod directed, under the gums, and then making for their own swag and quart-pot to brew up that ever welcome mug of tea. Jimmy and Tommo came in then, leading three fresh horses which they tied up under a couple of near-by saplings before making their way to their own fire, laying down their battered felt hats beside their swags, and getting out their quart-pots like everyone else was doing.

As they passed her, they gave Lindsay a puzzled glance, but showed their even white teeth in their customary friendly smiles.

The other men, too, kept looking over at Lindsay. She could see their eyes darting her way under cover of their smoko operations, but if Rod was aware of those furtive, peeping looks or the bouts of whispering that accompanied them, he gave no sign. He was obviously content not to notice. He seemed to be waiting for something.

When all the men had come into camp for the night, except for the horse-tailer out there with the cattle until the first ringer had had his meal and could take his place, and the steaks were beginning to sizzle and spit on the three different fires, Rod stepped into the clearing between the fires and called to Lindsay.

'Come here for a moment, please, Lindsay,' he said, with that old, familiar ring of authority. 'I wish to say something.'

Lindsay stood up and obeyed, just like everyone always did when Rod used that stern, commanding tone. She walked out of her own warm firelit circle, and into the clearing.

'Come here, Lindsay. Right here to me.'

All eyes were watching. Curiously, the quart-pots and pannikins ceased their chinking, and even the steaks seemed to sizzle more quietly than before, as she and Rod stood there together in the little pool of silence.

Then, with the eyes still gazing and the bush all about them, Rod took off his hat, tilted up her chin with steady fingers, and kissed her with a slow, deliberate tenderness, right on her lips. Then he put his hat under his arm, and turned to the firelight where Artie and Herb were kneeling on one knee over the steaks.

'*Now*, Artie,' he murmured deeply, 'you go and collect on the knockout stakes, eh!'

Rod took Lindsay's hand and led her gently back to her own little fire away from the rest, and as their feet crunched softly over the fallen gumleaves, they heard Art's voice, breathless with stupefaction—

'Well! If that don't beat all!'

Lindsay gazed at Rod.

'You knew?' she said wonderingly.

'I told you there'd be no point in you competing, didn't I? You were home and dry already, you see.'

'All *along*?' she whispered incredulously.

Just for one brief moment, Rod's teeth glinted in the firelight.

'It's up to every man to know what goes on on his own station, Lindsay,' he muttered huskily, before he gave her that second kiss.

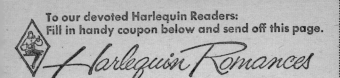

To our devoted Harlequin Readers:
Fill in handy coupon below and send off this page.

Harlequin Romances

TITLES STILL IN PRINT

51465 DAMSEL IN GREEN, B. Neels

51466 RETURN TO SPRING, J. Macleod

51467 BEYOND THE SWEET WATERS, A. Hampson

51468 YESTERDAY, TODAY AND TOMORROW, J. Dunbar

51469 TO THE HIGHEST BIDDER, H. Pressley

51470 KING COUNTRY, M. Way

51471 WHEN BIRDS DO SING, F. Kidd

51472 BELOVED CASTAWAY, V. Winspear

51473 SILENT HEART, L. Ellis

51474 MY SISTER CELIA, M. Burchell

51475 THE VERMILION GATEWAY, B. Dell

51476 BELIEVE IN TOMORROW, N. Asquith

51477 THE LAND OF THE LOTUS EATERS, I. Chace

51478 EVE'S OWN EDEN, K. Mutch

51479 THE SCENTED HILLS, R. Lane

51480 THE LINDEN LEAF, J. Arbor

〰〰〰〰〰〰〰〰〰〰〰〰〰〰〰

Harlequin Books, Dept. Z

Simon & Schuster, Inc., 11 West 39th St.
New York, N.Y. 10018

☐ **Please send me information about Harlequin Romance Subscribers Club.**

Send me titles checked above. I enclose .50 per copy plus .15 per book for postage and handling.

Name ....

Address ....

City .... State .... Zip ....

MAIL THIS COUPON TODAY